On My Honor

An Epic Medieval
Tale Told in
Irish Mythology

Genie Day

ACKNOWLEDGEMENTS

The book you hold in your hand did not start as a book. I had a job I hated before I finally got my college degree; I couldn't tell my unkind employer to take a flying leap because I like to eat and have a roof over my head, so I went to a counselor who advised me to journal; to pour my anger and frustration safely on paper, thus keeping me employed and out of trouble. As I journaled, the characters took on a life of their own, and over a period of years, "On My Honor" evolved into a book full of adventure.

I owe a debt of gratitude to my wonderful husband, Jeff, who listened so patiently while I whined and complained about my unkind employer (a lot!). My wonderful husband supported me, prepared meals, drove me to college so I wouldn't have to drive around endlessly looking for parking, paid the bills, kept up the house, paid for math tutors (a whole other story), and cheered me on while I got my degree and a better job. He is my real life knight in shining armor.

I also owe a debt of gratitude to Bryan Tsunoda, the best manager I've ever had the good fortune of working for. Unlike anyone I had ever worked for, Bryan took a sincere interest in the personal and professional growth of his employees. He was patient and kind and sometimes tough. Over the course of time, assignments he gave me, and many conversations that sometimes started with, "We must talk." – (never a good sign and comparable to being sent to the principal's office), I grew and matured in character as I learned to leave my immature and demanding ways behind. Looking back now, I don't know how he put up with me. As sometimes happens, the sad day came when the wonderful growth I experienced with Bryan led me to a different job better suited to my newly-earned college education, and personal and professional talents. Bryan is King Byron in the book, and in the sequel, and he is every bit the defender and protector of those around him in real life as he is in the book, as I'm sure his drop-dead gorgeous wife and little daughter can attest to. I hope that you, the reader, will nod your head in agreement when he is referred to as "Byron the Just."

A note to women: Finish school and go to college. I don't care what anyone says, it's still a man's world even though it's the 21st century and not the 17th century. Men still get paid more for the same jobs than women do. With divorce and single parenting on the rise, a college education is the best favor you can do for yourself; it opens doors of respect - self respect and respect from others. I would not have the job I do today as a technical editor if I hadn't finished college.

I owe a debt of gratitude I can never repay to Jesus Christ, my Defender and Champion, Who has never left my side since I asked Him into my heart and He claimed me as His beloved.

Enjoy your journey into the 17th century with Torey, the half-immortal, Simon the Brute, and King Byron the Just.

The Goddess Queen Danu

Danu perched, motionless, on the edge of the shallow pool, studiously watching the images of the mortal world. The trials and tribulations of man unfolded on the shimmering surface of a pool watched by the gods. On occasion the gods chose to walk in the world of mortals as a man, woman, child, or beast, and in subtle ways they toyed with the fate of empires.

As queen of the Tuatha de Danann, and as goddess of the Eire, Danu reigned as possessively and solicitously over her people as a lioness over her cubs.

Danu's exotic beauty belied her royal discipline. The queen's warrior Champions, and her Silver Riders knelt before their majesty, awaiting her next command. She ruled them as much by her exquisite loveliness as she did by her sage wisdom and sovereign authority.

The Tuatha de Danann were Celtic gods who tended and nurtured the people of the Eire. The gods had remarkable longevity, and seemed to stop aging upon reaching adulthood. They were skilled in art, science, and poetry, and possessed abilities to tap into certain elemental and cosmic energies in the form of Magic. They were not completely immortal, however, for they could be mortally wounded in battle. The Tuatha de Danann were also well known for their passionate allegiance to their enchanting queen.

Dian Cecht, great physician of the Tuatha de Danann, and Queen Danu's lover, strode across the verdant earthen floor of their lush mystical isle to join his queen in her vigil.

The de Danaan deities who reposed on couches with their queen on the island paradise known as Tir-na-nog, the Land of Youth, were amused by the goddess' preoccupation with the goings-on of the mortal world and the friction it sometimes created between the two lovers.

Dian was not happy when the royal enchantress didn't look up as he approached.

"You spend a lot of time watching over your earth-bound daughter," he whined irritably.

The goddess rolled her eyes and dismissed him with a wave of her hand. She knew that when she took a mortal lover, it made Dian jealous even though he lay with mortal women.

"You deceive yourself if you think a mortal man can give you greater pleasure than a god!" he retorted.

He needn't have hoped for the passionate banter of heated words, however, for it takes two to spar, and the lovely goddess was once again preoccupied with the image in the pool.

Queen Danu was the goddess of fertility and poetry. So exquisite was she that no mortal man could resist her when she chose to cast a spell on him with her arresting, emerald green eyes. So drawn was she to a ruggedly handsome and virile mortal man she had seen in the Pool of Mortals, that she had decided to walk upon the Earth and seduce him.

Daniel O'Rourke, he was, a coxswain, a swarthy commander of a ship that plied the seas off the coast of Ireland. He was a stout man of solid muscles and Celtic Irish charm. He was charming and virile, indeed, for he had impregnated her.

This was unfortunate, not because Danu was unhappy to find herself with child - nay she was ecstatic - but woe be to the queen mother because her baby girl was half-mortal. This was disastrous because the child could not live among the gods, but had to live her life among mortals. If the child's father had been one of the Tuatha de Danann, she would have had access to both worlds, the realm of the gods and the mortal world of men. But, alas, her father was an earth-bound Irish man. The queen was truly an Irish mother, for her heart was stricken, so much so that she gave her child many lives. The queen mother adored her girl child and vigilantly watched over her earth-bound babe throughout each of those lifetimes. The Immortals gave the child gifts to aid her survival.

In her third life the babe had grown up and became Rosalena, an exotic dancer for royalty. As Rosalena, she was summoned into the ruling king's presence, King Edward, his warriors, and his knights. The king and his assembly enjoyed celebrating after a victorious battle, and she was commanded to give them an evening of erotic dancing, followed by seductive pleasure. In this life as Rosalena, she was also called "Little Dancer." When summoned by the king she was escorted to the edge of the thick, red carpet where she dropped to her knees in submission.

Rosalena sprang to her feet in surprise as the boom of King Edward's voice broke the silence, "Dance! Dance for us, Little Dancer!" Her swaying hips entranced them, inviting them to play and forget their thoughts of battle.

The Little Dancer deliberately aroused in them an awareness of their strength and superiority as conquerors and warriors. Her dance ended with her undulating hips going in slower and still slower circular motions until she dropped suddenly and submissively before the king's throne, her flaming red hair flowing over the stone floor, her back pressed toward the floor with her legs tucked under her, caressing her own breasts, with her pelvis arched invitingly high, awaiting the king's command.

Any one of the men could have her for the night. King Edward would not question it. Indeed, she was a reward for those who pleased him. They were mesmerized as she lightly stroked the curves of her body, waiting expectantly until the king decided who would have her, unless he decided to take her himself.

Play was oft the serious business of the de Dannan deity. The goddess Queen Danu gifted her daughter while she was yet in her womb, saturating her pores and essence with sexuality, instilling in her joy and delight with all things pleasurable.

Danu gave her a small frame, like her own, easy to command and dominate, and a delicate face that could be either expressive and playful or quiet and attentive. Danu formed her to be petite, yet muscular, and she added to that a talent for athletics and gymnastics, knowing that this pleased kings, noblemen, and soldiers.

The goddess also gave her child white, satiny skin, irresistible to the touch, delightful to the eye, and tapered, slender fingers that were gifted with the ability to bestow breathtaking pleasure. The child had her mother's emerald green eyes and her father's fiery red hair.

The goddess' daughter was born, in each lifetime, with the inherited power of shapeshifting in the mortal world, and the ability to call upon her mother, and those in her mother's kingdom whenever she needed them. Danu knew her daughter would need her birthright of shapeshifting if she were to survive in the world of mortals.

Dian knew from watching mortal kings rule through the ages how difficult the challenges of rulership could be, and he knew Danu's earthbound child would be subject to kings. Therefore, as physician of the Celtic gods, he instilled within her mind a sharp intellect.

Dian smiled to himself as he recalled the many times he had visited the mortal world and had lain naked in the warmth of the afternoon in a tangle of damp, satiated limbs with a lover. There, in his private chambers, he could talk openly of the challenges troubling him. His lady would confide her ideas, which often proved to be useful, warning him of this thing or that.

Walking among men was easy for the daughter of Danu, for she was not directly involved in any of the castle intrigue, and this gave her unencumbered insight. She was given freedom of movement and became a fixture of little import so that conversations and intentions were discussed openly in her presence. She was loyal and sensuously playful, and she brought important informational tidbits back to her king.

Queen Danu peered into the images unfolding before her in the glassy surface of the Pool of Mortals, furrowing her brow with concern. The Tamlin, Queen Danu's changeling warrior-woman and personal bodyguard, met her queen's worried gaze with compassion. The two women bowed to each other, the changeling-warrior, extending her heartfelt aid, and her queen, declining the offer, for now.

The Tamlin had two small daughters of her own. Their father, Lugh Lamfada, was also one of Danu's immortal champions. The Tamlin's daughters thus enjoyed access to both worlds. Tam could not imagine the grief of being separated from her daughters and having to peer at them through a portal, so she pledged loyalty not only to her queen, but also to take care of the queen's earth-bound child.

It was the 17th century when Danu saw that King Edward's own folly was about to bring an end to his reign. It was time for the queen mother to grant her child another life.

Queen Danu Instructs Her Daughter

Queen Danu understood that the king whom prophecy foretold and her daughter needed each other. She had seen both her daughter and the stubborn, valiant king in the Pool of Mortals the night her daughter was born. In the dark shadows and watery depths of the Pool of Mortals the ancient, elder Kings Nauda, Lir, and Dagda had revealed the prophecy her half-mortal, half-goddess baby would fulfill.

Her child would, indeed, need his discipline, and he, her mettle. Danu was an immortal woman as well as a goddess, and she was well aware of what her child would be subject to in the medieval world of men and would not send HER daughter into that world without adequate preparation.

Danu and her daughter reviewed the lessons taught from the cradle, and again in each reincarnated life her little girl had lived. Together they talked about the young lady's training in sensuality classes where she learned from both men and women how to give exquisite pleasure. They talked about the young lady's days as Rosalena, the Little Dancer, and of her candid talks with King Edward during heated afternoons of sensual pleasure in his chamber.

Mother and daughter philosophically discussed self-respect, dignity, humility and veneration, and their respective and intricate balance.

They talked about practical things such as medicinal herbs, candle making, preserving vegetables, and child- bearing.

Danu told her young lady a funny story about her own mother, and how one day, when she was a little goddess, she wanted to practice making little fire-balls strike the rocks by the pond to see them explode, instead of practicing magic lessons with her tutor. Well, Danu's mother sneaked up on her at the pond, in the form of a bear, and just when she thought her little girl would pass out from her terrified screaming, she turned herself back into a goddess, rolling in the grass, laughing so hard she was holding her sides. That ended Danu's truancy! Danu and her mother giggled like two little accomplices.

Danu and her girl child talked about rape, bondage, and bloody sieges. Danu instructed her on when to be gregarious, and when to be demure, when to be bold and when to be quiet, when to stand and fight and when to flee. But, most importantly, Danu schooled her beloved child on those times when it would be necessary to call upon her goddess mother on the Isle of Tir-na-nog.

"Will you bring into remembrance all that I have told you, my precious?" Mother Danu asked, hoping her regal demeanor hid her motherly fears.

"Yes, Mother Danu, by the gods, I shall," she smiled, but the smile held tearful tremors.

"I pray, my darling, that you will fare well in the Time of Kings," said Danu, resisting the urge to bite her lower lip.

"Mother Danu," the girl pleaded as tears ran down her cheeks, "how will I know him, this handsome, stubborn, valiant king that prophecy says I shall serve?"

"You will know him, Child. He is known and loved for his character and by the way he wields his authority to uphold justice. The prophecy states that he is such an extraordinary mortal, that he is enchanted; a wizard king, who has the magical ability to decipher a man's heart, and therefore, his intent. This king's mortal sovereignty holds the balance of justice as the gods have given it to him. Because of this, his judgments are considered infallible." Danu gave her daughter a moment to digest that before continuing.

"But beware, daughter, though all kings tout strength of character, and have been taught by the great philosophers from ancient times to be convincing, only one wields true justice."

With a kiss to the top of her young lady's head, and a flip of her wrist, it was done. Danu called out to her in the girl's flight through time.

"Ah, I nearly forgot, my darling!" Danu's voice echoed after her.

"Your mortal name is Torey."

And so it began.

Childhood in King Alexander's Castle

Stephanie gasped in surprise as cold water streamed down her back, in her eyes, and down the front of her dress. This was washday, and the other servant girls laughed at Torey's prank on the older girl. The girls had watched Torey sneak up on Stephanie armed with a formidable looking bucket of cold water. They had to suppress their snickering so as not to give her away.

The two girls often played jokes on each other. Stephanie threw down the tunics she'd been washing to chase Torey, but, as usual, Torey was faster. Both girls were giggling as Stephanie chased her to the wood's edge.

"You can run away, you little sprite," Stephanie giggled breathlessly, "but I'll get you when you least expect it," she promised. Steph wanted to play the game a little while longer, but duties weighed heavily on both girls, for both were accountable to King Alexander.

"Come along, now, little one," Stephanie called out to Torey who was hiding behind a tree, obviously wanting Stephanie to come and find her. "We must finish the wash and get back to the castle to help in the kitchen before King Alexander and his hunting party return."

Stephanie stood with her hands on her hips. Torey reluctantly popped her head out from her hiding place behind a great tree for she knew that when her friend took that stance, there was no changing her mind.

Torey pouted, "you're a bloody bore," but left her hiding place behind the tree to join Stephanie and return to their tasks.

"That's not fair, or very kind of you! And such language for such a little lady!" Stephanie poked Torey's ribs, half-joking and half-seriously, and then said, persuasively, "I promise that if you help me finish our chores, we will play cards and tiles tonight with the other girls after dinner, we will, but only if you promise not to cheat!"

Torey grinned, her good humor restored. "I promise!" she said as she held her right hand over her heart. "Besides," the mischievous Torey added, "I can beat you easily by playing fair!"

Stephanie smiled at her young friend. "I can't very well argue when you're right, now can I?"

The remainder of the day was occupied with the wash and a myriad of other duties that were required to prepare the evening's feast.

Torey was one of King Alexander's youngest servants. She was a beautiful girl with flaming red hair and large green eyes. She had been brought before the king as a small child, after her village was besieged and her parents were killed, and he had decided to keep her for himself. He had only to wait until she was old enough. He never regretted his decision for he found her to be as helpful and sweet as she was lovely, and a delight to everyone around her. Full of curiosity, and lion-hearted, she loved to laugh, and play, and was altogether engaging. King Alexander found her most captivating.

And so it went for Torey, like a merry tune on a harp until she came of age.

From Child to Woman

Oanu gazed into the Pool of Mortals on the Isle of Tir-na-nog and was pleased to see that her child had blossomed into a beautiful young woman who turned the heads of kings. But she knew King Alexander was not the king of whom the prophecy spoke, so she kept a vigilant eye on her daughter, confident that Torey's path would eventually lead her to him. The goddess was not the only one who noticed that Torey had become striking to look upon.

In her fourteenth summer King Alexander noticed Torey had blossomed from a capricious child to a curvaceous young woman. He had waited a long time for her to come of age, watching her grow, and he burned with passion for her. The king ordered an extravagant feast with all the trimmings. He ordered that Torey be bathed, adorned, and seated next to him at dinner. She was a vision of loveliness that sparkled and shimmered as she supped beside him. Torey laughed as the court jesters and acrobats performed their daring and comical routines, and she applauded with exuberant amusement and enthusiastic approval as the fire breathers and dancers defied natural law with their precision.

Her laughter and joy intoxicated the king with desire for her. She was spicy and sweet, daring and demure, sassy and submissive, and he wanted nothing more than to take her to his bed and taste her. He wanted to show her that she was so desirable that a king would swoon at her feet if she would but grant him her favors. He knew she was as playful and spontaneous as a child, and just as innocent, for she was untouched by any man.

King Alexander clapped his hands to signify the end of the feast and festivities. He motioned for his personal attendants, "Take her to my chambers, paint her pudendum with henna, and prepare her for me." Torey blushed deeply, bowed to her lord, and followed the attendants.

Later that night, in the privacy of the royal chamber, King Alexander took Torey's maidenhead gently, being mindful of her petite stature, restraining his long-held desire for her until she healed before taking her again. His patience was rewarded, for Torey was the most passionate lover he had ever taken to his bed. King Alexander was delighted with himself.

Over time, the king took other concubines, but he kept Torey close at hand, enjoying her himself, and using her beauty and her talents to bargain for political alliances. Consequently, Torey became accomplished in the ways of political diplomacy in this life, using submissive sensuality as she had in her previous lives, while praying always to her goddess mother Queen Danu.

However, Torey had grown in maturity and wisdom, and she could sense that something was amiss. Sleep had claimed her as she sent her prayers to her mother, but in her spirit, she heard Ember, the fairy-woman Prism, beckon to her. The Prisms were a fairy people created by Queen Danu. The fairy women were about two feet tall, with the curvaceous body of a human, mortal woman, and the wings of a butterfly. Their wings were an electric, iridescent blue, with yellow veins that glowed like the sun running through each of the wings. They had two black antennae that sloped gracefully from either side of their forehead. Their antennae, designed to detect distraught, and other types of pheromones, were long and very thin, covered with a light layer of silky black hairs. There were many of Ember's kind and considered a wonderment of life.

Ember's beautiful wings folded behind her as she lighted upon the open windowsill. When Torey's spirit rose from slumber and walked to the window, she was alarmed to find Ember in an anxious state. Ember brought a message to Torey from the Queen Mother of the Ire that the Pool of Mortals had reflected dangerous and troubled times that were coming for Torey, but that the Pool was dark and shadowy and the Queen Mother could not see exactly what the cause of the trouble was.

Thus, her mother warned her that change was coming.

Visitors and Trouble

The other girls, who were all older than Torey, were gathered around Stephanie, the oldest. They were whispering but fell silent when Torey entered the room. Nothing had changed in the way the other servant girls related to Torey since she had become King Alexander's concubine. In fact, Torey's intimate proximity to the king often placed her in political intrigue that none of them envied.

"Why are you all whispering?" Torey asked, trying to sound casual. She was hurt that they were sharing a secret that didn't include her. All the girls looked down; none of them would meet her questioning eyes. This alarmed Torey, and she looked at Stephanie for an explanation.

"There are rumors around the castle that King Alexander has gotten himself into a bit 'o trouble, he has. It seems his fondness for gambling, expensive things, and impressing courtesans has run him into a bit of debt, it has. On top of that, the council is expecting foreign diplomats and traders from Spain to arrive soon. In fact," she said in a less calm voice, "it is rumored that King Alexander may make up the difference the treasury lacks by using his concubines to pay his debts."

One of the girls came forward to appeal to Torey, her eyes wide with fear. "Speak to him, lass, he favors you. He will listen to you. This is our home, none of us want to be traded and taken away!" The young girl fell to her knees throwing her arms around Torey's waist, wailing in despair.

Torey and Stephanie exchanged glances. Both of them were now young women, and they knew well the reality of their lives and those of the other girls, and there was naught to be done about it. But Torey, for all her youth and petite size, was strong and lion-hearted; she would not have those with whom she felt a kinship be fearful, so she consoled them as best she could. She put on her most convincing smile. "My elegant ladies of the castle, do you really think King Alexander would trade away the most beautiful girls in the kingdom? I think not!"

Torey watched them brighten as their fear and doubt subsided in the face of her persuasive façade of confidence. But, deep inside, she seethed in anger that King Alexander would let this happen to the most defenseless members of his castle household. "By Queen Danu," she thought to herself, "I shall request to speak with that errant king!"

The great gong in the castle sounded, indicating important news had arrived. Presently, a royal messenger came to the chambers of King Alexander's ladies and read from a parchment:

"At the end of the week foreign traders from Spain will arrive. There will be a great reception feast with much entertainment, and you will all dress in your finest, for you will be introduced to our visitors and seated at the king's table."

Apprehension filled the room, all eyes turned to Torey. She smiled with confidence and said with a wink, "Aye, then we will give them Irish hospitality, we will."

For the rest of the week the servants of the castle frantically busied themselves scrubbing, cooking, and making preparations. Armor was polished, floors were scrubbed, and hunting parties returned with pheasant and venison. The bakers prepared bread, cakes, and pies. The jugglers, fire-eaters, musicians, and dancers were engaged. Seamstresses sewed gowns for the ladies.

Finally, the castle and all its residents were in a state of readiness as the foreign ships sailed into King Alexander's harbor. Carriages delivered their foreign passengers to the steps of King Alexander's castle, as the king stood in his stately robes and crown with his ladies, council, bodyguards, and attendants next to him, ready to receive the visitors.

In all the time Torey had lived at the castle, she had never seen such a display of pomp and show like this day. The only exception, perhaps, was on the day that King Alexander claimed her maidenhead. But this was unsettlingly different. Torey felt a deep sense of foreboding as she smiled and curtsied appropriately as each of the foreign traders and diplomats proceeded through the receiving line and were introduced and seated in the formal dining hall.

When Lord Diego and Lady Alejandra, his favorite, were introduced, Torey caught her breath. She had never seen such a stunning lady. Her shimmering black hair was caught up in pearls and jewels. Her almond eyes were framed with velvet blue kohl, and her lips were crimson red. White blossoms danced on one side of her shiny tresses attached to combs arranged in her hair. Her perfect figure was wrapped in a modest red saya with embroidery of her Spanish homeland on it.

As the introductions were made, Lady Alejandra glanced briefly into Torey's eyes and smiled. Her smile was warm and sincere, not at all what Torey was expecting. How could this woman, who was so far from home, smile at Torey like she was her long-lost best friend? Her heart was touched and Torey decided at that moment to make this exquisite lady feel at home. Torey had no idea what that would mean for her, but she would soon learn.

At dinner, Torey, seated next to King Alexander, whispered discreetly in his ear, "my lord, if you must trade any of your ladies, trade me and spare my sisters."

"You may just get your request, against my own better judgment. It seems Lord Diego favors you above the others."

Torey fumed inwardly, incredulous at King Alexander's assumption. How could he not know this was not her wish? She kept her eyes down so she could better resist the urge to impale his majesty with the glare that burned in her eyes. She thought to herself, "this is not my wish, you self-indulgent king. I offer myself because you fail to defend and protect your women."

Torey could hardly contain herself. She glanced at Lord Diego as he, King Alexander, and Lord Simon, Captain of the king's guard, and one of the king's advisors, exchanged pleased glances in appreciation of Torey's loveliness. She wanted to stick her tongue out at all of them and run from the room, but she dared not.

"Lord Diego, Lord Simon, and I will be meeting with my council tomorrow morning to talk about trade, payment, and diplomatic measures," King Alexander informed her.

Torey's apprehension grew. However, she had no idea how daunting her life was about to become.

LORD DIEGO'S BIDDING

Torey gazed out the carriage window as the horses' rhythmic stride carried her along the narrow dirt road. The moon was full and bright, making it easier for the driver and the horses to see. The gardenias and jasmine were in full bloom; Torey closed her eyes and breathed in deeply, filling her lungs with their heady fragrance, trying to draw serenity within her mind. It was being elusive.

Despite how pleasant the night was, Torey was filled with foreboding. She tried not to think about it, but her thoughts kept wandering back to the conversation she had had with Stephen, the overseer of all the ladies. She had been going about her duties at the castle when he came to her. He had told her that a carriage would come for her that evening; she was to bathe and dress in an appealing manner, for she had been chosen by Lord Diego to entertain him and his guests. She had no idea what to expect. She asked Lady Alejandra, but the only reply she had received were simple instructions to smile and be hospitable.

Her escorts were two of King Alexander's most experienced men, Lord Simon and Lord Lawton, who were loaned to Lord Diego, as well. Lawton was tall, thin, and quiet. He paid her no mind, which suited her just fine.

Lord Simon, on the other hand, had always made her skin crawl the way he leered at her. As Captain of King Alexander's army, he commanded fear from those around him, for he took no prisoners and showed no mercy. He was known as Simon the Blackguard, or Simon the Brute. He was ruggedly handsome at 5 foot 10 inches tall with piercing blue eyes, dark brown shoulder-length hair; muscular and solid, with a powerful build. Just above his right eye he sported a jagged scar from a near-miss in a sword fight. He was disciplined and calculating, and practiced his warrior moves daily. The courtesans at court brazenly simpered and vied for his attention. Torey feared him. No one uttered a sound as the carriage made its way through the night shadows.

Torey could feel the sway of the carriage slow as the clop-clop of the horses fell into a more leisurely clippety-clop when the horses sauntered over a wooden bridge that led through the gatehouse into the outer yard and then to the guardhouse. The guards announced the arrival of the guests, and the driver was allowed entry into the stables. The castle was nestled deep in the woods, and was maintained by a small staff. The carriage slowed and then stopped altogether, and she could hear the horses snorting their impatience. The door was opened and a hand extended to help her down. Lords Simon and Lawton walked on either side of her as they reached the entryway of the royal apartments. Lord Simon knocked on the door and gently nudged Torey towards it. She was very surprised when Lord Diego, himself, opened the door.

He had a devilish grin on his face as he gave her a slight bow. He was rather portly with cheeks so pudgy that he nearly lost his eyes when he smiled. He was short, not much taller than Torey, and had a bald spot on top of his head that reflected the light when he bowed. Torey returned his bow as was the custom of his homeland. He leaned forward as if to kiss her cheek in welcome as was the custom of her homeland, but instead, surprised her by cupping her bosom in both his hands, bringing his face down and kissing her breasts. He was quite pleased with himself, smiling and chuckling as though he had just told the most amusing joke and fully expected her to appreciate his antics. Torey was not amused.

He took her by the hand and led her down a long hallway and into a large room befitting the status of a king, with Simon and Lawton close behind. He led her across the room to Lady Alejandra, who was engaged in conversation with several ladies and gentlemen. Lord Diego spoke to Lady Alejandra in Spanish, their eyes shifting briefly to Torey.

Lady Alejandra took Torey by the hand and led her into a side room. Crossing the elegantly furnished room to an armoire, she fumbled around in a drawer and pulled out several pieces of ladies' intimate apparel.

"You are to change into these," she instructed Torey in her heavy Spanish accent. Torey had noticed that the guests were very comfortably dressed. The men wore luxuriant robes and lounge pants; the women were attired in seductive under garments and corsets. Lady Alejandra helped Torey out of her traveling clothes. Torey stood before her quite devoid of clothing, trying hard to maintain her dignity. Lady Alejandra knelt before Torey holding green lace panties, indicating to Torey that she was to step into them. The panties were lace and fur trimmed, with a see-through bustle also trimmed in soft fur that went from hip-to-hip around the back, giving a short skirt effect when viewed from the rear. The corset was low-cut and too small, so much so that her nipples peeped out from over the top of the fur like small pink eyes peering up at Lady Alejandra; she eyed them back with a frown.

"Your neeples do not appear to be much 'ek-si-ted,'" her accent complained. Torey shrank within herself, a wildfire of dismay consuming her. She did not feel very 'ek-si-ted' anywhere.

Lady Alejandra crossed the room to a basin of water and dipped her fingers into it. She came back over to Torey and firmly pinched her nipples with her icy cold fingers, making them stand erect. Torey was incredulous.

"Much better!" Lady Alejandra exclaimed with a beaming, pleased smile. "Ek-si-ted neeples please Lord Diego," her accent crooned approvingly.

Torey wilted with dread as she looked down at herself, her face five shades of red, "I can't go out there like this!" She was so shaken she could hardly hear her own voice, her eyes wide with apprehension.

"You can, milady. You must. I will be with you. I will teach." Lady Alejandra tried to sound reassuring, but Torey was far from persuaded.

Lady Alejandra knelt before Torey, lifting first one foot, and then the other, slipping on soft black leather boots, then she drew black silk gloves onto Torey's hands that went up to her elbows. Lady Alejandra dabbed rose color on Torey's satiny skin, powdered a dab on her cheeks, and carefully colored her lips. She then applied brown kohl on her eyelids, which accentuated Torey's green eyes.

After leading Torey to a full-length mirror framed with ornately carved oak in the corner of the large bedchamber, Lady Alejandra smiled her approval. Torey gasped at the stranger who stared back at her. The young woman in the mirror was transformed into a vision of seduction, a plaything for the men who waited in the other room. But this was not lion-hearted Torey, and while her heart was still encased in fear and apprehension, her spirit rose in defiance.

An insistent bell sounded in the next room, Lady Alejandra brightened with anticipation, "now is time we must go to dinner, milady." Lady Alejandra was festive and bubbly as she hastened a reluctant Torey to the door.

Lord Diego was waiting for them at the archway by the great dining room. He wore his mischievous grin as he offered Torey his arm, with Lady Alejandra following behind them, as they walked into the dining room. He seated himself between Torey and Lady Alejandra. Lords Simon and Lawton were also at the long table, and Torey sighed with resignation as she realized they would also be there for the duration of the evening. Everyone ate and drank, and talked and laughed. There was a great, blazing fireplace in the common room of the castle, making it cozy. Musicians played well and lively in the great room, filling the place with merry tunes well suited for an evening of entertainment. Torey carefully glanced around making note of every room she was in, every archway, and at every door that led outside. Heavily armed guards were posted at every door. Lord Diego had many of his bodyguards dispersed throughout the castle, guarding every door, hallway, and exit. Even if she made her way outside, how far could she possibly get? And where would she go, back to the castle only to be beaten by King Alexander, and then returned to Lord Diego?

Lord Diego waited for a lull in the great dining room to signal that hunger for food had been appeased before other appetites became apparent. He clapped his hands. Everyone rose, with goblets in hand, and ambled leisurely toward the great room. Lord Diego hooked his arm in Torey's and escorted her. He had not been able to take his eyes off of her since she arrived. A very petite woman with a tray came by offering Torey more to drink. Lady Alejandra introduced her as Margarite. She was also a servant of Lord Diego. Torey gratefully accepted the drink, taking large gulps in an effort to reconcile herself to this new role. Torey noticed that Margarite kept a motherly eye on her, refilling her glass, and hovering close-by. This gave Torey a sense of kinship, softening the edge of her fear.

All the women there were dressed similarly to Torey; each outfit accentuating the wearer's best attributes, but above all creatures there, Lady Alejandra was the most exquisite. Her long, silky, black hair hung down to her waist and bounced like ripples across water when she walked. She had perfect creamy skin, high cheekbones and lovely dark almond-shaped eyes framed by arched eyebrows held in a question. Pretty, full lips that seemed to ask to be kissed framed her warm, contagious smile. She had full hips, a tiny waist and perfect, firm, round breasts creating contours that caused great appreciation of her symmetry. Torey could easily see why Lady Alejandra was Lord Diego's favorite.

Lord Diego spoke to Lady Alejandra again in Spanish. She rose from her place next to him, walked over to the harp, lifted the train of her lovely silk lingerie, seated herself, and began to play. Her fingers were long and graceful; she stroked the strings like a professional musician. The piece she played was so melancholy that it made Torey want to cry. Lady Alejandra glanced at Torey with a small smile and played a lighter tune. Lord Diego snapped his fingers for Lady Alejandra to rejoin him and Torey on the large couch. She took her place next to her lord, smiling at him. He kissed Lady Alejandra's lips lustfully, letting his lips slide down to her breasts, his hand wandering to the silky place between her thighs.

The musicians continued entertaining the guests. There was talking and laughter all around Torey as people enjoyed themselves, but she noticed that, gradually, the guests had begun to wander off to private chambers.

Lord Simon's eyes met Torey's as she gazed about the room; she immediately averted her gaze and looked instead at Lord Diego enjoying himself with Lady Alejandra. Simon crossed the room and came up behind Torey where she sat on the couch. Leaning over, he encircled her with his arms, kissing the side of her neck. He cupped both her breasts with his hands, twirling her nipples between his forefingers and thumb.

"I pray you, Sir, touch me not!" Torey recoiled, slapping his hands away, repulsed by his touch.

Lord Diego spoke sharply to Simon, heated words flared and volleyed between the two men. It ended when Lord Diego clapped his hands demandingly, and two women came over and each hooked an arm in Simon's arms. Simon hesitated for a moment, scowling, and then accepted Lord Diego's alternate choice. The three strolled from the room.

Torey had noticed a young boy at dinner, sitting next to Lawton, he and the boy were now seated by the fireplace. Lawton was feeding the boy sweetmeat, caressing the child in an intimate way. Lawton leaned close to the boy's face with a finger under the boy's chin, he tilted the boy's face up and kissed him lustfully, tenderly stroking the boy's face. Glancing back at Lord Diego with a bleary-eyed smile, he led the boy from the room.

Realization turned Torey's face crimson. Her heart ached for the boy, for she and the boy were walking the same thorny path in life. She wanted to murder Lawton, but was helpless to do anything.

Lady Alejandra had been watching Torey's expression and was afraid Lord Diego would notice her distress. She leaned over to Torey, with her hand on Lord Diego's knee, then she kissed Torey's mouth passionately, darting her tongue in and out, and then she giggled and played with Torey's hair. Torey looked into Lady Alejandra's eyes, even though Lady Alejandra was smiling, Torey saw pleading in them. Torey suddenly understood the meaning of Lady Alejandra's silent pleading and responded with a reluctant smile.

Lord Diego rose from the couch and led Torey and Lady Alejandra across the great room into the bed chamber in which Lady Alejandra had dressed Torey, and closed the door behind them. The fireplace was warm, casting a soft glow across the room, and taking the chill off the spring evening. Lord Diego spoke in Spanish to Lady Alejandra, and she pulled back the bed coverlet, fluffed the pillows, and laid across the bed. Lord Diego gripped Torey by her shoulders, turning her to face him. Again, Torey thought he wanted her to kiss him, so she tilted her face toward his. Instead, his grip on her shoulders pushed her forcefully down to her knees before him. He loosened the sash on the robe he wore and pushed it back, keeping it on his shoulders. He was quite nude beneath the robe. Realizing what he wanted her to do, Torey's head snapped up, and her defiant, "Nay!" punctuated the quiet before she realized she had spoken.

Lady Alejandra gasped, her hand covered her mouth. "Torey!" Lady Alejandra whispered her alarm and fear for Torey, trying to save her. The only other sound was the music as the musicians continued to play in the great room, their lively melody in odd contrast to the tension building in the bedchamber.

Lord Diego drew back his hand and backhanded Torey just hard enough to set her on her bottom on the skins that were spread on the stone floor, scolding her harshly in Spanish. Stunned, and tasting blood on the inside of her lip, she gathered herself back up onto her knees. Slowly, with loathing and resignation, Torey did his bidding. She was surprised when, after only a few moments, he pushed her back by her shoulders and drew her to her feet by her arms.

Torey tried to suppress a face of revulsion and wiped her mouth on the back of her silk glove. Lord Diego was, once again, in a jovial mood. He spoke to Lady Alejandra in Spanish. Lady Alejandra re-arranged the pillows on the bed, stacking them one atop the other, and patted the bed indicating to Torey that she was to climb onto the bed beside her.

Torey was filled with apprehension, but did as requested. Lord Diego, pleased with her apparent compliance, climbed onto the bed behind her, and grasped her firmly by her hips, positioning her face down, with her hips high across the pillows. He reached for a vial of rose water that was next to the candles on the bedside table, and slid the lacy silk down over Torey's hips. He poured the rose water in his chubby hands and caressed Torey's delicate womanhood, paying special attention to her forbidden, small, round orifice.

Torey was horrified when she realized where Lord Diego's hands were going, indicating what he intended to do. She dared not protest again, but instead beseeched Lady Alejandra with panicked, pleading eyes. Her knuckles were clenched white as she gripped the pillows, her terrified eyes told Lady Alejandra of her inexperience in such matters.

Lady Alejandra looked up into Lord Diego's eyes, she playfully licked her lips, and, in her sensual, exotic, Spanish way, spoke to him in a throaty voice. He paused, grinned like an adolescent boy, and pushed Torey off the pillows and waited for Lady Alejandra to position herself where Torey had been. While Lord Diego began to pleasure himself with Lady Alejandra, he spoke to her again in his native tongue. Lady Alejandra sought Torey's attention, making her watch as she stroked the side of her own breasts, then motioned for Torey to come close to her. Torey followed Lady Alejandra's lead, and, as they lay naked together, lovely and soft, they gave each other comfort with tender caresses and kisses.

Sympathy and comfort soon gave way to awakened desire as Lady Alejandra taught Torey the finer points of being a woman while Lord Diego watched. This pleased him greatly. Torey nearly melted with gratitude to Lady Alejandra for taking her place on the pillows, for that meant Lord Diego would not be hurting Torey this night.

Lord Diego heaved himself down on the bed, quite pleased with himself, and rang the chamber bell. Margarite, the servant woman, came into the room with a tray of sweetmeats and drinks. When he had quenched his thirst with deep gulps, he smiled his boyish smile, groaned loudly, and then quite soundly slapped both ladies across their backside. He spoke to Lady Alejandra in Spanish, and she smiled as though she had just received the highest praise. Still smiling, she took Torey's hand, and pressed gold coins into her palm.

"You have pleased my lord well this night. You will do even better next time!"

Torey's mouth dropped open in disbelief. Next time!? She thought she felt herself scream, but no sound was coming out! Her mouth was open, tears spilled down her face, her hands were clenched in white-knuckle fists, but no sound was coming out! Lord Diego and his lady only smiled back at her as though they were all having a grand time.

Torey realized the scream of livid protest had come from deep within - her soul had wailed against her bondage. But alas, a slave has no voice, only a spirit that cannot be fettered. The wail resonated and reverberated through the fibers of her being, her heart, her soul, her mind and spirit, igniting the rebellion of the exploited. A hot cauldron of rage simmered in Torey's gut, melting the icy dread that had, up to now, encased her heart.

She was consumed with loathing for King Alexander, Lord Diego, and Lord Simon for their exploitation of her. She had only to wait for the chance to escape.

The king's Women

Torey went about her duties at the castle, trying not to think about the events of the night before. She had been here for years, and up to now, life at the castle had not been bad. She had become part of the rhythm and routine of daily life in the castle with the other slaves and servant girls.

All of the king's servants went to the marketplace in the outer courtyard. The marketplace was wonderful. Pungent odors, sights, and sounds accosted the senses. Basket weavers, hemp workers, the metal smith and the clothier stood about hawking their wares. Fresh meat hung on hooks, chickens squawked and pecked the ground, sheep bleated, and goats in a pen were for sale. One could buy any food, apparel, or trinket one wanted.

Many of the merchants were women who lived throughout the local countryside and were permitted to bring their wares to town. In the course of the buying and selling, bartering and trading, friendships and loyalties also formed. Torey had befriended many of these merchants, they knew she was a captive servant and could not leave the castle, but friendships developed, nonetheless.

After that dark evening of having her status of concubine reduced to whore for Lord Diego, these ladies who smiled warmly as they spoke with her, occasionally touching her arm or hand reassuringly while making a point about this or that, were balm for her injured soul on this bright, sunny day that felt so gray and chilly to her.

There were two particular women who were warmer and more talkative to Torey than any of the other merchants, and showed her more compassion than any of the others; they were Leigh Thompson and Teresa Miller. The women were neighbors from the countryside. Leigh's husband, Daniel, ran a tavern, and Teresa's man, Matthew, owned a small farm, and a mill. They were Torey's strongest friends outside the castle. These warm encouragements gave Torey the determination she needed on this day to keep going.

Torey had just finished hoeing vegetables in the royal garden, and was carrying a large basket filled with potatoes, beans, and tomatoes. As she headed for the pantry in the kitchen, King Alexander himself blocked the doorway and prevented her from passing through.

"Come with me, Torey. We must talk." King Alexander, accompanied by two guards, led Torey to his chambers. Torey's heart sank, but she held her chin high, fighting the fear that clawed up her spine, threatening to betray her. Once inside the king's chambers, with the guards outside the door, King Alexander waited until she was kneeling before him, then he began. "Lord Diego tells me that you entertained him well last night. For this I am well pleased." For just a moment the king's eyes wandered to Torey's full breasts and small waist.

Torey had heard the gossip in the castle. The Spaniards were fascinated with her. Like their women, she was beautiful and petite, with satiny skin that was pleasurable to the touch, but they had never seen a woman with red hair and green eyes, and such creamy pale skin. King Alexander was pleased that he had a slave that the foreign emissary so ardently wanted to possess.

"As you know, the Spanish emissary has accompanied the merchants and wares across the seas to trade with us. The goods and political exchange are vital to the kingdom. I have granted them accommodations in the royal guest quarters." He hesitated a moment before going on. "I have given you to Lord Diego while he is here. You are to move into the chambers that are next to his entourage, and you are to do whatever he bids you. But you are not to leave with him and his company. You are still my property, and this has been made clear to him. If he makes his departure from my kingdom with anything that is not his, my archers will pierce him through." The king concluded his directives. "Do we understand each other, Torey?"

Torey curtsied lowly before him.

"Aye, milord," she replied, hardly above a whisper, having great difficulty getting the words past the lump of disbelief in her throat.

"Very well then, your king is well pleased," he said, approvingly. He took a deep breath. Moments passed. Torey could feel his eyes on her.

"Rise." King Alexander's voice was muted, but held the hard edge of steel. This was not a request.

"Milord?" Torey nearly blurted out, WHAT? But knew that would displease him.

"Rise," he said again, the hard edge of steel threatening her. He pulled her up to her feet to stand before him, leaning his head against her thigh. He breathed in the earthy smell of the dirt from the garden, the pungence of her sweat, and the light fragrance of soap from her freshly washed hair. His senses came alive; his blood pumped faster, his pulse raced. The conqueror within him stirred. He felt mean, and the need to dominate overcame him. He reached down and slipped her sandals from her feet, then slid his hands underneath her skirts, hooking his fingers on her undergarments, caressing her thighs and shapely calves as he slid her pantaloons down.

King Alexander leaned back with his foot extended, indicating that she was to pull off his boots. He stood and hastily climbed out of his trousers. Facing Torey, he slid his hands under her skirts, grabbing her bare backside, crushing her to him, kissing her hard. She cried out, his forceful embrace taking her down. Torey knew resisting the king's advances was out of the question, that she must submit to him as she had so many times before. A small whimper of protest escaped her lips. The king, mistaking her anguished whimper for pleasure, became even more aggressive.

She closed her eyes and visualized the tavern Leigh had told her about. Torey was there now, with Leigh, Teresa, and Anne the dancer, enjoying ale, and flirting with men of her choosing. She promised herself not to notice while the king took her.

Torey could hear the door close behind King Alexander as he was leaving, and the thud of his boots on the stone corridor floor as he and his guards made their way down the long hallway. She pressed the clean cloth that she had retrieved from a nearby drawer between her thighs to her flower. Rolling over on her side, her tears trickled down the bridge of her nose, unchecked.

There was a gentle knock at the door. Torey startled, jumped up, and hurriedly searched for her undergarments. With her heart pounding with apprehension, she hoped the king had not returned for another round.

Thankfully, it was Anne at the door, she opened it just a crack, "I beg to enter." She called out timidly. Torey nearly collapsed with relief, opening the door just enough to pull Anne in, and then fell into her arms, sobbing.

Anne was a dancer, she was not one of the king's slaves or servants so she could come and go as she pleased. Anne owned a small farm in the countryside with a vegetable garden, chickens, goats, and cows. She danced for the king and the royal court when the king entertained, and she also danced at a local countryside tavern. It paid well and helped her maintain her independence, entertaining men on her own terms. She had become fast friends with Torey during their haggling over goods in the courtyard.

"Ah, now, lass, cry not, you know how he is. He didn't hurt you, did he? The king is not known for hurting the wenches he dallies with."

"Nay," Torey sniffled and dabbed her tear-stained face "I wish I were just a wench he dallied with. Tis bad enough I live in fear of Simon the Blackguard. The ladies in the court whisper about him, it seems he has a cruel streak. He has been in pursuit of me since King Alexander claimed me. I've always feared him, and now I've made an enemy of him because I would not submit to him last night, and the king has given me to Lord Diego, for a time." Torey's voice was calm even though tears ran down her cheeks in rivulets.

"Anne, do you know what that means?" Torey sniffled.

Anne knew. Lord Diego knew, too. Torey was at his mercy.

"How long, my friend?" Anne took care to keep her concern for her friend from her voice so as not to alarm her.

Torey wailed, "Until Lord Diego is finished trading with King Alexander's merchants, and finishes the business at court. Who knows how long that will take, maybe all summer." "I am fearful, Anne. I fear Lord Diego, and even more so, I fear Lord Simon."

"Ah, lass, sorry I am for you." Anne held Torey until her friend's tears subsided.

Night of Pain

Several weeks had passed since that terrible night when Torey had been whisked away to the castle that King Alexander had so graciously offered Lord Diego for the duration of his visit. Lord Diego was sure King Alexander did not know the nature of the dinner parties that were being held in his royal highness' country home. Lord Diego was also sure King Alexander wouldn't care enough to stop him, especially since the "entertainment" was not mistreated. He also never kept the women long enough for them to be missed. The women were, under threat of death, never to speak of their clandestine evenings.

The only one whose heart was wounded by this most unexpected change in rank from concubine to whore was Torey. The other servants and slave girls considered themselves fortunate to have won the favor of a wealthy and powerful lord who rewarded them so handsomely for their favors. They even scolded Torey and tried to shame her for not being grateful to Lord Diego and for not submitting to him completely, as he wished. They complained that Torey angered Lord Diego, and that he became disagreeable, moody, and more difficult to please. They implored Torey to swallow her pride and bow to him, but Torey would not.

King Alexander owned her, and took her for his pleasure whenever he wanted, and he loaned her to others, but he could not dominate her spirit. She was determined that he would not overwhelm her courage.

Torey had been summoned to the castle many times since that first terrible night. She had continued to be blatantly rebellious to Lord Diego, even as he forced her to her knees, grabbing a fistful of her red hair and making her kneel, naked, before him. He became very agitated when her stubborn resolution to oppose him drove him to use persistence and aggression to force her into the submission he desired of her. They both knew it was a battle of wills. She had taken the sting of his backhand across her delicate cheekbones many times.

Once the appetites of the guests had been appeased, the musicians were instructed to play seductive music, and the attentions of the guests were now turned to assuage other, baser appetites. Lord Diego's favorite initial gesture, indicating that playtime had begun, was to order Torey on all fours before him, like a dog. He would bend over her and pull her head straight back by a fistful of her red hair, pulling it so hard tears stung her eyes. He usually came away with strands of red hair caught around his pudgy fingers. With his other hand, he smacked Torey's backside with such force that her body jerked with each blow. It gave him great pleasure to see her flinch when she knew the next smack was coming.

When Lord Diego went into a rage and punished Torey, Lady Alejandra would coo to her during the punishment, stroke her face, and gently kiss her lips and stroke her breasts to soothe her. Torey knew Lady Alley, as Torey now called her, was only doing those things to help her get through these nights.

Torey had been summoned to the castle many times, but this time was different. Something wasn't right. Stephen, the castle's domestic overseer, always came to her to tell her that her presence would be required at the castle.

Torey loved Stephen because he was sweet, sincere, and tried his best to protect the women in the castle. She loved him for the same reason all the women in the castle loved him, his ardor for his wife and baby daughter never wandered and never wavered. Every woman in the castle dreamed of having a man like that for her own. When word came to Torey that she was going to be summoned to the castle, she could not find Stephen to confirm the message. Lord Diego's messenger stood, impatiently waiting for her decision.

"What say you, wench?" he growled, raising his hand palm up. His impatient gesture urged Torey to reply, and implied that she was no one important he need waste time on. Torey knew she must not decline. With a reluctant shrug of her shoulders, she dropped her head and nodded her consent without meeting the messenger's eyes. If she declined, she would be severely punished. She could take Lord Diego's backhanding her, and his other cruelties, but she doubted she would still be standing if her back were being striped by his whip. Torey felt dismayed at the gooseflesh that crept up her spine. The hairs on her arms and the back of her neck stood up, as she watched the messenger take his leave to carry her answer to Lord Diego.

Torey didn't recognize the guards who escorted her to the waiting carriage that evening. They avoided eye contact and carried themselves in a furtive, cautious fashion, their eyes darting about as though they expected to be attacked by the king's army at any moment. When Torey tried to make light conversation with them, they looked at each other and then at her and said it would be better if she kept quiet. It caught Torey by alarming surprise to realize that their manner was suspicious and guilty, not authoritative and confident, as had been the demeanor of the guards every time before as they carried out Lord Diego's orders to escort her.

They gave her a hand assisting her into the lofty carriage. As soon as the wooden carriage door slammed shut behind her, the horses were off at such a fast trot that Torey yelped as she was thrown back against the seat. Even the nighttime sky loomed ominous and foreboding with the moon hiding behind the cloud cover and no stars to be seen. The inky blackness of the night matched the dread that hovered over Torey's heart as she peered out the window. Apprehension gnawed at her stomach.

Soon she could feel the carriage slow and then stop as they arrived at the castle. The wooden door was thrown open and an unfamiliar hand was extended out to her to assist her descent. She accepted it as a matter of course and, flanked by the two guards, was soon knocking on the door of King Alexander's summer home.

Torey gasped in shock when the large double doors swung open and Simon the Blackguard himself stood before her.

"Good evening, Torey." He bowed sarcastically in mock admiration. With an evil grin he looked into her eyes, delighted at her fear and shock, and attempted to kiss the back of her hand. He smelled strongly of wine and sweat, and he resembled a vulture to her. She tried to snatch her hand away, but he grabbed her arm and pulled her inside. The guards stayed outside and posted themselves at the door.

Torey looked past Simon as he gripped her arm. Only the fireplace in the main hall was lit. There were no delicious smells or laughter coming from the kitchen or dining hall. Lady Alejandra was nowhere to be seen. There were no serving women and no musicians, only a few other women that Torey recognized as prostitutes who were often chased away from the royal market in the outer courtyard of the castle. Several of Simon's men were there.

"What is the meaning of this?" Torey demanded, with her hands on her hips, enraged.

"Torey, my dear Torey. You look so lovely tonight. I have delightful plans for you." He placed his hand on her back and crushed her to him. "You're going to be a good little slave girl and do whatever I tell you. Do you think anyone would notice or even care if one little slave girl went missing? Hmmm? I'm giving you a chance to make it up to me for all the times you snubbed me and wouldn't look my way. You think you're too good for me? Ah, my little whore, you will pay for shaming me in front of my men and Lord Diego. You - a lowly slave," he laughed and corrected himself, "no - a lowly whore, humiliated me. I think you need a lesson, Torey, on how to please your masters."

"By order of King Alexander, I was paid for my services to Lord Diego - I am not a whore, you vile bastard!" Torey defiantly corrected him.

Simon laughed, sincerely amused that semantics mattered to Torey.

"You will not think yourself so clever," he growled, wrenching her arm behind her, and kissing her mouth hard, "when I am done with you." Apprehension washed over her like a cold, ominous wave.

"Take her into the bed chamber and dress her for me," he instructed two of the other women. "You go with them and guard her," he pointed to one of his men, "but you are not to have her - yet." The man nodded and shoved Torey ahead of him.

Torey was taken into the bedchamber where she had been many times before. Hostile female hands practically ripped her clothes off and snatched her around, dressing her in the delicate lace that Simon had brought for her. She was escorted back into the main room and seated on the same large couch where she sat that first night when she rejected Simon's aggressive advances.

"Ah, my little whore," Simon circled the couch, slowly, taking her in with his eyes, until he was behind her like he was that night weeks before. He leaned over her until his chin rested on the top of her head. He gripped her arms with his hands, immobilizing her, placing his mouth next to her ear, and whispered obscene things to her. She tried to turn her head away from the vile, whispering lips.

"Beg me, Torey," his whispering voice was vicious in her ear, "Beg me to take you." He slid one hand up to grasp her throat. When she struggled, he clamped her windpipe harder. He slid his other hand down inside the front of her panties, down, until he was cupping her flower, sliding his middle finger inside her womanhood. The men chuckled, finding the entertainment quite amusing.

Torey screamed, "NAY!" Kicking her legs up and twisting her hips from side to side, she tried to wrench his finger from within her. She struggled to fight the fear that clawed at her stomach when she heard his deep, threatening laughter in her ear.

"Think you not, for a moment, my little whore, that I will not choke the life from you on this very couch if you continue to fight me." His ominous warning fell heavily on her spirit, like manacles on a slave, his whispered threat hot on her neck. He felt her shudder with terror and disgust, and he laughed.

Torey strained against his grip and whimpered, but fought back her tears.

Simon's men formed a circle around Torey and slowly closed it.

Torey screamed for Danu, her goddess mother. To Torey's unbelievable horror, nothing happened; there were no bright lights, no shapeshifting into a fox, no prisms. Nothing. All her senses turned cold with panic, "Mother Danu, where are you? I need you!" Torey screamed in terror in her abandonment from the floor where Simon had dragged her, as aggressive male hands held her down, and tore the delicate lace from her body.

The men had their way with Torey until her senses reeled and she slid in and out of blackness.

"Beg me, Torey!" Simon demanded in his lustful madness. "Beg me to take you, or my men and I will take you until you breathe your last." He clamped his hand down on her throat. Her eyes went wide as she struggled for air, her hand went to his around her throat, and struggled hard, trying to pull his hand away. He ground his manhood deeper within her flower until he moaned uncontrollably as he reached the apex of his storm. His spent body pulsated as he clutched her beneath him until his satiated limbs gave way. Simon the Brute pushed her away from him, kicking her, causing her to double in pain, naked and bruised, on the floor.

"That's for not begging me, your master, to take you," he panted venomously.

"You are not my master." Torey hurt all over and her breath was short, but she managed to breathe the words to him through gritted teeth in barely a whisper. By the look on his face, she knew he had heard her.

Torey then bore the stripes from Simon's whip. It was almost worth it to her, knowing how much she must have infuriated him.

Her flesh was wounded and bleeding, but he had not broken her spirit.

The Nurturing Healer

Torey's body hurt with every to and 'fro motion of the carriage's mad dash as it careened back toward the castle. The horses' driving hooves churned the dirt road, leaving a ribbon of deep shadow striped with sand-colored dirt, shimmering eerily in the pale moonlight.

She could not hold her eyes open to stave off the throbbing blackness that lurked behind her bruised, swollen eyes like a menacing bird of prey, circling, closer, and still closer, wanting to envelop her, to swallow her whole. The cruel jostling of the carriage-turned-wild-animal seemed hell-bent on dismembering her beaten and bruised limbs with its invisible gnashing teeth.

As she moaned with the intense physical pain of her broken body, and listened to her angry, ravaged spirit beseech Danu for the brutal theft of her dignity and humanity, the bird of prey mercifully carried her into the blackness.

After what seemed an eternity, the carriage came to a halt. The wooden door was thrown open and a hand was hastily extended to her, but as much as Torey wanted to flee from her captors, she could not compel her limbs to move. Big, meaty hands attached to great, muscular arms reached in and forcefully pulled her from the carriage. The guard threw her over his shoulder like a small sack of potatoes. Though Torey grunted in pain, the guard only marched onward. He eventually stopped at the door of her apartments; opened the door, carried her in, and after depositing her on her bed, turned, and left the room.

The sun had not yet risen, so she had been returned to her rooms unseen. King Alexander would certainly not be looking for her.

Torey rolled over on the bed, wrapped her arms around her stomach, curled her legs up under her, and wept. She shook uncontrollably, her face contorted into inexplicable expressions as her soul and body cried out in anguish against the injustice that had been done to her this night. She didn't think the little girl within would ever heal again.

Torey startled at a noise she heard coming from a dark corner of the room.

"Who goes there?" Torey leaned up on one elbow, and fearfully inquired into the darkness.

"It is I, Lady Alejandra." The lady stepped out of the shadows as she whispered her reply. "I was frantic with worry when I couldn't find you at dinner, and no one, not the guards, or the sentries, or the other servants or slaves, had seen you all night. I was afraid of what might have happened to you. I can see that my worst fears have been realized."

Torey fell back on the bed and moaned softly. Lady Alejandra came over to her.

"My beautiful lady, what have they done to you?" Lady Alejandra lay down beside Torey and stroked her hair. "My pretty little girl, my poor, pretty little girl. I made you a warm bath, and I brought you bread and meat and wine. Come, my poor little girl, come to the bath and I will bathe you and feed you, and dress you in a clean, comfortable sleep shirt."

Torey wrapped her arms around Lady Alejandra and clung to her as the beautiful mistress-turned-healer carried Torey over to the wooden tub and let her down, gently, into the warm, fragrant waters. She laid Torey's head back against the top of the tub and lifted her long red hair over the top so it draped over the side. Lady Alejandra dipped a washcloth into the water and slowly washed Torey's bruised face. She dripped warm drops of water on Torey's swollen lips, and down her bare breasts. She planted gentle, loving kisses on Torey's forehead, the tip of her nose, and her cheeks.

Lady Alejandra's anger burned as she watched the bath water turn red with Torey's blood. She gently held a cup of wine to Torey's swollen lips. The wine contained a mixture of healing and sleep herbs to ease Torey's pain and lull her into a deep, healing sleep. She lovingly washed the petite, dejected young woman, squeezing warm rivulets of fragrant water on her from the washcloth until she saw the furrowed lines of pain and grief ease from Torey's brow. She carefully lifted Torey from the water, wrapped a blanket around her, and carried her to the bed and gently laid her across it.

Lady Alejandra lay down next to Torey, smoothed her red hair away from her face, brushed her tears away, and held her, as the bird of prey, holding true to its threat, mercifully swallowed Torey into the depths of its blackness.

LADY ALEJANDRA COMFORTS TOREY

O ays passed as Torey healed under Lady Alejandra's vigilant care. Unbeknownst to Lord Diego, Lady Alejandra visited the local healers and herb shops to gather the best herbs and potions for healing that the lord's money could buy. Lady Alejandra resolutely vowed to herself that she would nurse Torey back to health, and then plead with his lordship to put Simon to death to avenge Torey's terrible mistreatment.

Lady Alejandra bought poultices to soothe Torey's angry purple bruises, ointment to rub on injuries yet oozing, and catgut to sew the cut above Torey's eye, the one on her mouth, and the gash on her thigh. She mixed the proper leaves in hot water to make tea that soothed Torey's injured body and her defiled spirit.

The tea also helped Torey sleep a dreamless, restful sleep, lest her rest be haunted by nightmares of cruel ghosts from that night. Lady Alejandra rubbed lavender in Torey's lovely red hair until she earned a small smile from the crestfallen girl.

"Are you feeling better, milady?"

Torey's eyes had just fluttered open from a long night of restful slumber. She sleepily gazed up into Lady Alejandra's eyes and smiled, suddenly realizing how very comforting it felt to have Lady Alejandra's arms around her, holding her close. Lady Alejandra kissed the top of Torey's nose, encouraging her to respond. Torey's smile faded as the memory of the desecration she had suffered flashed like a lightning bolt through her mind. A tear slid down her cheek.

"It is I who should be calling you milady. I might have died had you not..." Torey's voice trailed off, as the painful, ugly scenes jolted through her mind. She caught her breath, making her broken ribs stab her like small, sharp knives, causing her to catch her breath again. Lady Alejandra gently held her close and shushed her.

"Little lady, while you were in your fevered sleep I heard you cry out to your mother, the great goddess, Queen Danu. I am sure there must be a reason she could not deliver you in your moment of need. No mother would willingly abandon so precious a child." Lady Alley smiled and gently stroked Torey's cheek and brushed her tears away. "Little lady, I have something else to tell you." Lady Alejandra spoke in her not-so-broken adopted tongue. She was loath to tell Torey of Lord Diego's decision.

"I pleaded with Lord Diego as I promised milady I would." Lady Alejandra continued, "Torey. My lady," this time the honorable title was spoken in a voice laden with sincerity, pain, and sorrow. "I laid bare my body and my soul to him, I wooed him, I soothed him, I pleased him, I begged him." Lady Alejandra stopped, fought back her own hot, angry tears, and mustered the courage to go on, and then blurted out the words, "But he would not honor my request. He said I am his slave already, I have nothing he doesn't already own. He said he cannot execute Simon because Simon belongs to King Alexander. He will not go to King Alexander and plead for a slave." Lady Alejandra struggled to get her own hurt emotions under control.

She thought she was Lord Diego's lady. He himself had given her the title and took her everywhere with him, even to the chagrin of his wife. She enjoyed privileges the other mistresses and concubines did not. He had given her expensive clothes and jewels and lavished her with his attention. She had become over-confident and had forgotten her place, and he had reminded her of it, breaking her heart and causing her shame as word got around to the other mistresses and concubines.

Lady Alejandra rushed on in an effort to allay the sting of Torey's disappointment.

"Torey, I have been praying to your goddess Mother, Queen Danu, on your behalf, and she has answered me. She is angered because Lord Diego will not avenge you. You must forgive the goddess and have faith in her, for she will reveal her reasons to you in due time."

At that Torey gave Lady Alejandra a weak hug. A tiny spark of hope ignited against the heavy gloom of despondency that hung like a thick fog in Torey's heart.

A Promise
for Torey

From the depth of Torey's healing slumber in Lady Alejandra's arms, Torey heard Mother Danu calling to her. She felt herself rise and sit up on the side of the bed. She looked down at her sleeping form, considering it for a moment.

"Torey, my precious daughter," she heard her goddess mother and was drawn to the window. The moonlight shone very brightly this night. Torey gazed intently at the edge of the forest, barely making out a luminescent glow from deep within the forest.

"Come to me, my darling," came the sweet, gentle voice again. Torey quietly slipped into the hall and out into the courtyard. She headed down the courtyard path between rows of fragrant gardenia and rose bushes that were so intoxicating that she was tempted to tarry there. The sound of wings whooshing in the air froze Torey in her tracks. She hunched down in protective instinct, throwing her arms up to shield her eyes. She scanned the night sky and saw a figure flying toward her. As recognition dawned on her, she straightened up and stared hard into the moonlit night. "Sparkle!" Torey called out.

"Nay, it is I, Ember. Sparkle is with the goddess mother. Sparkle and Ember belonged to a people called Prisms who were created by the goddess to lend beauty and grace to the world of gods and magic.

"I have been sent by the goddess mother to give you the gift of flight and guide you through the time passage to Tir-na-nog where the goddess Mother Danu awaits you." Sparkle spun faster and faster, high in the air, over Torey, covering her with a luminous dust. She took Torey by the hand. Together they took flight and breezed their way into the forest and high up into the mountains. Finally, they came to a wooden door in the side of the mountain. Ember spoke in Prism, the door creaked open, and they stepped through a time portal, entering Queen Danu's sidhe, which is a mound or hill in which fairies live, on the Isle of Tir-na-nog. It was breathtaking. All around them there were lush fruit trees, vegetable gardens, and flower and herb gardens. A light breeze greeted them carrying with it the delicious smell of baking bread.

Torey could hear her goddess Mother Danu in an argumentative exchange with Dian. Danu and Dian sat together at the Pool of Immortals, obviously disagreeing about something. Upon walking to the edge of the gardens of Danu's home, Torey harrumphed to get her mother's attention.

Danu was delighted to see her daughter, and had a plan for making amends with her angry woman-child. "Come, my darling, come! Sit with your negligent mother." Patting the seat next to her, Danu spoke lovingly and apologetically, penitently emphasizing the word negligent, all the while glaring at Dian.

When Danu offered her cheek for Torey to kiss, Torey gave her a cold, perfunctory peck.

"Yes, you are negligent!" Torey accused peevishly, still being mindful to whom she was speaking.

Danu tried fussing with a strand of Torey's hair that had fallen out of place, fawning over her, but Torey would have none of it and pulled away and withdrew in her hurt and anger.

"Those men nearly killed me, Mother! Where were you? Why didn't you allow me to shapeshift or send Sparkle to turn them into ash?" Tears filled her eyes, but her anger kept them from spilling over.

"Torey, my darling, if your wish to shapeshift into the fox had been granted, Simon would have put you in a cage that was bound by a spell, forever trapping you as a fox. That Simon, such a nasty fellow." Danu fussed with her elegant robes while she spoke to keep herself from stroking Torey's hair. She knew Torey was angry and would have none of the goddess' fawning at the moment. "Had Sparkle turned them to ash, Lord Diego and King Alexander would have sent their assassins after you, further complicating things. But if you think Simon will go unpunished, my darling, then, you have much to learn about the lioness within your goddess Mother. Dian has assured me that he has the situation in hand," she cast him a glaring sidelong glance and rolled her eyes, "and that you shall have your revenge."

Torey was so pleased to hear this that she threw her arms around her goddess Mother and kissed her whole face until Danu was laughing for her to stop. Then she bowed before Dian and kissed his hand. He cupped her face and gently kissed her brow.

"Go back now, Torey, with Ember. Finish healing and know that I am watching over you with Danu. Be patient. Soon you will have your vengeance." He tapped Torey's nose in a fatherly manner, and gave her a comforting wink of sure intent. Dian, assuming his noble station, offered Torey his cheek for her to kiss in farewell.

Ember took Torey by the hand and soon they were gliding over the tops of the trees back toward the castle. Ember delivered Torey to the open window, pressing her finger to her lips, indicating quiet, and took flight from the window into the night sky, turning briefly to wave farewell to Torey. Torey walked soundlessly across the stone floor and climbed into bed, her spirit lying back down into her sleeping form.

The Potion of Vengeance

Lady Alejandra stood nervously in the witch's house, waiting for her to finish mixing up the potion. The strange little house was set far off from the main road among heavy dense forest and weeping willow trees with large, gnarled branches and roots twisting up from the ground, curving protectively toward the house much as the old witch's gnarled, aged hands were now curved around the hissing, foaming potion.

It had taken Lady Alejandra nearly a half-day of travel to reach the little house. Keena, the old witch, muttered to herself in rhyming singsong fashion using words only she herself could understand. She looked ominous as she stood before the oil lamp, the light filtering through her thin, straw-like hair, throwing spider-web like shadows on the walls. Keena suddenly stopped muttering and turned around, focusing her attention on Lady Alejandra.

"Mix this potion," she instructed in a raspy voice, "in the gentleman's tea or ale in the blackness of night after the moon has risen. The magic of the spell will be done by dawn." Keena held her hand out for payment before handing the glass vial to Lady Alejandra. The Lady dropped a gold piece in the witch's outstretched hand, bringing a snarly smile to the old witch's lips, and then she handed the vial to Lady Alejandra.

"Remember," the sage icon of spells warned, "not before sundown, or it renders the magic impotent."

Lady Alejandra nodded and had to exert control over her legs so as not to be rude and run from the witch's house.

Lady Alejandra Teaches Torey

Torey answered the knock at her chamber door and was rewarded with relief from her worry to find Alley standing there. She threw her arms around her, kicking the door shut with her foot, for there were guards, soldiers, and servants walking about in the great hall outside the door.

"Where have you been all day?" She asked. "I have been so worried about you!"

Alley smiled and hugged her back.

"I have some dinner for you, come to the table." Torey said as she took Lady Alejandra's riding hat and cloak and laid them across the dressing chest. The two women seated themselves at Torey's small wooden table. Torey heaped both their plates with mutton, chicken, and bread. Alley noticed that there were beans and apples from the castle garden.

"Torey, I told you to stay hidden in your chambers until I returned," Alley said gently, not wanting to wound Torey with too strong an admonition. She had to suppress a small smile of approval as she watched Torey stuff her mouth with a chunk of bread and tear off a piece of chicken. "Word will get around that you are healed now," said the Lady with concern that bordered on alarm.

Torey glanced up, chewing on a mouth full of chicken, holding an apple in one hand, and a chunk of bread in the other.

"I was hungry and I wanted to hear the gossip going on in the castle." Torey hesitated and added haltingly, "Simon is asking for me. The scullery servants made excuses for me today, but how long will that work?" Torey's eyes were wide in near panic at the thought of being alone with him again.

"I will take care of it, Torey," Lady Alejandra looked imploringly into Torey's eyes as she placed her hand on her shoulder. "You must trust me!" Torey reluctantly nodded.

"You've been to see the witch in the wood, haven't you?" Torey asked quietly, but she already knew the answer. Alley nodded with a small, grim smile and finished the remnants of food on her plate. Both women sat back, sipping their wine.

"I beg you, Alley, don't get yourself beheaded or banished because of me." Torey pleaded anxiously.

Lady Alejandra laid a reassuring hand on Torey's knee.

"It is by the hand of your goddess Mother Danu and Dian, the great physician. This night I shall answer Simon's call and serve his evening meal and wine." A grim, determined smile curved the corners of the Lady's mouth.

Torey hugged her in thanks for the risk she knew the Lady was taking on her behalf, even though she didn't know exactly what it was.

Lady Alejandra looked deeply into Torey's eyes and gently stroked her face. "Milady," cautiously, she posed her question, "have you ever melted under a man's touch, and felt your passion burn from within you, and longed for him to take you?"

Torey dropped her eyes and leaned her head to one side, almost imperceptibly shaking her head.

"Oh, milady," Alley murmured softly and compassionately, "Being with a man is not what it has always been like for you." The Lady spoke tenderly. "In Spain, my mother always said 'passionate spirit of young woman needs to spread wings and fly, but not always know how.' Your passion burns, Torey, like magnificent horse with bad master." Desperately wanting to show Torey the delight and wonder of the fettered desire that the Lady knew simmered within her friend, she added in an urgent whisper, "I am good teacher for you, Torey, I am woman, like you. Men do not understand body of woman."

Torey turned her face away and withdrew from her friend's out-stretched hand.

Undaunted, the Lady rose, "I will prepare a bath to soothe you and keep you company before I serve Simon, yes?" Torey brightened at the idea.

Soon the wooden tub in Torey's apartment was filled with steamy fragrant water. Torey insisted that Alley join her. Even though both women were very petite, there wasn't much room, so Alley sat behind Torey, wrapping her beautiful shapely legs around Torey's middle. She mixed crushed lavender in the suds she had made in her hand with the soap and washed Torey's back. Torey arched her back first this way, then that, enjoying the back washing and encouraging Alley not to miss any spots. Torey melted against her, resting the back of her head against the Lady's bosom.

Torey laid her arms atop Alley's arms and wrapped them around her small waist in a hug. "I thank you, Lady Alley, for being an ever-present friend." Torey turned her head slightly so she could look up into Lady Alley's eyes.

Alley saw the love and gratitude in Torey's eyes, and squeezed her tight. She gently kissed the side of Torey's face and neck and nuzzled her, much as she had done when they had entertained Lord Diego, but this time it was in heartfelt compassion that her friend's sexuality was always shrouded in shame. It was time to awaken Torey to her own loveliness and passion.

The sensation delighted Torey. Her pulse quickened. Alley traced Torey's ear with her tongue and playfully sucked her ear lobe, tugging at it with her teeth. Torey giggled. Alley cupped Torey's bosom, slowly and seductively moving her thumbs in circular motions over the tips of their peaks, and squeezed and caressed the round fullness of Torey's lovely breasts. She caressed Torey's bosom, stomach, and inner thighs with the lavender scent, and kissed her neck, telling her all the while how beautiful she was and how silky soft her skin felt. Torey's legs relaxed, the sides of her knees resting on the sides of the tub. Torey slid her tongue into Alley's warm mouth and kissed her deeply and longingly. She slowly guided Alley's hands down to her flower.

Alley's hands hesitated, "Milady, my lovely lady, I long to do your bidding, but only if it is your wish." The intimate plea was spoken in a voice husky and tender, washing over Torey in a compelling torrent of passion and healing emotion.

Torey had said those words so many times to her many masters, that she had never realized how much she needed to hear them herself. She had said them from her knees, prostrate, kneeling partially clothed or stripped naked before whichever king owned her, or whichever nobleman had summoned her. She had said those words in the night, at dawn, in the middle of the day, in private chambers, and at the throne.

Torey turned her face so she could return Alley's hot kisses, her tongue exploring Lady Alley's warm inviting mouth. The Lady's delicate tapered fingers found Torey's flower, but instead of sliding her fingers deeply between the petals, she gently and insistently probed the engorged strawberry shape protruding just now from the top of Torey's petals. She delighted herself by caressing Torey's firm, full bosom, and stroking her satiny skin, then slowly back to Torey's swollen petals. Lady Alley's fingers became very busy very quickly, taking Torey's breath away.

Torey gasped for breath at the exquisite delight she had just experienced and started giggling. "That was wonderful!" Lady Alley started giggling, too. Torey hugged the Lady's arms tight, turning her head and gently kissing her, conveying to her understanding and mutual appreciation of their shared intimacy.

The Lady smiled into Torey's eyes and stroked her face, her smile affirming the lesson.

Torey realized that she was shivering now as the water had grown cold, she stood up and reached for towels, handing one to Alley, and wrapping herself in one.

Suddenly, both women were rudely startled out of their very pleasant repose, their attention riveted by a firm knock at the door.

The Reckoning

The knock at the door confirmed Torey's worst fear: it was Simon's messenger. Lady Alejandra went to the door and greeted the messenger in Torey's stead. Simon had sent his messenger to summon Torey to serve him his evening meal and wine in his private chamber. Alley convinced the messenger that Lord Diego had issued an order that Torey be given ample time to heal and that she would serve Simon in Torey's stead. The messenger had been reluctant to carry this message back to Simon, but didn't wish to bring a whipping down on his head for questioning Lord Diego's favorite. To further persuade the fearful messenger, Lady Alejandra pressed a gold coin in his palm, and sent him on his way.

Torey suddenly couldn't bear the thought of Alley going in her stead or leaving her alone in her apartments. What if something went wrong? She would never forgive herself if anything happened to her friend because of her.

Alley read Torey's fearful face and touched her hand to Torey's arm in reassurance.

"Who am I, Torey?"

"You are Lady Alejandra." Torey replied, unsure of why the question had been posed.

"I am the Lord Diego's favorite. If ever there was a time to capitalize on that title, it is now."

Lady Alejandra crossed the room to a dresser and opened a small drawer, withdrawing from it a glass vial, which she slipped deep between her bosoms.

Even though the hour was late, the Lady dressed herself carefully, adorning her hair, arranging her beautiful black tresses and her skirts attractively. She wanted Simon's eyes to be drawn to her, arrested and distracted by her beauty so he would not pay attention to what she was doing. Torey watched Alley's every move, her eyes still wide with fear for her friend. She had never seen the Lady dress and prepare herself with such purpose.

Swallowing back her own fear, Lady Alejandra said matter-of-factly, "Mother Danu goes with me this night, Torey. I do her bidding." She better be with me this night, Alley thought to herself, or it could very well be my last.

With that, she slipped out the door, waiting a moment to listen to make sure Torey latched it behind her.

The Lost Jewels

Blood-curdling screams shattered the serenity of the new day's dawn. Hurried footsteps and the clatter of armor could be heard in the hall outside Torey's apartments. Torey threw back her blankets and started to rise from her bed to see what all the commotion was about when Lady Alejandra's frown told her to wait without uttering a word. Torey didn't remember falling asleep, so frightened was she for her friend. Torey squeezed Alley's hand to express her relief that she had returned from the evening's activities unharmed. The castle's alarm was sounding, booming voices were giving orders, and soldiers tromped through the hall in great haste. Whatever was going on certainly had the castle in an uproar.

The minutes crawled by as Torey and Lady Alley listened a long while until at last the melee of activity died down. In their fright following the screams, they clung together, staring at each other and then at the door, wondering if they should get up and try to find out what had happened. What did you do? Torey wanted to ask as she stared into Alley's eyes.

Hunger soon pressed them both with the need to get up; they certainly couldn't hide in fright in Torey's apartments forever. Alley pressed a finger to her lips to signal quiet; they rose, dressed, and prepared a simple breakfast.

After eating, Alley went to the door and cautiously opened it a crack, peering down the hall, first one way, then the other. There were no more guards or soldiers in the hall except the usual sentries. The alarming activity seemed to have settled down into the every day rhythm of mundane tasks being done and people going about their daily business. Lady Alley took Torey by the hand, and she and Torey slipped out the door; they took the long way least traveled, down a flight of stairs and around the back of the castle to the kitchen.

There were several servants in the kitchen going about their duties when Torey and Lady Alejandra came through the door.

"It's good to see you up and feeling better, lass," said one of the servants to Torey. All the servants exchanged furtive glances, for word had gotten around as to why Torey had not been able to attend to her duties. Not all of them liked her because she was spirited and beautiful. She aroused their envy, but they would not have wished ill fate upon her, either.

"Did you hear what happened?" another one asked, "Did you hear what happened to that ol' pompous Simon," she asked again, gloating. Before anyone could ask what happened, she went on. "Seems ol' Simon awoke at dawn, he did." The servant could not hold back her amusement, and she started giggling as she told the story, "with his whore in the bed with 'im when his manly urgin's stirred," more laughter, "there weren't enough there to do the job, there weren't." By now she was guffawing. "His whore went to laughin' hysterically, she did, and 'im screamin', he was! The 'larm was sounded and soldiers come runnin'. When they got there, there was Simon, butt naked, screamin' in his bed, lookin' down at his withered manhood with his whore pointin' and laughin'. Now Simon is the butt o' all the jokes ot the court, he is, and all the fine noble ladies that simpered after 'im are laughin' at 'im." The scullery maid guffawed anew at her own joke, and then, straightening herself up she said, "'Ol Simon is na' so pompous, now!"

Torey gave Lady Alley a small knowing smile as all the servants in the kitchen agreed.

A Dangerous Enemy

J ames stood at rigid attention by the heavy chamber door, in full guard's uniform, eyes forward, weapon at the ready. He cautiously stole a glance now and then at the enraged captain who paced before the fireplace, and occasionally responded with an "Aye, Captain" to Simon's rantings.

James was Simon's personal guard and had witnessed many of Simon's rages, and the ensuing violence visited upon the perceived perpetrator, but none of his rages had been like this. Even James dared not try to calm his lord. He most especially dared not chuckle, even though he wanted to. He dearly wished he were the guard on the other side of the chamber door. He had to force himself not to think of the scene that he and the other guards had been summoned to when the alarm was sounded, but he couldn't help himself.

Never had anything so bizarre and so fitting beset the proud and intimidating Simon. The ladies of the court who had simpered after him were snickering behind his back and avoiding him. He was the laughing stock of all his men and the nobles in the castle. Even King Alexander had accused him of being a poor sport. A poor sport! Simon's face had gone purplish-red with rage at the jesting that even King Alexander suffered him. When Simon reached for his sword in the Great Hall at dinner, the king's guards rushed forward, and the Great Hall had grown ominously quiet as everyone waited for Simon's next move. The Captain had enough wits about him, even in his rage, to recall that his mother had been banished to the Underworld for the mistake she made in losing control of herself. He would not make that error in judgment. Nay, he needed time to think and cool off. He had tried to laugh it off, snorted in derision, and stormed out.

James tried to ignore the pleading in the eyes of the poor lass that Simon had ordered brought to him. Frankly, James couldn't see the point of Simon having ordered a wench. She whimpered and her eyes pleaded to be allowed to take her leave. James frowned and tried to shake his head "nay" to her. He tried to warn her with his eyes to be quiet, for her whining only angered Simon more.

Simon continued to pace and rant, while James continued to steal glances from the corner of his eye. James watched while the muscles in Simon's jaw hardened in his anger, his eyes were wild and had a far-away look in them.

"I will find a way to restore my seed," Simon vowed, "even if I have to visit my mother's old arch enemy." Simon's lean, muscular frame was taut with rage, the hardened sinew in the enormous arms flexed each time he brought the riding crop down across his own open palm. Simon seemed unaware that his hand was purpling under the relentless crop while his mind raced.

The sound of laughter and music wafted across the courtyard to Simon's ears. James rolled his eyes, of all times to hold a ball, he thought to himself. There was a grand ball being held this night and Simon, in his condition, dared not attend. Knowing that there was gay celebration going on in the Great Hall attended by luscious ladies that had once simpered after him, that the best wine flowed, and there was cash to be gained from the gambling tables only agitated him more; he struck his riding crop across his open palm again.

The wench, cowering on the bed, screamed in frightened surprise as the crop cracked across Simon's palm, and she began to weep in her fright.

"That redheaded whore, who does she think she is!" he ranted and paced, striking first the table that held the burning candles, and then the bedpost. The cruel sound of the riding crop terrified the wench and she wailed in her fright. Her frightened wailing drew Simon's focused attention to her, and he raged, "Shut up, you stupid whore!" Simon brought the riding crop down hard across her shoulders and commenced to beat her with it.

"Who does that whore think she is!" Simon again demanded wildly as he flailed the little wench. Simon was not seeing this wench, but another, in his mind's eye. He ripped open her corset and laid bare her creamy breasts and slender back. Seeing her naked loveliness only enraged him more. The poor girl screamed and rolled off the bed and crawled across the stone floor to escape the lashing as she begged for mercy.

James could contain himself no longer. He threw himself on Simon, wresting the riding crop from his grasp. "Captain, cease from this violence, I beg you!" He implored. James looked at the wench as he held Simon fast, quickly tossed the coverlet that had been neatly folded at the foot of the bed to her so that she could cover her nakedness and said, "Be gone with you, and speak of this to no one!"

"Unhand me, knave!" Simon gruffed as he elbowed James off of him. Simon cared not as the wench made a swift and terrified getaway.

"Be at peace, Captain, I beg you."

"I cannot be at peace in this degradation and humiliation that I suffer at the hands of that worthless whore who thinks overmuch of herself. And neither shall she have any peace, James, I swear it."

Hell Hath No Fury

"You summoned me, my lord?" Lady Alejandra asked, hoping her fear would not betray her voice. She knelt before Lord Diego's throne, her forehead pressed against the backs of her hands on the stone floor. At least he could not see the fear in her eyes.

"Aye, milady Alejandra," he let out a deep sigh; his tone was filled with passionate resignation.

What? She thought to herself as her brows knit together. She was completely baffled by his intimate address of her.

He rose from his throne, clasped his hands behind him, stepped down in front of her, and began to pace. She realized he was troubled, so she waited patiently for him to speak.

"Our negotiations with King Alexander, his lords, and his knights are not going as well as expected. The king invited the Trio of Kings from the north to join in the negotiations without consulting with the Spanish Tribunal. King Francis, King Serrell, and King John II are arguing with each other and with King Alexander about the pricing of the goods, and the taxes, and how the profit should be divided up. There is heated disagreement about the pricing of goods and exorbitant import-export taxation. I fear the Trio of Kings may seize our ships and goods and take what they want. King Alexander will not sit still for such an affront. I fear there may be war."

"My lord, you summoned me to give me a report on the negotiations?" The Lady sat erect, as she remained kneeling before him. She folded her hands in her lap and looked up at him. She was still hurt and angry.

Lord Diego stood before her and put his hands on his hips and considered her. He rubbed his hand over his chin and then scratched his bald spot. At that moment he reminded her of a confused, but sincere little boy, caught with his hand in the cookie jar, unable to understand why he couldn't have the delicious cookies. He let out a deep sigh and sank down upon his throne.

"Nay, I did not." There was a pause. The Lady waited for him to continue.

"While I am concerned about the possibility of war on foreign ground, this concern has only hastened my decision for our departure."

Lady Alejandra's eyes widened in surprise, "We are leaving? We are returning to Spain?"

"Aye," he replied, searching her face for her reaction.

Lady Alejandra's brows knit together, her face took on a troubled expression, reflecting her thoughts. Her eyes searched the room as though the words she needed would suddenly appear on the wall.

"Nay, my lord!" she declared, fearfully but angrily.

He became agitated and sat erect on his throne. "I am your Master, you will do as I say!" He demanded.

"Nay, my lord, I will not!" Upon realizing that she had told her master nay again when he was already annoyed, the Lady turned her face away to avoid the anticipated rebuke. After a moment, when it didn't come, she looked up at him. He just sat there, looking dejected.

"Milady," he asked gently but urgently. "What are you saying?"

"I want to stay! You can sell me or offer me to King Alexander!" She said anxiously. Then she stated in a quiet, desperate voice, "Torey needs me." She broke their intense gaze, dropping her eyes to the floor so he could not see the hurt he had caused. "And she is never unkind."

"Aw, milady," Lord Diego drawled gently, trying to sound persuasive. "I am well aware of what you wanted and I know how you feel. You know I could not put to death a subject of King Alexander's kingdom!"

"You could have asked King Alexander for justice!" Lady Alejandra insisted, her mouth firmly pursed and her eyes fierce with anger. She didn't realize that her hands were on her hips, which looked decidedly comical in contrast to the rest of her, which was still in the subservient kneeling position. But then, this was a lover's quarrel.

"To plead on behalf of a servant?" he asked incredulously.

"Nay, milord! To plead on behalf of my dear friend!" she began to cry.

He grabbed the sides of his head in exasperation.

"By the gods, woman! Be reasonable!" and then, in a placating attempt to reason with her, he added, "A man of my position does not plead for a servant."

"Then, I will not go with you." The Lady stated quietly and stubbornly. As far as she was concerned, the matter was settled.

"My beloved, angry lady, King Alexander wanted me to put YOU to death for compromising his soldier. A soldier is the property of the king. Compromising the king's property is an indirect intent to harm the king, which is treason."

Lady Alejandra's eyes widened with fearful surprise at this bit of news. She opened her mouth to speak, but before she could utter any words, Lord Diego rushed to speak first.

"I told him I would not sentence nor even punish my woman, my Lady."

Lady Alejandra looked at him in astonishment. He'd risen from his throne and was now standing before her.

"King Alexander demanded two of my male servants as recompense for Simon, in exchange for your death sentence. They will live out their lives as his slaves. I have already signed them over to him. Preparations are being made for our departure. You must return home with me, Lady Alejandra." He smiled down at her, lifting her chin to look into her eyes, and emphasizing the title he had given her that elevated her above his other concubines. "You are the Lord Diego's Lady."

She brought his hand to her lips, kissing it. He pulled her up to him, off of her knees, cupped her face and kissed her mouth ardently and passionately.

"Simon is said to have sworn vengeance on whoever did that to him. He knows it had to be you and Torey. He knows magic was involved. I can whisk you back to Spain, to safety, but I cannot protect Torey, and King Alexander will not. Do what you wish to help Torey."

At this, Lady Alejandra smiled and returned his passionate caresses. He picked her up and cradled her in his arms. As he laid her across his bed and began to disrobe, he smiled wistfully, "Ah, poor Simon, he should not have been such a pompous ass. It is most unfortunate for him to learn in this way that, slave or not, hell hath no fury like a woman's wrath."

Escape

orey awoke to the sounds of utter chaos. The day had not quite dawned, the alarm had sounded, and there were pounding footsteps of soldiers running in full armor in the hall. She could hear the clang of weapons and the rattle of chain mail. Captains were yelling orders. The castle had experienced alarms before, but this was different. The entire castle was being called to alarm to set emergency defenses. That could only mean one thing. The castle was under siege. Those pesky Kings, Torey thought to herself, why couldn't they learn to get along?

She had to find Alley. She knew the Lady had been summoned to Lord Diego's chambers the evening before, but nothing else. Torey sprang out of bed and dashed to the door to answer the urgent knocking. She had no sooner cracked the door open than Lady Alejandra burst in with two big, well-armed guards. Torey gave the guards a questioning look. Alley pointed a thumb over her shoulder and explained, "they're for my protection! Torey, the castle is under siege; you must make your escape before Simon comes looking for you! King Alexander will not miss you!"

The Lady had brought a traveling bag to give to Torey, and she began stuffing Torey's things in it. She shoved Torey towards the dressing chest. "Put the riding clothes on I gave you, make haste, and catch your hair back in a ribbon."

Torey glared at the two guards. They turned their backs so she could change her clothes while Alley flew around the room gathering only the most important of Torey's things.

They lit candles to light their path down the long, dark hallways. Alley grabbed Torey's hand. They raced with the guards, out the door, down the hall and down the flight of stairs at the back of the castle where the servants' quarters led to the kitchen. The passageway was dark; in their haste they had to take care not to extinguish their candles. Lady Alejandra led them out the kitchen door, and into the courtyard that led to the royal gardens. Beyond the garden towered a high stone wall that surrounded the entire castle. A sentry walked the top of it, and another guarded the door that led out to the guard's station. On the other side of that station was an outer door that opened to the road, and the city lay just beyond.

"I will distract the sentry on the wall, Torey."

Alley handed Torey two small packages that she had been holding under her cloak. One held gold and silver, the other held food.

"Offer the door sentry a gold piece to let you through while I'm busy with the wall sentry. If he tries to detain you, use your powers of persuasion. My guard will be watching. If the sentry blocks your flight, my guard will kill him."

Could this really be happening? Torey felt as though she were watching someone else escape from the castle during a siege.

"There will be a horse, saddled, with a water skin, ready to go. Ride to the country, Torey, past King Alexander's country home, ride through the valley of mountain passes and through the forest to the village where the peasant women live who come to the market in the castle courtyard. They will take you in. Torey, you have enough gold and silver to last a long time if you are careful." Lady Alejandra pressed the bags into Torey's hands, holding her hands for a moment.

Torey tucked the coin purse and bag of food into the inside pockets of her cloak, and then threw her arms around Alley in despair.

"Come with me, Alley, please!" Torey pleaded. Her heart was breaking at the thought of saying farewell to her dearest friend.

Lady Alejandra shook her head sadly, her eyes blurring with tears. "My place is with the Lord Diego, Torey." The Lady extended her hand to Torey, showing off the most beautiful emerald and diamond ring Torey had ever seen.

"He has made it official," she said with beaming eyes, but a weak smile, a little afraid of Torey's reaction. "I am Number One Favorite, and soon to be Number Two Wife."

Even though Torey hated his Lordship, she knew her friend must make her own choices, and it was obvious that Alley was thrilled with this unexpected turn of events. Torey nodded her understanding and bowed to Lady Alejandra in congratulations, kissing her hand.

"Forgive me, milady, but I shall despise him for all time."

The Lady pressed Torey's hand to her cheek in understanding and compassion.

"We are sailing for our homeland, for Spain; we have been granted amnesty and an unmolested departure by the warring kings in exchange for all of our trading goods. I must hurry, for the ships are being readied for our departure."

She buttoned Torey's cloak and pulled the hood over her mane of red hair. "Now flee. My guard will hide here and watch. I will go up and distract the sentry on the wall."

Torey hugged Lady Alejandra tightly to her and fought back the hot tears that stung the back of her eyes. Now was not the time to grieve, there would be time enough for that later. Now they needed to survive.

"Run not, Torey; try not to seem alarmed."

Torey nodded her understanding, turned, and started out across the courtyard in a purposeful, but not frightened, gait. She bit her lower lip as she made a concerted effort not to let her quaking legs break into a dead run.

If they were to successfully distract both sentries at the same time, she must not make it to the sentry on the ground before Alley made it to the sentry on the wall. Torey glanced up. Alley was almost there. She watched as the sentry put his arms around Lady Alejandra and led her inside the sentry station on the wall.

"Who goes there?" The ground sentry was eyeing Torey suspiciously. She smiled politely, as she knew would be expected of a servant.

"I must travel to the city today to do King Alexander's bidding," she declared, thrusting her chin forward trying to make herself sound more convincing. Torey had seen him once or twice around the castle, but King Alexander had many soldiers, guards, and sentries, and she didn't know them all. He didn't recognize her, which was all the better. She held a gold coin tightly in her hand.

"Where are your orders?" The sentry demanded.

"I wasn't given any written orders." Torey hesitated; she hadn't expected to be questioned.

"All persons on official business for the king must have written orders with the king's seal, or they may not pass." He stated, quite resolutely.

Torey fought the panic threatening the pit of her stomach.

"Maybe this will help." She pressed the gold coin into the sentry's outstretched hand. He jammed the coin into a coin purse tied to his waist by a leather strap and looked into her face. He cupped the side of her face with an open hand, stroking her cheek with his stubby, fat thumb. Torey's eyes dropped and she reddened under his scrutiny.

"I think this will help, too." He slid his arm around Torey's waist, crushed her to him and kissed her mouth hard, leaving no question as to what he thought would help.

Torey tried to pull away, "I haven't much time; if I don't return soon King Alexander will send someone for me."

"Then I'd better be quick about it." He said, leering as he pulled her into the sentry station.

While Torey fumbled to set her undergarments to rights, the sentry opened the door that led to the dusty road for her. He kissed her, swatted her bottom, and pushed her through the door, closing it behind her. She heard the great latch on the heavy wooden door slide through and lock into place.

For the first time since childhood, she faced her life unfettered by the rule of king, lord, or nobleman. The magnitude of what that meant had not dawned on her yet; her only thought at the moment was to escape.

She mounted the horse that Alley had promised would be tethered there, dug her heels hard into the horse's sides and galloped away from the castle toward the countryside, praying to her goddess mother that Alley got away safely too.

Torey could not see that another lone rider also fled the castle.

DANIEL'S TAVERN

Lady Alejandra's words rang in Torey's ears, 'don't run, Torey, try not to seem alarmed,' as she slowed the horse's frantic gallop to a trot. The castle was so far behind her now that she could no longer see it when she looked back. The horse whinnied its appreciation of the less arduous pace.

"I don't even know your name," Torey said to the horse as she patted its neck, "but you certainly are handsome."

The horse snorted and nodded its head, as though agreeing with the compliment.

The stallion was a deep, rich chestnut flecked with black throughout its lustrous coat. It had a bright reddish-brown patch on its left hind quarter that Torey had noticed when she had so hurriedly swung her leg over the saddle. She thought this was one of Lady Alejandra's personal horses, probably a gift from Lord Diego. The animal had been well cared for. Now it was Torey's.

"I will call you Patch," she said to the horse.

Patch once again enthusiastically snorted his agreement, tossing his head and shaking his beautiful deep brown mane as if telling Torey she had correctly guessed his name.

Now that the urgent need to flee the castle and its dangers had subsided, Torey felt a strange sense of excitement and exhilaration. It was still early morning, and a long road lay ahead of her. She wasn't even sure how far away from the castle Leigh, Teresa, and Anne lived, but she knew from past conversations that it was several hours' ride by wagon.

She had never been allowed to leave the castle, or to go riding in the country with Lady Alejandra. Slaves and servants were not allowed to come and go as they pleased. Even though Torey could not come and go at will, she had often helped the stable hands curry and exercise King Alexander's prized horses, so she knew how to ride. At least that was not one of the problems she had to worry about right now.

She had a general idea of where she was going and who she was to look for, but what would she do once she got there? Torey smiled to herself when she realized what she would NOT have to do. Suddenly she was aware of how bright and sunny this new day was, how cheerful the chirping of the birds flying overhead sounded on this early morn, how majestic the trees seemed, and how luscious and green the world around her looked as she rocked rhythmically in the saddle with Patch's powerful strides.

She felt confident that Leigh, Teresa, and Anne would help her figure it out. For now, she just needed to get there.

After riding along for some time without seeing any other travelers, Torey caught her breath with alarm at the sound of men and horses approaching from a distance up ahead. Pulling back on the reins, her eyes darted from one side of the road to the other while she quickly tried to decide what to do. Patch, seeming to sense his petite rider's alarm, made the decision for her, turning off the road to the right, and trotting into the trees until they were well off the road and out of sight. Patch's rich brown and black-flecked coat blended into the woods like camouflage.

Torey quickly dismounted, covered her red hair with her cloak, and stood behind Patch, holding her breath and listening. She could hear the riders passing at a leisurely pace. Torey judged, by their conversation, that they were soldiers from another province. They were bragging about their last battle, the blood they had drawn, the booty they had won, and the women they had taken. Torey imagined that the soldiers' stories of their conquests would grow at the retelling of them by twilight of this day when they stopped for lodging and the ale began to flow. She shuddered at the thought.

As the men's voices grew distant down the dusty road, the sound of splashing water caught her attention. She walked Patch to a stream that was a short distance down a slope from where she had been hiding. The water felt good on her face as she splashed it on herself.

With a firm, powerful nudge, the stallion nearly pushed her into the stream.

"I am so sorry, my friend," Torey said apologetically, "how thoughtless of me, you're thirsty, too." She took the bit out of the horse's mouth to allow him to drink more easily, and retrieved a snack for him from the bag Lady Alejandra had prepared for her.

Sadness suddenly clutched at her heart as she handled the bag that, only hours before, Alley had thrust into her hands. She leaned against the saddle and briefly closed her eyes. I'm not going to be sad, she told herself, I'm going to forever remember my friend and all her kindnesses to me. At that, Torey brightened and took some bread, carrots, and dried fruit out of the bag, fed Patch some treats, and sat down on a large rock next to the stream and ate. She could not know that Queen Danu lovingly gazed upon her through the Pool of Mortals, and guided her path. It was calming to watch Patch graze. He looked up at her now and then with his large, soft, brown eyes, like a friend would over a mug of ale.

When she was finished, she replaced the leather bridle for Patch and hugged his muzzle, stroking the soft, dark brown nose. He whinnied gently and nudged her as though returning the hug. Torey pulled herself up by the pommel of the saddle and swung her leg over.

"I think we'd better stay off the main road but keep it in sight until we get to the valley on the other side of this wood, Patch," Torey said to the horse.

He snorted his agreement as he swung his head around and gazed up at her reassuringly with his large, soft brown eyes.

In some places it was difficult to navigate the woods alongside the road, but Torey felt it was safer, even though it was slower. She was in no hurry as long as she reached the village in the country before dark.

The sun was high in the sky now and it was very warm. Torey could feel droplets of sweat run down the back of her neck and between her breasts, but at least they were traveling at a pace that was comfortable for Patch. She had taken off the cloak and laid it across the saddle in front of her to give herself some relief from the midday heat. The terrain had begun to change so she knew she was getting closer. The forest was less dense, the brush was greener, and the few travelers she heard on the road appeared to be simple country folk going about their business, so she decided to take to the road again. Even though it was dreadfully hot she again donned her cloak, taking care to cover her red hair so as not to draw attention to herself.

After riding for several more hours, she began to see a house here and there with smoke coming from the chimneys, as well as country folk tending their gardens, working in the fields next to the houses, or driving their wagons on the road.

The tavern that Leigh and Daniel ran could not be far away. When she made the next bend in the road, she saw an unassuming, sturdy looking two-story building made from stone and wood. As she drew closer she could see a heavy wooden door, which, at the moment, was nearly closed. Above the door hung a sign that said, simply, 'Daniel's Tavern'. Torey drew a deep breath of both relief and apprehension. After all, no one knew she was coming.

Torey decided to go around to the back. A wagon was hitched there, and a young boy and his father were preparing to leave. The man was scolding the child, yanking on his ear and slapping him. Torey's temper flared. She heard the man scold the boy for dropping eggs on the ground, and how they lost the profit for those eggs because of him. The child began to cry. From atop her horse, Torey grabbed the man's wrist, as he was about to box the child's ears again. Without saying a word, she shook her head emphatically. She accomplished her intended purpose, for when she let go of his wrist, he gently lifted the boy into the wagon, glancing furtively back at Torey.

When the man finally pulled his wagon away from the back of the tavern, Torey dismounted, only to find that she was confronted by an indignant, bossy goose. The goose gave her a terrible startle, charging at her heels, honking and flapping her wings, and making quite a fuss stirring up the dust. Torey danced about to avoid the nipping beak, flailing her arms and hollering, "shoo, shoo, goose, leave me be."

Seeing his mistress alarmed, Patch drew back his lips over his long teeth and bawled his disapproval of the goose's bad manners, and stamped his hooves at the feathered creature.

When the goose finally decided Torey was not a threat, she wagged her tail like a school teacher shaking a finger at an errant student, scolded Torey once more, and waddled off to her sentry duty.

Torey caught her breath as she stood with her hand over her pounding heart, gathered her courage, threw her shoulders back, and knocked on the door.

"Hell's bells, no need to knock, just come on in," called a brassy female voice from within.

The door stood slightly ajar. Torey pushed it open, and timidly stepped inside, her hand still on the handle as though undecided whether she was going in or staying outside.

A very tall, slender man wearing a white apron stood behind the bar stacking freshly washed mugs. A short, pretty blonde woman Torey knew to be Leigh was sweeping the floor. Both of them stopped what they were doing when they realized it was she. Leigh dropped her broom, and it landed with a thud on the wood floor. Leigh and the tall, slender man exchanged glances and then looked at Torey. They both knew something formidable must have happened for Torey to be standing at their door.

Torey was put off by their obvious surprise, and felt unwelcome.

"I should not have come here," she said to their shocked silence.

"Nay, silly child, come in, come in," Leigh insisted, quickly recovering and taking Torey into her arms. "I'm happy for you that you're away from that terrible place." She waved a hand at the aproned man behind the bar. "This is my brother, Gregg."

Torey grinned and slid her cloak off, freeing her thick mane of red hair. Gregg was unusually tall with a lean but muscular frame. He was handsome with an outdoor ruggedness that was very appealing, and his manner was confident and disarming. His intimidating height was topped with a head full of curly red hair like Torey's. He had sharp, gray-green honest-looking eyes.

He grinned back at her. "Aye, pretty little lady," he said, as he took her in.

Torey blushed.

Leigh looked from Torey to Gregg and back again. "Now that's sump-thin', it 'tis! The two of you look more like brother and sister than we do!"

Torey wrinkled one side of her nose, gave Leigh a quizzical, comical look that asked, "how did that happen?" and playfully tugged at the woman's long, blonde hair.

Catching on to Torey's amused curiosity, Leigh rolled her eyes, smiled, and shrugged. "We never asked our mum." Both women smiled at the resemblance that Gregg and Torey shared.

Now that the introductions had been made, Leigh took a more serious tone. "Are you alright, lass?" Her concern was sincere. Leigh had heard bits and pieces about life in the castle when she had come to the market place in the outer courtyard. She knew it had not been easy for Torey, but she had no idea just how difficult it had been. Leigh ushered Torey over to sit down at one of the tables.

"Would you like some ale?" Leigh asked as she waved a hand at Gregg who brought over three mugs of ale before Torey could answer.

It was late afternoon now, and she was grateful to have a rest and something to drink. Torey told them about the siege and how Lady Alejandra had helped her escape, being careful to leave out the humiliating details about King Alexander, his noblemen, Lord Simon, and Lord Diego's "festivities."

Leigh and Gregg sat open-mouthed and sympathetic. Torey finished by saying she had a few coins and would work at whatever they wanted her to do if Leigh would let her stay.

"I can't make any promises, Child. My man, Daniel, is on the road for a few days to get supplies for the tavern. I will talk to him when he comes home, but I must tell you, I don't want any trouble from King Alexander's soldiers." Leigh was trying hard to be reassuring without giving Torey false hope or empty promises.

Gregg interjected without taking his eyes off of Torey. "I'll protect her." He grinned at their fair, red-haired guest. "I could use the help with the chores, the customers, and the cooking."

Torey blushed again. "I was a servant at the castle, and I worked very hard. I am willing to work hard to earn my keep." She looked pleadingly at Leigh. Gregg copied, and then exaggerated, Torey's expression of pleading, sticking out his lower lip to make a piteous pout-face at Leigh.

"Alright, alright, you two, but we still have to talk to Daniel," said Leigh, rolling her eyes and conceding to the two of them.

Torey hugged Leigh so hard her chair nearly toppled over.

"Yes, but everyone knows who the real boss is." Gregg gave Leigh an affectionate nudge and a knowing wink. "Come with me, Torey, we'll stable and water your horse, and then I'll show you around the place." Gregg took the three empty mugs and placed them on the bar, and grabbed an apron for Torey and motioned for her to follow him.

As Gregg led Torey outside to show her their chickens, livestock, and the vegetable garden, she smiled up at him. He was more than a full foot-and-a-half taller than she, with freckles across his nose, and the most mischievous gray-green eyes she had ever seen.

"Did you really mean what you said about protecting me?" she asked timidly. "And where did you get that red hair?" she added with an amused grin.

He tousled hers with one of his big hands. "I might ask you the same!" he answered with a wondering smile.

TOREY MEETS GERTIE

As Gregg and Torey approached the barn and the pens where the animals were kept, the testy goose once again assailed her as though she had been hiding behind the side of the barn just waiting for Torey to pass by. Torey was so startled she nearly climbed up Gregg's lean, muscular frame. He laughed so hard he almost dropped her on the ground into the animal droppings. "I'm not a tree!" he managed to say.

"I'm so sorry! And I'm so embarrassed. That's the second time that nasty goose has scolded me! I'm afraid she really doesn't like me at all." Torey exclaimed, as she gathered her composure.

"I think it's just a misunderstanding," said Gregg good-naturedly, reaching into his pocket. "Here," he said, reaching for Torey's hand, "you need to be properly introduced with a little bribery." He placed some grain and clover in Torey's palm. Kneeling down on the ground with his open hand outstretched, he called to the goose. "Come here, Gertie, there's someone I want you to meet, but you have to be nice."

The goose quickly waddled over to Gregg, and began nibbling the succulent leaves of clover from his palm. Gregg took Torey's wrist and slowly placed her hand on his, palm up, so that the goose was eating from her hand instead of his. "Gertie, this is Torey, she lives here now, you'll be seeing her every day, and if you're nice to her, she'll give you treats, too." He glanced at Torey. "Talk to her, Torey, say her name, tell her she's a good girl for guarding the barnyard so well."

Torey smiled, I guess if I can talk to a horse, I can talk to a goose, she thought to herself. She crooned to the goose for several minutes while the feathered creature finished the bits of grain and clover from the palm of her hand. Satisfied that Torey had paid her proper respects and was now considered 'family', Gertie honked her thanks for the treats and waddled away, back to her guard duty.

"Why does Leigh have a goose?" Torey asked as they walked into the barn.

"Believe it or not, Gertie is a great watch dog and gardener. We can hear her honk from upstairs if something upsets her, and she eats the weeds from the garden without disturbing the vegetables. As if that weren't enough reason to have her around, she mothers all the other animals, like a mother hen," Gregg said with a smile.

Gertie had followed them into the barn and was standing with one webbed foot on one of Gregg's massive boots, looking up at him and making goose sounds as though she were agreeing with every word he said about her. He leaned down and stroked her neck; she leaned into it like a puppy getting its ear scratched.

"Gertie has green eyes! I've never seen an animal with green eyes!" Torey exclaimed in surprise. Gertie preened and primped herself, obviously enjoying all the attention. Torey laughed, "If I didn't know better I'd say you were being very prissy for a sassy little goose." She stroked Gertie's neck.

"Well, I'd say the introduction went very well." Gregg was encouraged. "Every morning and afternoon when you come out to tend to the chores, give Gertie a treat and talk to her and you will be surprised at how faithful a friend she can be."

Gertie followed the two around close on their heels as though she were being shown around too, stopping just for a moment to scold the pigs and chatter with the chickens.

As Torey listened to Gregg's instructions, she couldn't help but notice just how lean and muscular he was and how very handsome, but there was also something vaguely familiar about him.

Gregg found Torey to be the most ravishing redhead he'd ever seen. He wanted to hold her close, and protect her. But he felt conflicted, for he also found her strangely familiar. But how could that be? They had never met.

CHORES AT THE TAVERN

It didn't take long for Torey to win the admiration and affection of Leigh and her brother Gregg. By dawn of each new day Torey had gathered the eggs, milked the cow, and started breakfast.

Gertie met Torey in the barnyard every morning, waited patiently for her treats, and waddled in front of Torey, looking back to make sure she was close behind. If the chickens pecked at Torey's hands when she took the eggs from the straw nests, Gertie scolded them. If the pigs rushed the gate of their pen and frightened Torey, as they seemed to enjoy doing, Gertie gave them a good talking to, as well, flapping her wings and kicking up the dirt just to let them know she really meant business.

"Aww, now, they're not so bad, Gertie, I'm getting used to them." Torey smiled as she talked to her feathered friend.

As Torey perched on the wooden stool to milk the cow, Gertie paced back and forth, crooning, fussing, and conversing with the large four-legged creature. Whatever the content of the conversation, it always seemed to have a calming effect on the cow and made the task of milking easier.

Gertie was Torey's constant companion as she went about her chores, waddling alongside her, honking and talking to her. Torey found herself looking forward to the company of her feathered friend as she went about her work.

By the end of the first week she had learned how to make bread, which was no easy task, laboring with the dough, kneading it, and then baking it in the huge wood-burning stove in the cookhouse behind the tavern.

Torey stripped the beds of their soiled sheets in each of the guest rooms of the tavern. After carrying them in a woven basket to the washing well behind the tavern, she slapped the soap-lathered linen against the rocks until her arms ached, getting them clean and ridding them of the musty smell, and the bedbugs. Next, she twisted and wrung the sheets and hoisted them upon a line to dry in the sun, with Gertie alongside, honking her approval.

The chore that impressed Leigh and Gregg the most, though, was when Torey emptied and cleaned the chamber pots in each of the rooms, including Daniel and Leigh's and Gregg's rooms. That was a foul job no one liked, some people didn't do it when it was needed, and fewer still voluntarily did it. Even Gertie kept her distance, craning her neck and turning her beak away until Torey finished.

"I'll bet if you had hands, you'd be holding your nose right about now." Torey said ruefully to her down-covered friend.

By midday Torey was famished. Basking in the warm sun with a full stomach, the barnyard animals napped this time of day. Gertie was no exception, tucking her webbed feet under her and settling herself comfortably in the fresh straw Torey had lain down for her in her square wood box bed next to the barn. Her large, green eyes drooped, but the vigilant goose managed to keep watch on any goings-on.

Torey headed for the back steps to the kitchen to check on the stew that was simmering on their wood-burning stove. She was just spooning up stew for the midday meal when Gregg came in, drawn by the enticing aroma of stew and biscuits.

"You know if you keep working this hard, you'll work yourself into an early grave and we won't have to ask Daniel if you can stay." Gregg joked with Torey, but she caught his concern.

Leigh nodded her agreement and added with gentle concern, "You're not a servant here, Lass."

Torey's back ached, but she smiled at Leigh as she sat down to join them at the table. "Aye, it's certainly a different and wonderful feeling."

"Besides, we need you rested for tonight." Gregg said with a mischievous smile. "The end of the week is always a big night at the tavern. People come from all over to lift a mug of ale, have a bite to eat, tap their feet to the music of the lute and the tambour, and make merry with the ladies." Gregg winked at Torey.

Torey wasn't sure what Gregg meant by that, but rather than risk alienating herself and maybe finding herself on the streets at the mercy of marauding soldiers, she just smiled and ate her stew, telling herself she would find out soon enough.

With a glint in his eyes, Gregg told Torey about the musicians that frequently came to the tavern. They played their flutes and tabors for a meal, tips, and a room for the night.

Regulars, soldiers, farmers, and travelers came to the tavern on these Saturday nights to raise a mug or two of ale, get a bite to eat, enjoy the music, try to persuade the ladies to a dance, and more, if the gents were lucky. Gregg obviously enjoyed the festivities even though he still had to work serving ale.

Torey rose to clear the dishes when the front door burst open. A travel-weary man laden with packages trudged in. Leigh screamed, making Torey jump and reach for a kitchen knife, only to see Leigh throw herself into the bedraggled man's arms, sending packages tumbling to the wood floor.

"Daniel, you're home! I was going to send Gregg after 'ya, truly worried for your safety, I was!" Leigh smothered him in hugs and kisses, and, judging by Daniel's reaction, the feeling was mutual. "What took you so long?" Leigh wanted to know.

Gregg and Daniel clapped each other on the back in their mutual joy that Daniel was home and safe. It was obvious the two men got along well.

"And you," said Daniel with a warm smile, emphasizing 'you', "must be Torey." She smiled and blushed, so taken by surprise that she could only nod in acknowledgment.

Leigh motioned to Torey, just as she had to Gregg when Torey had arrived, indicating that a round of ale was needed. Torey immediately filled mugs while everyone settled themselves at a table to talk. She plunked down four full mugs of ale, and set a heaping bowl of steaming stew in front of Daniel, followed by a large basket of freshly baked bread.

Daniel drank deeply from his mug of ale. "Aah," his baritone voice rumbled from deep within his chest, "'tis good, lass, and 'tis good to be home." He dipped a chunk of bread deep in the stew and hungrily popped it in his mouth. He leaned his head back and closed his eyes, savoring the flavorful stew, the dark, strong ale, and the familiar feel of the wood bench beneath him.

Swallowing the last tasty bite and licking his lips, he opened his eyes as if coming back to the present moment. He smiled as he studied them for a moment, relieved beyond words to be home. Then his gaze settled on Torey.

"I ran into a bit of trouble, I did." He said, finally, his studied gaze still resting on Torey, who suddenly felt nervous and a little scared.

"Let's hear it, then, my lord," said Leigh anxiously.

His gaze shifted to Leigh. "The trading went well, and I got supplies for the tavern that will help us through the winter. I got candles, grain, and linens, among other things." Then he smiled at her, "I also got lavender for your bath, bar soap, bonnets, and cloth."

Leigh squealed and hugged him. "But what of the trouble, my love?" her brow creased with concern.

His smile faded and he looked again at Torey.

Before Daniel could say anything, Gregg spoke up, challenging him, "Whatever happened, it wasn't Torey's fault."

"Now hold on to your temper and that red hair of yours." Daniel said, motioning to Gregg to calm down. "No one has said anything is Torey's fault. I had a row with some soldiers. They were from King Alexander's lands."

At that news, Torey's face went ashen. Her eyes grew wide with fear. She stood up and backed away from the table.

"I won't go back there!" She declared.

Daniel took a deep, patient breath, his eyes resting sympathetically on Torey. He could only imagine what she had endured that could cause such fear.

"Child, I would not have you go back there. Now sit down, little lady, drink your ale, and I will tell all of you what I found out."

Torey, convinced she was safe, at least for now, sat down, lifted her mug and drank deeply, fixing her eyes on Daniel so she would not miss a word.

Daniel went on. "The soldiers said there was a siege and that King Alexander has been deposed. There is much civil strife between the kings and the common folk. The king's young son, Nicholas, has been placed on the throne. He is a child, under the control of the First Minister and the king's own advisors. It appears there was a conspiracy going on right under the king's nose. Who knows what will happen now. The soldiers are everywhere. They're hostile and confrontational, looking for a fight. I convinced them that I was a simple merchant, unarmed, and peaceful. They were drunk. I pacified them with cloth and food, and they went on their way. The soldiers are raiding farms and businesses, setting some on fire, and taking what they want. I fear this will get worse before it gets better. I think there will be skirmishes and possibly civil war. I was very glad Gregg was here with you," he said to Leigh, placing his hand over hers on the table. Daniel's worry for his woman was reflected in his eyes.

"What do we do?" Gregg rose and paced for a moment, his brow knit in concern.

"I think we need to spread the word to the people, other merchants, farmers, and anyone else who lives in this province that's interested, that we need to stick together. We need to come to each other's aid if our businesses, homes, or farms are attacked and raided by marauding soldiers. Here at the tavern, we need to keep our pikes and swords at the ready." He looked from one to the other as he shared his grim news.

"Aye!" Gregg said forcefully, plunking his mug of ale on the table for emphasis, the muscles in his large forearms flexing.

"Are we still set for the festivities tonight?" Daniel asked Leigh and Gregg in a lighter tone.

"Aye, aye!" they both said.

"Our lute player and our drummer will be here to entertain the customers? And the rooms upstairs are ready for lodging?" He asked, knowing full well that all the preparations were done before he asked.

"Aye, my lord, but of course!" Leigh replied with a playful slap on the side of Daniel's arm. Then she winked at Torey affectionately. "Thanks to Torey's labors, every room has fresh straw in the bed, freshly scrubbed linen, swept floors, and even clean chamber pots."

Daniel smiled at Torey, obviously impressed. "Little lass, you make a fine addition to this family. Your labors are greatly appreciated."

"Then I can stay?" Torey dared to ask.

"Was there ever a doubt?" Daniel winked at her. "Torey, can you help Gregg and Leigh serve the ale, take orders for dinner, and have a merry dance should the gentlemen ask? I think you have earned a little fun for yourself."

Torey smiled, blushed, and nodded her head. "Aye, my Lord, I can do that."

Then Leigh rose, taking Daniel by the hand, and turned to Torey and Gregg. "Me and my man are going upstairs and get reacquainted. Gregg, perhaps you could help Lady Torey," she winked at Torey and smiled, "to fill her washing tub with hot water for a bath in lavender before tonight's festivities."

Torey brightened.

Gregg stood, smiled, and in mock reverence, with one arm behind his back, bowed deeply to Leigh, sweeping his hat in an exaggerated arc. "Aye, Lady Leigh."

 Torey giggled and poked Gregg's ribs, making him lose his irreverent bow. When he nearly fell over, they all laughed.

Leigh smacked Daniel's bottom, urging him up the stairs. She turned back and said to Torey, "When you are ready, I have just the right dress for you. It's fit to serve ale and have a whirl or two."

When Torey saw that the couple was well lodged upstairs, she turned to Gregg and, blushing, smiled timidly. "You don't have to fill my bath, Gregg." Torey felt embarrassed that Leigh made such a bold suggestion. "I can fill my own."

Gregg bowed deeply, making a wide arc with his hat, clicked his boots together, and said quite sincerely, "It would be the highlight of my day, Lady Torey." From his deep bow, he looked up at her, his handsome face in a wide grin.

Torey had never seen a gesture quite so endearing.

"Aye, my lord," Torey agreed in mock obedience, returning his smile, "But I insist on helping you."

"As you wish, milady." Gregg said as he came up out of his bow.

As Torey started for the kitchen, Gregg came up beside her with a playful glint in his eyes and started bowing like a jester. "I am at your service. I am at your beck and call. I live to hear your commands."

Torey giggled at his silliness and pushed him ahead of her into the kitchen. He moved just fast enough to avoid her playful aim at the back of his head with her open hand.

Together they carried enough buckets of hot water up the stairs and into Torey's room to fill the wooden tub in the corner. Torey stood expectantly looking at Gregg when the last bucket had been poured, and she was ready to indulge.

Gregg suddenly realized the awkwardness of the moment. With his hand on the door, he turned to her.

"Torey," he said with concern in his voice, "I think it wise to teach you how to use weaponry. You should also know how to hunt and bring down small game and how to prepare your kill for the meat house out back. I will teach you about the forest, what you can eat and what is poisonous. It is uncertain times we are in. You need to know how to survive."

"Aye," Torey agreed softly. She understood fully the gravity of what he was saying.

He smiled as he reached for the door, "Rest a bit, little lady, you owe me ale and a dance tonight."

Then he bowed in his jesterly way just to see Torey smile as he pulled the door closed.

Dancing and Festivities at the Tavern

The musicians were playing a merry tune, and Torey found herself bouncing to the music as she, Gregg, Leigh, and Daniel waited tables and carried mugs of ale. A handsome customer with a lean build dropped his money in Torey's apron and patted her bottom as she plunked down his third mug of ale. At least she thought it was his third mug, she may have lost count. He was certainly paying handsomely for it, giving Torey tips that were very generous.

Torey felt lovely in the blue garments Leigh had loaned her, the typical peasant blouse drawn tight with a corset that tied under Torey's bosom and fell low on her shoulders, with a full skirt that fell just below Torey's well-toned calves, showing off her small ankles and tiny waist. The locket that Leigh had fastened around Torey's neck hung teasingly between the round fullness of her breasts.

The handsome gentleman had taken quite a fancy to her. As she politely tried to discourage him, the tavern door burst open and a cheer and a roar went up from the crowd, "It's Anne! Anne the dancer is here!" They all cheered.

Torey was beside herself with delight. She had not seen her friend since that night, long ago, when she learned she had been given to Lord Diego and Anne had comforted her.

Leigh and Gregg hurried over to make her welcome, and everyone in the tavern wanted to buy her a mug of ale. Anne was an exotically beautiful woman who shimmered in her dancing costume. Her black hair hung in curly spiral ringlets with black shiny combs sweeping thick dark locks to one side. She carried herself with an air of seductive mystery. The men in the room fell over themselves in hopes of getting her attention. Torey's eyes widened as she watched Anne and Leigh race to see which one could gulp a mug of ale the fastest.

Anne glanced around the room and screamed, "Torey!" when she saw her. With a dancer's grace she swept across the floor to Torey, encircling her waist and announcing loudly to everyone, "This is my beautiful friend, Torey, and she dances, too!" Torey's mouth dropped open, but before she could protest, Anne assured her, "follow my lead, it'll be fun!"

Torey quickly glanced at Gregg across the room. He smiled his protective smile and nodded his approval to her, setting her at ease.

Anne took two mugs of ale off a nearby table as everyone clapped to the music, encouraging the two women to dance for them. She handed one to Torey, they clinked their mugs together and then faced the crowd raising their ale high in the air.

"A toast to all, for good health, happiness, and long life," she stopped a moment with her mug held high and scanned the crowd, briefly exchanging familiar gazes with a few of the men. Then she smiled wickedly and added, "and many great loves!" Everyone downed their ale to the toast, and then Anne led Torey by the hand in a dance. They danced from one end of the tavern to the other until the song ended. A gentleman grabbed Anne by the arm, pulling her away to the bar. The musicians immediately struck up another merry song.

The same handsome gentleman who had been trying to get Torey's attention all evening stepped up, encircled her waist and whirled her across the floor to the bar where Gregg stood keeping an eye on things. The gentleman plunked down a gold piece on the bar and looked at Gregg, whose expression became serious, but not threatening.

"Tis the lady's decision," he stated matter-of-factly, without looking at Torey.

Torey's dear friend, Anne, winked at her as she and her fellow ambled up to the counter. The fellow plunked his gold piece down in front of Gregg. Anne giggled and playfully swatted Torey's bottom as she headed toward the stairs. Anne squealed with delight as her man caught up with her, and hoisted her over his shoulder and carried her up the stairs to the rooms.

Torey watched as the playful couple disappeared into a room at the top of the stairs. Her face turned crimson with comprehension.

"Oh!" She cried in surprise to the handsome gentleman who still stood beside her, awaiting her decision, his unclaimed gold coin still lying on the counter. Torey stammered. "Oh, good Sir, forgive me," she pleaded in her embarrassment, her eyes flitted about the room, "I knew not that ..." Torey's voice trailed off in astounded disbelief at herself. How could she not have known? She could not bring herself to meet the gentleman's gaze and see the disappointment in his eyes.

Gregg suddenly realized that Torey hadn't understood when he told her about the Saturday night festivities at the tavern. He knew from what Leigh had told him and Daniel that Torey had belonged to King Alexander. Gregg knew full well what that meant. Gregg suddenly felt like a black-guard when he saw the panicked, embarrassed look on Torey's face. He put his hand on the gentleman's arm to soothe his bruised ardor.

"Mayhap next time, good Sir."

"Very well, then, Sir." He bowed tactfully to Gregg, and then turned his attention to Torey. "Milady," the gentleman bowed deeply to Torey, kissed the back of her hand, and straightened. Gazing deeply into her startled eyes, he gave her his most charming smile, and then turned and reluctantly walked away.

His gallant demeanor captivated Torey. Her mouth dropped open as she watched him take his leave of her. She hadn't noticed 'til this moment how handsome he was, how broad his shoulders were, how his hair curled at the nape of his neck, and how proudly he carried himself.

"I think a breath of air is needed, I do." Gregg led her by the hand out the back door of the kitchen, and into the barnyard.

Gertie had been dozing and softly honked her annoyance at being startled by the sudden appearance of her two best friends. Gregg spoke softly to her until she settled down again. Gertie looked curiously at both of them, but stayed quiet.

"Torey," Gregg began slowly, taking her hands in his, drawing her close to him. He spoke with earnest sincerity, "no one expects you to go upstairs with anyone if you choose not to. And no one will think less of you if you do. Anne is a free woman. She loves life, she loves to dance, and everyone loves her. Her husband died years ago, and she has one child, a daughter, who helps her run her small farm. Anne's mother taught her how to dance, and she has done well for herself. As you know, she dances for kings. She takes whom she pleases to her bed. When she dances at the tavern, a percentage goes to the tavern. Anne and Leigh have been very close friends for years, but it is the same for any of the women who go upstairs with the gentlemen. But, Torey, lass, it is your choice," he continued gently, "none of us is a king that would force you to our bed. If a man tries to have his way, I promise you he will be swiftly reckoned with."

At that, and to his great relief, Torey coquettishly smiled up at him.

"Very well then, my knight in shining armor, 'tis well with you that you have chosen to be a knight, and not a king, for I hate kings!"

Gregg bowed deeply in his comical jester way, making a wide, sweeping arc with his hat. He smiled to himself at the sweet sound of Torey's laughter.

"It would be the highlight of my day to buy the lady a mug of ale, and to collect on the debt of a dance." He said, making his voice deep in exaggerated chivalry. It pleased him greatly to hear Torey giggle at his antics, for it was in these moments that the veil of shame she wore lifted briefly.

They went back in and joined the festivities. As the evening wore on and the crowd began to thin out, Torey shyly approached the musician banging on the tabor when the musicians took pause.

"Good Sir, I have watched you all evening, your music and your sentimental folk songs have captured my fancy. Would you think me shameless if I asked if there be interest in a lady?"

Speechless, the musician stood, bowed, and kissed the back of Torey's hand. He took a deep breath and gazed fondly into her green eyes, "My Lady Fair, you have honored me greater than words can express. But alas, lovely lady, I have no gold piece. I am but a poor musician."

Torey nodded her understanding.

Then he added, "but I shall never forget that a lady fair as you desired me." Torey smiled and bowed, and, with her cheeks flaming, returned to the bar.

This had been a night of wonderment for Torey. This was the first time since King Alexander had taken her maidenhead that she could choose to decline a man's desire of her, and her choice was respected as though she were a noblewoman.

There had been times when the men who had summoned her to their beds had stirred her, evoking her desire. She had learned early on, after surrendering her innocence to King Alexander, that she could favorably influence her masters by demonstrating a passionate desire to please them. It was fortunate that she was a woman of ardor. It was also the first time she had made an overture of her own to someone SHE desired, and had been declined because he felt that he was not worthy of her.

Torey had never felt more liberated or empowered as she did this night. She walked a little taller and stood a little straighter. Gregg smiled to himself as he watched her climb the stairs when the last customer had gone home, his heart and his desire burned for her. From the top landing she turned and said, "Thank you for the best evening I have ever had."

She was the most alluring woman-child Gregg had ever seen. "I think 'tis the ale talking, lass," he said with a wink, grinning. She smiled the most innocent coquettish smile he had ever seen, her beautiful red hair flowing over her creamy shoulders, the lovely locket cradled between her full bosoms. He looked up at her, standing there, on the top landing. With her flushed face, being slightly out of breath, and a little sweaty, she looked like a lover in the after-glow. She was so ravishingly desirable to him at that moment that, had she not seemed so vaguely familiar, he would not have been able to control his want of her.

"Careful, lovely lady," he warned good-naturedly, nearly overcome with his desire for her, "I haven't a gold coin, either."

Torey blushed and smiled, ran back down the stairs, kissed him on the cheek, and ran back up the stairs to her room. As his eyes followed her backside up the stairs, he realized she had a disarming and frustrating ability to endear herself to him like a child and stir his ardor at the same time.

"Aye, lass, I think you came here to steal hearts," Gregg said to himself as he sighed deeply, shaking his head.

His smile faded as his thoughts turned to the more serious matters at hand, the growing unrest among the king's soldiers, the lords, the nobility, and the peasants, and how he was going to protect the tavern, and most of all, Torey. The civil unrest had already turned violent a number of times.

Tomorrow I shall start teaching you, little lass, how to survive. He put the broom away and made ready a bow and a quiver of arrows, a short blade, a dirk, and a sword. He would teach her more weaponry when she mastered those. He went to bed feeling encouraged at the thought of better equipping Torey in her quest for survival.

CRACKING

The hulking figure on horseback made his way at a steady, unhurried pace through the dark wood of dense weeping willow trees, being careful to avoid the gnarled roots twisting up from the ground. They seemed to reach for him as though they were trying to impede his progress. He struck at the branches that were trying to claw him, grab him, and knock him off his horse. He cursed the Forbidden Forest.

The witch's black crow, Uta, cawed threateningly from the trees warning the rider to turn back, for this was his mistress' forest. The lone rider knew the crow was an extension of Keena, the witch, and he knew she could see through the eyes of the crow.

"I am not afraid of you, old woman. It is you who should beware," he thought, unaware that his hand had dropped down to his side checking that his sword was in place and at the ready.

"The things a man must do," he grumbled to himself, "to claim what is rightfully his." The exact location of the redheaded wench who escaped King Alexander's castle was unknown to him. He knew the general direction of the villages of the marketplace women who had befriended her, and he knew they all lived in small villages beyond the great forest in the vast valley far to the east of the castle, so he would begin his search there.

The witch would grant him his tracking spell so that he could find the red-headed whore and then track her comings and goings so he could set a trap. The icon of spells would give him the antidote to restore his bewitched manhood, and then he would find the girl and claim what was rightfully his. Why shouldn't he have her, he reasoned to himself, he had been one of King Alexander's most powerful advisors, which entitled him to many things.

He was strikingly handsome and menacingly commanding. He could have any noblewoman in the king's court that he wanted, the way they all fawned over him, bowing and curtsying and demurely brushing their full luscious bosoms against him.

The one he wanted, though, the one he had always wanted, was the king's spirited, little redheaded whore. She should have been his whore all along. He knew only he could teach her about real men, tame her, and break her spirit.

He deserved to have her nude, silky flesh pliant in his grip, and have her he would. Then he would teach her to submit to him. After all, he was a powerful wizard, a Prince of the Underworld. He smiled to himself at the thought of her, nude and helpless, groveling and pleading at his feet. His lustful thoughts compelled him onward.

Finally reaching the macabre little house, he dismounted and tethered his horse to the rail, walked across the wood porch, and swatted at the crow as it flew at his head, harassing him while cawing raucously. Without knocking, he pushed the door open and walked inside.

"Have you no fear of the magical power of the Underworld?" Keena asked without looking up from her study of the Book of Spells. Uta the crow continued to caw harshly, scolding him.

"Have you forgotten that my mother is a Princess of the Underworld?" His smile turned cold and dangerous.

"Have you forgotten that it was I who sent her back to the Underworld?" Keena cautioned him in an equally threatening manner, her smile just as cold and dangerous.

"I was a boy. My magic was not yet strong enough to stop you. But that, old woman, is a battle we will fight another day," said he, through clenched teeth. His patience tested, he drew a deep breath, gathered his composure, and continued. "Today, I need a tracking spell and an antidote, and you are going to concoct both for me."

"I am a witch. I know what you want, but it will cost you," she rasped begrudgingly.

The big man reached in his cape and withdrew a bag of gold. Keena snatched at it with her bony, gnarled hands.

He withdrew it for a moment.

"Half now, the other half when the spell and the antidote work. If I come to harm, I will come back and cut your heart out and feed it to Uta."

Keena winced, her grim weathered face grew even grimmer at the thought, but she held her ground. She would not let him intimidate her.

Keena hissed her instructions through crooked yellow teeth. "So be it. But the spell will only work if the tracking crystal is mixed with a drop of blood and a lock of hair from the person you wish to track. You must get those things and bring them back to me."

"Agreed. But mark my words, old woman, if this is a trick, you will not live long enough to brag about how you deceived Simon the Brute," he threatened as he headed for the door.

"Many a wizard more powerful than you has fallen by their own arrogance," Keena said to herself in a raspy whisper. She shook her head and watched the evil wizard mount his horse and gallop away with urgency to begin his quest. "And this woman you must possess is protected by Queen Danu herself, mother of the Tuatha de Dannan, her loyal Champions, and her Silver Riders." Keena thought to herself.

Keena's words riveted against the walls of her tiny enchanted cottage as though a terrible and mighty force had been unleashed by Lord Simon's relentless pursuit. Though an eternal fire burned brightly in Keena's hearth, a chill crept through her old bones. She shivered uneasily and quickly closed and bolted the door.

ARCHERY LESSONS

Very early the next morning, just as the first hint of the sun's rays crept across the valley where the tavern was nestled, Gregg rapped on Torey's door.

"Hey, rise and shine, you long-eared galoot!" He called out playfully.

When the door opened within moments, and Torey stood before him fully dressed and ready to go, Gregg was surprised, pleased, and impressed.

"You long-eared what?" She teased back with a wide grin. Torey adored him and loved that she could be silly with him.

Gregg appreciated that she was so bright and sunny early in the morning. He handed her a knapsack, a skin of water, and hung a quiver of arrows over her shoulder, placing the bow over it.

"Think you can handle that?" he asked, making small adjustments to balance the weight on her shoulders. With the rest of the weapons and his own knapsack thrown over his back, he looked like an armed renegade.

"That sounds like a challenge to me!" She said in mock insult. "Lead the way." She pushed him down the hall ahead of her, following closely behind. They walked out the back door of the kitchen quietly, taking care not to wake Daniel and Leigh or those who had sought lodging the night before.

Gregg and Torey waited while the stable boy brought out Patch, Torey's horse, and a horse for Gregg to ride. Gertie greeted them with her usual affectionate honking, waddling circles around Torey, and crooning her approval. "You have to wait for your breakfast, poppet." Torey said. Leigh had agreed to do the early morning chores in Torey's stead, as Gregg was eager to begin the lessons.

As they headed out on horseback, Torey took a deep breath of the crisp fall air.

"Where are we going?" She asked, as excited as a child.

"I want to show you a part of the valley you haven't seen." Gregg replied with a pleased smile.

"That task shall be easy, for I haven't seen any of it."

They rode along in silence. Gregg wanted to give Torey a chance to see the beauty of the surrounding countryside. Soon they came within hearing distance of a waterfall and Gregg motioned for her to stay quiet and dismount. He tied their horses to a small tree, took her by the hand, and walked quietly toward the lake where several pheasants and a small deer drank furtively at the water's edge.

Gregg drew an arrow from the quiver and showed Torey how to nock it into the bow and line up her fingers and the arrow to her target. He thought she was going to have trouble pulling back hard enough on the bow, but her arms were strong, and she pulled back firmly. At his signal, she let the arrow fly. Queen Danu hovered between the two worlds and guided Torey's arrow, so it was true to target. Feathers flew, and the rest of the game scattered. Torey nearly yipped out loud she was so proud of herself, as this was her first hunt. Gregg gave her a smiling thumbs-up as they went to collect her prize. Though Torey was unaware, her goddess mother smiled her approval, as well.

Gregg tied the pheasant to Torey's horse and spent the rest of the morning teaching her how to move about soundlessly in the wood, how to wield the knife, and how to practice with the sword. He was impressed that she could throw the knife so accurately, and he could tell that, with a little practice, she would be pretty formidable with the bow and arrow. The sword, however, proved to be too large and heavy for her small frame and she was unable to wield it effectively.

By midday they were hungry so they stopped, watered the horses, and ate the biscuits, cheese, and dried strips of meat Gregg had packed for them. The sun was high and warm in the sky, and they both knew there was work to be done at the tavern, so they mounted up and headed back.

They sauntered along in silence when Torey decided to voice her curiosity about him.

"Do you know of your origins?" she asked him in a gentle tone. He never talked about himself and she didn't know if he would be put off by her question.

"Aye, lass, I have, or rather had, a mother and a father." He smiled, always the jester. This time, though, instead of amusing Torey, it hurt her. She felt he was keeping her at a distance. Gregg could see it in her face, and, in an effort to make amends, he said, "I don't remember anything about being very young, lass, only that Leigh was always there. She has always been a loving sister. And what about you? Were you born at the castle?"

Torey's brow knitted in her effort to remember. She couldn't have been more than three or four when her village fell under attack. There was fire everywhere, familiar voices weeping and begging for mercy. She remembered crying and screaming and pulling on her fallen mother, begging her to get up and run. Then suddenly a soldier in chain mail scooped her up and carried her to the castle on his horse. She remembered her immortal mother, Queen Danu, coming to her in her dreams. She remembered a kindly, older, jovial woman named Matilda who took care of her and the other children until King Alexander summoned her the first time.

"Nay," she finally answered. She understood now why he hadn't wanted to talk about the past. "I wasn't born at the castle. My village was besieged. Soldiers murdered my parents, and I was taken to King Alexander. When I came of age he told me he fancied me, and that it was to my good fortune." She looked down, her face turning red. "I think you know the story from there."

Gregg hated to see the veil of shame that was so often on her face despite her sunny disposition. He tried to cheer her. "I can understand why you hate kings, I can, but if it makes you feel any better, milady, if I were King Alexander, I would have summoned you to my bed, too, I would."

Torey smiled wistfully. "I am grateful to you, I am, for showing me a different life."

Gregg welcomed the change of subject and brightened. "We must practice as often as possible so you can become an accomplished archer and help me hunt game! 'Tis a challenge, it is, to keep the tavern in a good supply of meat." He smiled in the endearing way that melted her heart.

Gertie's honking and scolding announced their return. They stabled the horses and were laughing and recounting the hunt as they brought Torey's prize into the tavern to show off. They were greeted with somber stares from Daniel and Leigh, who looked at each other and then back at them.

"What?" Torey asked, suddenly feeling very uneasy. "What is amiss?" Torey was beginning to feel scared.

Leigh insisted that nothing was amiss, but she kept staring at Gregg and Torey as though she'd seen a ghost. "I'm going to go visitin'. You two take care of Daniel and the tavern, and keep yourselves out of trouble. I'll be back as soon as I can."

Gregg was immediately suspicious. He asked Torey to tell Leigh all about their day as he poured ale for himself and Daniel, and then strong-armed his brother-in-law outside to talk. "Are you and Leigh having a row, my friend?" Gregg pressed him to talk.

"Nay, nothing like that, Leigh has some family business to take care of." Daniel tried to sound reassuring, but Gregg couldn't shake the feeling that something was amiss.

Cupid's Arrow

Torey tried to enjoy the Saturday night festivities at the tavern with Anne and Teresa, but her thoughts kept wandering back to Leigh, and pondered her friend's mysterious journey. Torey stood up straight and resolved to enjoy herself as she watched Anne and Teresa entertain the gentlemen.

The dashing lord whose company Torey had declined came back. His name was Liam, he was a nobleman, and he was smitten with her. He was tall, with a lean build, piercing blue eyes, and handsome, rugged looks that sported a full mustache. There was no mistaking his station in life for he dressed as meticulously as any wealthy nobleman. He was a ladies' man, and quite the courtly gentleman.

As time went on, Liam took Torey for picnics in the forest in his magnificent carriage. He brought her flowers and new dresses and combs for her hair. He made her the envy of all her friends. The handsome nobleman gave Gregg so many gold pieces for Torey's undivided attention that the tavern more than prospered for the season.

Liam was a tender lover, awakening in her depths a fiery, brazen passion that made her blush. He coaxed her into teaching him what pleased her, and then he executed those moves slowly, building her passion until she felt she might die from the sweet agony of it, before finally giving her release.

"Torey." Liam said softly, early one morning, as he cuddled her delightful nakedness, stroking her satiny skin, and burying his face in her soft, fragrant, red hair.

"Mmmmhh," Torey murmured, stirring slightly, still half asleep. Captivated, he looked down into her green eyes as they fluttered open; he could stare into their emerald depths endlessly. She gazed back, his blue eyes were serious, bringing her fully awake.

"Aye, my lord, speak your mind."

"Torey, you have done well with your archery lessons with Gregg, and I know he would give his life to protect you, but I fear your involvement with the Rebellion."

"Aye," Torey agreed.

"You must take care, Torey. This is not your battle. You are not one of these peasants, little lady. I know who you are, and the deposed king's court knows you did not take your leave with Lord Diego and his Lady."

Torey's eyes widened with fear. Liam continued, "Worry not, my beautiful lady, the court will not discover you through me. But my love, if I discovered you, others might also. I must leave to attend to business. I shall return when I can, and when I do, I will expect you to dismiss whatever gentleman you are dallying with and make yourself available to me." Liam patted her silky bottom.

"Aye," Torey smiled mischievously, and kissed him most wickedly.

THERE BE DRAGONS ABOUT

Liam left at dawn, bidding Torey a fond but reluctant farewell.

Gregg and Torey made ready their weapons and knapsacks for their early morning hunting and archery lesson.

They started out earlier than usual for Gregg wanted to take Torey to a different part of the forest that was a greater distance away so they could explore new hunting territory. Just as Torey began to wonder if they had lost their way, Gregg motioned for them to dismount and tether their horses.

They walked for a while until Torey heard rustling noises. She held up a hand for Gregg, pointing in the direction of the noises. She drew an arrow from the quiver on her shoulder and nocked it on the bow, squeezing her fingers around it to hold it in place until she was ready.

Gregg followed a dozen or so paces behind.

Torey came to the edge of a clearing, across the clearing, a small pond reflected the cliff face and the trees above it. She grinned and motioned to Gregg as they spotted a buck drinking at the pond. The buck would provide an excellent supply of meat for the tavern.

Just as Torey was about to let her arrow fly, guided by Danu, a dragon as black as onyx stepped into their midst, somehow appearing from between the reflection and the rock face, and snapped up the buck in its jagged jaws. It turned and considered them with its hungry eyes.

Torey screamed in terror, dropping her bow on the forest floor and stumbled backward, landing on her backside. The ring of steel sang as Gregg drew his sword and stood between the dragon and Torey. The dragon gazed at them intently for a moment, narrowing its dark eyes as though pondering them, and then took flight with the buck in its long, toothy snout. Gregg was about to replace his sword in its scabbard and offer Torey a helping hand up onto her feet when she screamed and turned away, throwing her arms up to protect her head.

A brown-shouldered falcon with a great beak and long, sharp talons dove at them. Gregg sliced the air wildly with his sword trying to keep the falcon away from Torey. It dove at her again and again, with razor sharp talons scratching her arms, and its knife-like beak tearing at her hair. Gregg brought his sword around in a graceful arc and caught the ridge of the falcon's wing, sending feathers flying. It cried out in an ear-splitting shriek and struggled to fly over the top of the cliff face whence the dragon had so suddenly and mysteriously appeared, and then followed the dragon's flight path.

Torey was lying face down on the forest floor with both hands over her head, screaming and crying hysterically as Gregg lifted her up and hugged her to his chest, keeping his sword ready in case the attacking falcon returned.

On the other side of the forest, the falcon fell to earth. Simon, the evil wizard, lay naked on the forest floor, his right arm bleeding heavily from a most unfortunate introduction to steel. He carefully wiped a drop of blood from his fingertips to the tiny vial he carried around his neck, adding to that a lock of Torey's hair. He crawled over to where the dragon was feasting on the buck and climbed upon her spiny back, wedging his arms over her wings.

"Fly!" He commanded.

Keena Conjures a Spell

ta danced in alarm on his perch next to the witch's Book of Spells, flapping his large wings and cawing raucously.

"Calm yourself, Uta, I know they are coming, and I know why. Worry not, we are not in harm's way."

Keena heard a great rush of wind and the macabre little house shook as the dragon, bearing her wounded passenger, landed with a heavy thud in the clearing in front of the house. Simon released his grip on the dragon's wings and slid to the ground, his arm still bleeding heavily. The dragon bade Simon farewell, spread wide her leathery wings and took flight over the tops of the trees, and then disappeared deep into the Forbidden Forest to hunt.

Simon gathered himself and staggered to Keena's front door and pushed it open, once again without knocking, and stumbled in and fell into a heap on the floor. Keena, seeing him naked and bleeding, fished through a trunk of very old clothes and found a man's tunic and breeches.

"Simon the Evil Wizard, you have earned your title," she said in her raspy voice through gnarled teeth. "It would have been better for you if Gregg's sword had sliced your throat instead of your arm."

Simon grimaced and turned his head away, not wanting to look into eyes he knew could see the future.

"Don't get any ideas, old woman. Keep your advice and stitch me up. I trust my messenger delivered the balance of my debt."

Keena nodded. She did Simon's bidding, knowing the sooner she fixed him up, the sooner he would be on his way.

Once she finished the stitching of his arm, he sat before her on a wood bench, leaning on a small table eating mutton and bread and drinking Keena's wine. He watched her prepare the spell using Torey's hair and a drop of her blood. The witch worked in a singsong murmur that only she understood, mixing the strands of hair into a thick, black concoction, and moving her hands and arms in the air over the small iron pot that boiled and hissed. She held both her hands over the pot as though to warm herself, and recited an incantation in the language of the Underworld.

Suddenly the house shuddered, blue sparkles of light like tiny lightning bolts flashed in the house around the pot, moving in an ever-increasing circle until the whole house was filled with bright blue energy. The house shuddered again. The black, bubbling concoction in the witch's pot had been transformed into a fine, black crystal sand.

"I have to admit, I am impressed." An admiring Simon shook his head in approval as he finished the last of the mutton on his plate. He rose and held out his hand, the desire to be on his way burning in his eyes.

"There is one more step," Keena informed him. She took the vial over to a cabinet that held countless small bottles, labeled and arranged neatly. She removed the stopper from a bottle filled with fragrant, shimmering blue liquid. Allowing two drops to drip into the vial and mix with Torey's blood, she then poured them into the fine black crystal sand. The sand came alive with flashes of electric blue lightning bolts. Keena opened a small locket and filled it with the living black crystal. She snapped it shut and handed it to him.

"The conjured crystal has been charged with a living tracking spell from the Underworld, with the aid of witch's brew and the girl's own blood. Sprinkle the black sand on any looking glass or body of water and it will show you whom you seek."

"There is one more matter of business, old woman," Simon reminded her. Keena did not try to hide her gloating smile; she was proud of her magic when a spell worked as well as the shrinking potion had on Simon.

She had also been impressed with the Lady Alejandra's bravery and resourcefulness.

"You needn't be so proud of yourself, old woman. I want the antidote to the shrinking potion, and I want it now."

Keena knew by the threatening edge of Simon's voice that he meant business. Leaning on her cane, she shuffled over to shelves filled with bottles, vials, and potions. She searched for a moment and finally reached for a small vial filled with bubbly, blood-red liquid. She handed it to him saying, "When you see a woman whom you desire, drink the potion. You must sieze the woman and take her to your bed. Bind her with rope. Cut the palms of her bound hands and rub her blood on your manhood. The re-growth of your staff and seed will be immediate and painful. To complete the spell, you must then burn her clothes. You must ravish her while the fire rages."

Simon smiled an evil smile as he anticipated carrying out Keena's instructions, and then bowed in a way meant to be an insult rather than a show of good manners.

Keena returned the insult with a snarly smile and said with heavy sarcasm, "Uta, call the dragon to take this gentleman away."

Discoveries

Once Torey calmed down and stopped crying and shaking, Gregg took her to the water's edge and washed her wounds. He took ointment from his saddlebag and rubbed it on the deeper scratches and tied strips of cloth on her arms to stop the bleeding.

"Bloody hell, Gregg, that would have been ample meat for the tavern!" Torey quipped light-heartedly, in an effort to take the edge off both their fear.

"You worry about the darndest things, girl," said Gregg with a forced smile, finding Torey's effort at bravery most endearing.

Then, in a more serious tone she asked, "You've hunted these woods for years. Have you ever seen a falcon act like that, or a dragon appear from out of nowhere?" Torey's voice was still quavering.

"Nay, lass, I have not. I heard that a dragon had been awakened from its sleep, but I thought it was a tall tale to scare travelers." The attack had left Gregg shaken, too, but he didn't want her to know that. He helped Torey into her riding cloak and then helped her onto her horse, and decided to walk awhile, holding on to both horses' reins. They passed the clump of trees where the falcon had attacked Torey, and Gregg stopped and gathered several of the winged predator's feathers from the forest floor and tucked them inside his tunic.

When they finally reached the tavern Gregg helped a frightened and wounded Torey off her horse. Gertie waddled around Torey, fussing and scolding, expressing her concern more than usual. Gregg wished he could reassure Gertie that everything was okay, but he wasn't sure of that himself. Instead, he crooned to Gertie, telling her how good it was to be home and that she did a good job guarding the barnyard, while he scratched her long neck reassuringly.

Leigh and Daniel were sitting at a table talking over mugs of ale when Gregg and Torey came in. Gregg was alarmed at the air of seriousness that hung between his sister and her husband. Torey was delighted that Leigh had returned home from her journey. Leigh patted the wooden bench she was sitting on, indicating to Torey to sit next to her.

Gregg poured mugs of ale for himself and Torey and sat next to Daniel after exchanging a warm greeting with the big man, then looked at his sister apprehensively.

"Torey, lass, what do you remember of your mother and your family?" Leigh questioned gently. Torey's brow knit together in a worried look. "Worry not, Child, there's nothing wrong," she patted Torey's hand reassuringly, "but there's somethin' I must tell you." Leigh looked into Torey's eyes, "Try to remember, lass. Did your mother have a sister?"

It was a painful question for Torey. She looked at Gregg. His eyes were filled with sympathy and concern for her. She tried hard to remember her village, but all she could recall was that terrifying night of fighting and soldiers, of fire and death, and of herself as a small child. She remembered screaming in terror and being carried away on horseback in the arms of a soldier, away from her mother who lay still and bloody on the ground.

"Please don't make me think about it." Torey pleaded, tears welling up in her eyes. "Please don't make me try to remember."

"Must we do this?" Gregg demanded angrily.

"Aye! 'Tis important, you'll see." Leigh insisted as she continued. "Torey, your mother had a younger sister, her name was Juliana. She was a lovely little thing, she was, with sky blue eyes and flaming red hair. She married a man from another village that was far away. You were but a wee babe when your aunty left your village to be a wife."

Leigh's gaze left Torey for a moment and settled on Gregg.

"Juliana died bringing her baby boy into the world on the same night Torey's village fell." Tears were streaming down Leigh's face; she sniffled, but kept a steady voice. "The father could not take care of the child by himself so he gave the babe to my mother." Leigh closed her eyes against the pain of the truth, tears sliding unchecked down her cheeks.

Hearing the story a second time from her own lips was no easier than hearing it the first time had been.

"It wasn't long after that the baby's father died in a battle defending the peasants." Leigh could not go on, she looked from Gregg to Torey. Gregg and Torey looked at each other and then at Leigh as they began to understand what it was she was saying.

"So, you're not really my sister." Gregg sat astounded. With tears still on her cheeks, Leigh playfully boxed his ears.

"Aye," she said in her bossy, big sister way, "I'm as much your sister now as I have ever been!" she declared, then added sorrowfully, "but not by blood, lad."

Gregg hugged Leigh fiercely. "You will always be my sister, so I'll have none of this talk."

Then he playfully tugged on Torey's hair, resorting to humor to lighten the mood, as he so often did.

"And you! No wonder you always seemed so familiar to me!"

Leigh smiled at last, looked at Daniel, and gestured toward Gregg and Torey.

"That explains why their mannerisms are so much alike. We should have known something was amiss the first day Torey stood in this room looking so much like him!"

Torey smiled and blushed and boxed Gregg's arm.

"'Tis a good thing I desired you not!" she teased.

"Aye! I bet you didn't!" Gregg teased her back.

Then he looked at his sister and Daniel with great concern clouding his face. "There's something we must tell you. Stand up, Torey, take off your cloak."

Torey rose and slid the cloak off her shoulders, exposing her wounds.

"Oh, sweet Jesu!" Leigh gasped, covering her mouth.

Daniel became alarmed. "Did the two of you have a scrap with soldiers?"

The atmosphere in the tavern suddenly became serious.

"Torey was attacked by a strange falcon," Gregg began.

"And that wasn't the half of it," he continued. "The dragon I've heard whispered about made an appearance. It came out of a solid rock face, and snapped up Torey's game. I think the dragon and the falcon are somehow tied together by magic. What's worse, I think Torey is in real danger."

They all looked at her with great concern. No one wanted to utter the words that hung in the air for fear their utterance might give them life: Torey's past was looking for her, and they couldn't stop it.

At that, Torey stood up, reached into her waist belt, and pulled the short blade from its sheath. She plunged the knife in the table with conviction, determination in her face.

"I'll not have your pity! Do you hear? I'll not have it!" Torey looked at them and her heart caught in her throat, as she realized how much she loved them. "We are family now, and we will defend ourselves, and this tavern that is our livelihood and our home." Torey raised her glass of ale, inviting them to do the same.

All four of them clinked mugs together. "Aye! Aye! Hear, hear!"

Leigh chimed in with her agreement. "While I was visitin' other villages and seekin' out folks I thought was long dead and pokin' my nose around, and askin' questions about family history, I learned that soldiers are maraudin' and pillagin' where they want since King Alexander was deposed, and the Regent has little power. Since the king was sent into exile, there's no ruler, no order. Country folk and those in villages and provinces alike want to band together for protection against the plunder and arrogance of the soldiers. The people want to raid the soldiers' encampments before the raids can happen." Leigh looked from one set of intense eyes to another.

"Are you saying you want us to join the uprising?" Daniel asked, unsure of where Leigh was going in the recounting of her recent journey. "Aye, and nay." Leigh replied.

"Well, which is it?" Gregg questioned. "Any citizen, servant, or slave who challenges a soldier can be charged with treason. There is no offense more serious."

"Treason against what sovereignty?" Leigh raised her voice in frustration and fear. "We have no reigning king in our country! We must defend our home, our business, if we are to survive these uncertain times!"

"I agree!" Torey declared. "Gregg you know the woods and the countryside where the soldiers are known to camp and where they are likely to fight. We can organize raiding parties, strike while they are sleeping, and when they least expect it. I lived in the castle. Kings, lords, noblemen, and their soldiers are arrogant and over confident. They do not expect commoners, peasants, or merchants to defend themselves."

"Aye," Daniel agreed. "I cannot afford to have soldiers pillage my tavern, or steal my livestock, or take my women," he added with a grave tight-lipped smile as he gazed fondly at Leigh and Torey.

Gregg was not pleased, however, "This is not what I had in mind for Torey when I taught her the survival skills of archery and hunting and how to be a woodsman. But if this must be, then at least I know there is no archer that I know of that can best her, she never misses."

With a lump in his throat, Gregg's intense gaze held Torey for a very long moment, as though he might never see her again, before he finally lifted his mug.

The Skirmish

Summer was over, and the mornings were brisk as winter kissed the earth in earnest with her cold embrace of death.

Soldiers would not attack in the dark of night when their human targets were more difficult to see and their horses stumbled over uneven ground, so skirmishes and attacks occurred in the cold mists of dawn.

Torey thought it grievous that the birth of any new day would be greeted by death. She wondered what her goddess mother, Queen Danu, was thinking, as she must surely be watching from the Isle of Tir-na-nog. Torey trusted that Danu knew that her spirited daughter was doing what she must.

Just before dawn Torey watched for the signal from Gregg as their small band of rebels surrounded the encampment of soldiers who were preparing themselves for battle. Gregg watched Torey closely. He worried about all of them, that they were such a small group and so greatly out-numbered. What if they were captured? What if one of them were felled? How would he tell their family? He knew their purpose was to pick off a few soldiers, reduce their numbers, harry them, and slow them down. Their purpose was not to win the struggle against tyrannical kings and their noblemen, for they knew they could not. To hamper them, and to champion the peasants' rebellion against the nobles' practice of taking a new bride to their bed on her wedding night, these were their goals.

Gregg could not forget why they risked their lives in this daunting endeavor, not even when he became weary. He saw it burning in Torey's eyes every time he was about to give the signal. Her passion to right wrongs, and her abhorrence of kings and nobility frightened even him sometimes.

They had done this enough times now that Torey knew when he was about to give the signal. He held her eyes for a long moment each time, memorizing their unique sparkle and determination, and the soft contours of her face, so that if one of them did not return, he could carry the memory of her, whether still in this world, or the next. He loved her, she was his family, and he didn't think he could bear losing her again, so he protected her fiercely.

His heart pounded wildly as if it were going to crash through his chest; he couldn't help but smile to himself as he looked at her dressed like a peasant man. He was grateful she had been willing to listen to reason and disguise herself. She looked elfin in the getup, but he knew it would make her safer.

Once Gregg gave the signal, they each had a job to do that had to be done quickly and precisely. Each of them had to finish simultaneously to insure their chances of a clean getaway. The supply and food wagons were to be set on fire. The water supply had to be poisoned. The horses were set free, depending on how much time they had and how great the rebels' own numbers. All the while Torey and three other archers would pick off soldiers from the perimeter where they could avoid hand-to-hand combat. Her arrows always found their fatal target, flying straight and true, for her goddess mother guided her aim.

The battle was raging now, men were screaming and dying, acrid black smoke and ashes filled the air, burning their lungs and stinging their eyes. Horses were snorting and bawling and running blindly, hysterically trying to escape the chaos.

If Gregg and his small band of peasants and commoners, merchants and servants were very lucky, the ground would be littered with bodies of soldiers, and the rebels would suffer few, if any, losses.

Ironically, it was this part of the battle that frightened Gregg most, for it was at this time, when the battle was done, that Gregg and his people sometimes lost track of each other in their haste to get far away from the scene of the battle. During those times when he could not find Torey, he knew she would be given safe refuge in the surrounding countryside and province, but the not knowing until he could know for sure was always torture.

This was one of those battles he dreaded. He could not find her. Nor could he very well go about from door-to-door to search for her, for that kind of activity would only bring dangerous, if not fatal, attention. He would have to wait for word.

TAKING REFUGE

The battle had been particularly brutal this time. A sentry that Gregg's scouts had somehow missed had come upon Torey in the bush and had nearly run her through with his sword. Torey was caught by such deadly surprise that her spirit had cried out for help. There had been a burst of blinding light and Ember, the Prism, already whirling and exuding her black dust, had appeared above the sentry, quickly turning him to ashes. But not before he had dealt Torey her first flesh wound in battle, slashing her tunic and drawing her blood. Worse yet, she had lost the mask that Leigh had made for her and she was sure she had been seen. It had all happened so quickly that Ember was gone in a whirlwind of flashing light before Torey could thank her.

Toward the end of the battle Torey knew she had been found out, for she had drawn more than the usual amount of attack. Her goddess mother had taught her to know when to stand and fight and when to run so that she might fight another day, and run she did. In her retreat, however, she became separated from the others and thought it wise to seek refuge at Teresa's farm. She traversed several miles on foot to reach her friend's farm.

Even though it was only mid-morning, Torey was tired and hungry, and her wound, which ran down her side and across her backside, was bleeding and throbbing.

As soon as Torey knocked on the farmhouse door, it burst open and Torey was quickly pulled inside as though Teresa knew she was coming. Teresa tried to mask the concern on her face when she saw that Torey was wounded. She knew that her tiny, red-haired friend had gone out with the raiding party many times, but in all the times Torey had sought refuge with Teresa afterward, Teresa had never seen her injured or bleeding. Suddenly, the life-threatening danger of it became frighteningly real.

Teresa firmly bolted the door, and then peeked out the only window of the small, dark farmhouse to see if her friend had been followed. Satisfied that Torey was not being pursued, she helped her out of her torn, bloody clothes, and gently tended to Torey's bloody wound. Teresa made Torey comfortable, and prepared food for her. After they both ate, Teresa helped Torey wash up, and get dressed in the typical peasant's blouse, corset, and skirt, with an apron tied at her waist.

Teresa and Torey lay upon the straw high up in the hayloft of the barn. Teresa's husband, Matthew was out tending their farm when Torey appeared on their doorstep.

Teresa fussed over Torey, barely able to mask her very real concern with a light-hearted scolding.

"If I thought my refusing to mend your disguise would keep you from doing your dance with death, then I would shred it myself!"

"You didn't complain when I brought you a fine young pig from the last battle, or the laying hen from the battle before that," Torey argued, playfully punching Teresa's shoulder.

"Oww!" Teresa pretended to howl in pain, grabbing her shoulder and rolling over in the hay.

Torey, forever the woman-child, needed very little encouragement to play or to hide her feelings behind humor. She stood up in the hay with her hands on her hips, proclaiming, "Behold! With a mere touch I conquer all that I survey! I am immortal!" She fell back in the hay, giggling.

Suddenly Teresa was uncharacteristically serious.

"But you're not immortal, Torey, and all of us are so frightened for you that one of these times you won't walk away from the battle."

"Well, I'm half-immortal. Does that help?" Torey reasoned petulantly like an innocent child, her smile fading.

Teresa, in an effort to keep the mood light, widened her eyes and added, "Helping, hmmm, I heard about a most unusual king who rules with absolute justice given to him by the gods themselves!" Teresa made her voice sound mystical, talking about this new sovereign power, as she mended Torey's garments, casting sidelong glances at her.

Torey gave her an exaggerated yawn of disinterest.

Teresa took the hint but decided to bait Torey's feminine curiosity. "Know what else?"

Torey gave her another exaggerated yawn.

"I heard," Teresa smiled and her eyes got wide, but she didn't get a chance to finish before Torey caught on to the game. Teresa had a way of dealing with serious things without stating the obvious. Torey appreciated that quality, and found it endearing.

"You heard what, you silly goose?" Torey tumbled onto Teresa, held her down, and tickled her until she could hardly talk.

When the girls' giggling finally subsided, Teresa blurted out, "I heard he is a gifted, seasoned lover with many mistresses!" Gales of laughter filled the hayloft.

"You just couldn't help yourself, could you?" Torey accused good-naturedly, "Remember me? I'm the slave who hates kings and noblemen. It's a contradiction of terms! There are no noble men!"

There was a pause between the two women. Teresa feared she had gone too far and offended Torey, but she had been intrigued by the talk about this king and had wanted to share her inquisitiveness with Torey, her incorrigible girlfriend, and had not been thinking about Torey, the mistreated slave.

Teresa breathed a sigh of relief when Torey, her fun-loving, passionate girlfriend, said, without looking up, "So, how many mistresses does he have? And what's your idea of handsome? I know handsome!"

Then Torey grinned at Teresa as though she had not been engaged in her dance with death only hours before, her mind already entertaining thoughts of this mysterious king, purported to be the Just, and the Seasoned and Gifted Lover.

Simon Visits His Mother in the Underworld

"Mother, to what do I owe this unprecedented summons to the Underworld?" Simon was surly and aloof, behaving not at all in the way she had expected, and indeed, had wanted him to, after not seeing him for such a very long time.

Isabella, Simon's mother, the banished Princess of the Underworld, said plaintively, "can't a mother wish to see her child?"

Simon had no patience for this. He wanted her to come to the point, so he decided to hasten her getting there.

"We would not be having this conversation in the Underworld if you had not gotten yourself banished. You could have trifled with the affections of any king, lord, or nobleman. You could have had a crown and a throne by now for me to inherit. I could have been a rich, ruling king with a bedchamber full of beautiful whores. But nay, you had to trifle with the affections of the one wizard king whose magic allows him to know a man's heart and, thus, his intent. You, of all people, had to trifle with him. I could have been a king with subjects groveling at my feet. It's your fault I'm not, and now you want me to be overcome with heart-melting melancholy at not having seen you? I think I need to take my leave, now, Mother, have a pleasant day." He sneered sarcastically, and rose to leave.

"Wait!" Isabella pleaded to her son's back. He stopped, but didn't give her the courtesy of turning around to face her. "Simon, my son," she reached out to him tearfully in a helpless gesture. "I know of your heart's desire, but you are about to make the same mistake that you hate me for."

"And what mistake is that, Mother?" He asked sarcastically, rolling his eyes and tilting his head back, resting his hands on his hips impatiently, with his back still turned to her.

"You wish to possess a woman who is protected by the gods. She is the daughter of the goddess, Queen Danu." Her voice held the very real fear of the danger her son was flirting with. She did not want him to suffer the same fate she was bound to for all time. She finished with fearful finality. "You will die in your quest."

With a wicked grin, Simon the Brute turned halfway around.

"Ah," he said thoughtfully, "no wonder she is as intoxicating as wine, the conquest shall be sweeter still. Danu is no champion," he declared. "She was nowhere to be seen the night I possessed the slave. Just when I was going to purchase her from King Alexander, the wench escaped." He paused for just a moment. "Worry not, Mother, I shall not be as stupid as you were. I am a wizard, I shall cheat death and avoid being banished to the Underworld." He strode from the dark, mystical chamber.

"You will die in your quest." Isabella whispered through her tears as she watched her arrogant son disappear through the thick darkness that always encroached upon her chambers, her sadness making the darkness of the Underworld seem even more somber.

With the living, black crystal sand in a locket around his thick, muscular neck, and his manhood restored, Simon was more confident than a strutting peacock. He was not in a hurry now that Torey was as good as his. He decided he could treat himself to some rest and entertainment during his quest.

With money he had taken from King Alexander's treasury, he sought lodging at the most expensive taverns and bought the most expensive whores. He sank his head deeper into the pillow upon which he rested, with two naked voluptuous women that he had brought to bed with him the night before.

After the wenches had sated his desires, he would try out the tracking spell and call upon the daughter of Danu. "Hmmm, he thought, "whom should I get to announce my arrival, King Alexander?" The thought was so amusing that Simon chuckled out loud. Imagine the look of shocked surprise on the wench's face when she opened the door to find Simon the Brute standing there, in the flesh, come to take her home with him.

Torey's Surprise

The two women froze in fear at the sound of the knock at the door. Teresa was sure no one knew where Torey was. The women nearly melted with relief when they heard, "Tis I, Gregg, open up!" Teresa threw the door open and both women nearly knocked him over with their embraces. Gregg sighed with relief himself when he saw that Torey was safe, and he hugged her fiercely.

"Hey, now, easy on the ribs!" she teased him with mock caution.

"Why, lass, are you hurt?" He held her away from him with great concern, examining her torso.

"Nay, but made you look!" She grinned up at him with that mischievous grin that he adored.

"You know you're nothing but a long-eared galoot, you are!" He scolded good-naturedly. "I could wait no longer," he explained, "I had to come and see if you had taken refuge here."

"She lies, you know." Teresa gave Gregg a sly look, motioning toward Torey. "She was wounded in the battle."

Gregg frowned in earnest this time, his expression demanding an explanation.

Torey stuck her tongue out at Teresa for giving her away. She hated to worry him, she was always afraid he would be so distracted with concern for her that he would not take caution for himself.

"Hey!" Teresa protested Torey's gesture, pretending to be insulted. "We'll have none of that, unless you can do that better than my five-year-old!"

"Get your things, Torey, I'm taking you home, I am. Leigh and Daniel are very worried about you, too, they are." He turned to Teresa, "Thank you, milady, for everything." His voice was heavy with sincerity and emotion.

"Thank you!" Torey mouthed the words to Teresa as Gregg escorted her to their wagon. Teresa, now painfully aware of the dangers of the Rebellion, gave her dear friend a somber smile and pressed her fist to her heart in Celtic oath. Torey nodded her head in understanding.

"You're most welcome, my lord!" Teresa called after Gregg. After seeing Torey wounded and her clothes torn and bloody, she had a deeper respect for what the rebels were doing, and for the heartache she knew Gregg was enduring because of it. She bid them farewell as Gregg helped Torey into the wagon that he had brought for her.

Gregg turned to Teresa as he took up the reins in the driver's seat of the wagon. "Please come to the festivities this Saturday night, Teresa, and bring your daughter, Katy. We're having a surprise."

"I shall!" Teresa called after them, smiling back as she caught the hint of conspiracy. Torey turned and waved at her, sincere gratitude shining in her eyes.

"What's this about a surprise?" Torey asked Gregg as she squeezed his arm in her delight at seeing him again after the skirmish.

Gregg could not hide his relief and hugged her back. "What surprise? He teased her. Did you hear something about a surprise?"

"Aye, you long eared galoot, I did! From you!" She playfully boxed his arm.

Suddenly his playfulness changed to grave concern.

"Torey, quickly, don the cloak Teresa gave you and pull the hood over your hair," he ordered with calm but deadly seriousness. She immediately obeyed him. Within moments a cadre of soldiers rounded the next bend, spotting them immediately. There was no time to get off the road and hide.

"Do not look them in the eye, Torey. Keep your eyes and your head down," he instructed her.

The lead soldier, who wore the rank of Captain, blocked the road, motioning for his men to position themselves on either side of the wagon. Gregg resisted the natural impulse to drop his hand down to the hilt of his sword, but he positioned himself so he could move quickly, if challenged.

"Is there a problem, Captain?" Gregg made his voice sound casual.

"Seems there's a rebel movement afoot, some country rebels going about stealing from soldiers and the king's noblemen." The Captain's scrutinizing gaze rested on Torey as he said, "Have you any knowledge of that?"

"Really? Nay, I had not heard. I'm a merchant and my wife and I are just coming home from a trading journey."

Gregg didn't skip a beat. He was so convincing Torey would have believed him if she had not known otherwise. She was shocked the Captain was not convinced. He came up alongside the wagon and flipped the hood of her cloak off her head with the end of his short sword, surprising her so badly she jumped, sending her long red hair cascading over her shoulders.

"Rumor has it that one of the rebels is a female archer with long red hair. There aren't very many red-headed women in these parts," he said as he lifted her chin with the point of his short sword, and glared at her.

"Maybe we should take her in and question her," suggested one of the soldiers.

Gregg's heart was pounding as he furtively squeezed the hilt of his sword. He could sense that Torey was on the verge of panic. He didn't know if he would be victorious against this many soldiers in an attempt to defend Torey's life, but he was willing to try.

"Captain, I assure you, my wife is no archer. Sometimes she is disobedient. Aye, you know what they say about redheads." He smiled as though taking the soldier into his confidence, hoping this ploy would work. "But then I've never seen a truly obedient wife." He shook his head in consternation.

The other soldiers smiled and exchanged glances in agreement. But the Captain was not amused. "I would not know about wives, sir, since I have not one, and I would not waste my time." Then, looking straight at Torey, "I find that whores serve a man's needs just fine." Torey turned crimson, but kept her eyes down.

Gregg thought of a new tack.

"I must insist that you not disrespect my wife, Captain." He met the Captain's glare with a piercing glare of his own. Then, without taking his eyes off the captain, he addressed Torey, "cover your head, Wife." Torey's heart was pounding, but she immediately pulled the hood back up over her head and pulled the cloak around her.

The arrogant Captain with his leathery, battle-scarred face, brought his horse around to Gregg's side of the wagon and said in a threatening voice that carried teeth, "You may take your leave, but if I find you have deceived me, I will find you, and I will burn your house down. I will take everything you own, run you through with my sword, and ravish your lovely wife. Do we understand each other?"

"Aye." Gregg did not so much as flinch as he met the Captain's glare. Thanks for the warning, you son of a whore, Gregg thought, I will be ready.

The Captain shouted, "Onward!" and he and his company of soldiers continued on down the road. Gregg clicked his tongue at his horses and the wagon lurched forward.

Torey was so frightened they couldn't get out of there fast enough to suit her. They rode along in silence until Torey asked softly, "Gregg, how did he know I was a ..," her voice trailed off, her head hung down, she couldn't bring herself to say the word, and she couldn't look at him.

Gregg reached over and squeezed her hand reassuringly. "He didn't know, lass. It was what men call a lucky punch." Gregg glanced over at her, his heart wrenched for her. He hated the veil of shame she sometimes wore.

In desperate need of cheer, he smiled his jester smile, and boxed her arm. "Hey, aren't you curious about the surprise?"

Torey, fighting back tears, gratefully squeezed his arm and nodded, not yet trusting her voice.

"You can't tell Leigh I said anything," he continued conspiratorially, smiling confidentially, "but she has knowledge of your birthday, at least approximately."

Torey grinned, for this was wonderful news.

"And all of us are giving you a surprise birthday party," Gregg said. "So act surprised, will 'ya, you long-eared galoot!"

Torey bounced in the seat like a child.

"Really, a birthday party for me? Will there be presents?" She tugged on his arm in her excitement.

Gregg rolled his eyes heavenward in mock annoyance.

"Now she wants presents!" He put his arm around her and, with a big grin, hugged her tight.

When they finally reached the tavern, Torey helped Gregg unhitch the horses, stable them, and water them, with Gertie honking and fussing exuberantly. Leigh and Daniel came out into the barnyard and hugged Torey as fiercely as Gregg had.

"I hear we're having a party for me!" Torey was worse than a child, for she could not contain her excitement. She also did not want to talk about the raid, or the soldiers and how close she had come to meeting with disaster. Leigh and Daniel took the hint and didn't ask why she and Gregg seemed so shaken.

Leigh gave Gregg a scolding look with raised eyebrows, "The party was supposed to be a surprise!"

"I am surprised!" Torey exclaimed emphatically.

"Come, lass," Leigh said as she ushered everyone inside, "There's work to be done for the festivities, and the Birthday Girl has to help, too!"

Torey was so happy that she and Gregg were home and safe that even work was welcomed.

That Saturday night Leigh and the ladies outdid themselves decorating the tavern for Torey's party. They made garlands of wild flowers and hung them on the walls and the staircase. They hung sweet smelling spices on the doorposts and around the bar. The tavern was filled with the soft flicker of candles, throwing a romantic glow over the tables. Earlier, Leigh had baked a cake, and then put the finishing touches on an impressive black and green dress that she had been working on for Torey to wear.

As people arrived, Torey insisted on helping to wait customers and serve ale, even in her lovely dress. Teresa arrived with her husband, Matthew. They gave Torey a beautiful locket of her own to wear, so she would not have to borrow Leigh's anymore.

"Where's Gregg?" Torey asked Leigh anxiously when she realized she had not seen him for a while.

"He'll be here." Leigh smiled reassuringly.

Torey's friends and family were all there now, except Gregg. His absence was unsettling to her. She was carrying a tray full of mugs of ale above her head when Gregg came in the door. Leigh took the tray from Torey so Gregg could present his gift, and everyone gathered 'round.

Torey giggled with delight as Gregg stood before her with a long, narrow, wooden box in his hands. He opened his mouth to speak, but couldn't. For the first time, Torey's loveable jester was speechless. He took off his hat, bowed to her in that playful way of his, and handed her the box. She stood there, her eyes already brimming with tears, and she hadn't even opened it yet.

Leigh's impatience got the better of her. "Well, don't just stand there, 'ya long-eared, red-headed galoot; open it!"

"Aye, open it!" Everyone in the tavern raised their mugs and cheered her on, chanting, "Open it! Open it!"

Torey rolled her eyes in mock annoyance, "There's no relishing a moment here!"

She untied the decorative ribbon he had wrapped around the box, took the lid off, and lifted the gift from its lined box. She could not believe her eyes. She grasped the hilt of the most ornate, well-crafted sword she had ever seen. It was made of solid steel, the hilt was black with three round insets that looked like coins. Upon careful examination, she could see that the round insets were wrought into the likenesses of Gregg, Leigh, and Daniel. It had been constructed smaller than the average sword to fit Torey's stature perfectly.

Her eyes were shining with tears as she looked up at Gregg. "You remembered!"

Leigh looked puzzled, "Remembered what?" She had no idea what Torey was talking about.

Gregg nodded to Torey in affirmation.

Leigh elbowed Torey. "Remembered what?" She insisted.

Torey looked at Leigh.

"When Gregg was training me in weaponry we couldn't find a sword small enough for me to wield. I mentioned at that time that I wanted one of my own even though I'm a better archer than a swordsman."

Then she looked at Gregg, "This must have cost you a fortune to have made specially for me!" She threw her arms around him in a heartfelt hug. He wrapped his arms around her, swept her off her feet, and twirled her around onto the dance floor, signaling the musicians to begin playing again. They danced until Torey was breathless, then she and Gregg took a seat at the bar.

Anne came up to Torey with a big smile, "It's my turn!" She announced, "I have a gift for you, too!" She handed Torey a small, lovely wooden box and waited for her to open it.

Torey smiled and lifted the lid, squealed with delight, and hugged Anne, then took one of the lovely combs out of the box and handed it to Anne. "Here, put this one in my hair!" Anne fixed the comb firmly in Torey's tresses, sweeping her long locks away from her small face. "Now, dance for us!" She encouraged Anne with a wicked smile.

"Aye, milady. I have a special dance just for you." Torey beamed at her and clapped her hands, making everyone stand back to give Anne room for her dance.

Anne turned to Gregg, "May I?" she asked, reaching for the sword.

"Of course, milady" He bowed to her in his jester way.

Anne balanced the sword on her head and danced gracefully and sensuously, as though the sword was not there at all.

When the dance was finished, she handed the sword to Torey, bowed to everyone, and turned back to Torey. "Let's have some ale, lass, and I will explain the significance of the sword dance."

The two women seated themselves at a table, and Leigh and Teresa joined them. Anne clasped Torey's hand in hers.

"Remember the day I was with you in the castle, Torey? I admired you because you were brave even though you were very frightened. The dance is called the Dance of Defiance. It means, 'You control my life, you hold the sword over my head, but you do not control my spirit.' It reminded me so much of you that day that I've always wanted to show you."

Torey's heart was touched. This held great meaning for her. "Will you teach me to dance like that?" She asked in earnest.

Anne smiled, rose, and held out her hand to Torey. They danced and drank ale, laughing like children.

Torey was breathless from dancing when Leigh caught her eye, smiled, and motioned toward the front door.

Liam, the nobleman, was making his way across the tavern. Torey squealed as he closed the distance between them, wrapped her in his arms, and twirled her around. He was as handsome as she remembered, and she loved the way his moustache tickled her. Torey could not be more delighted, for it had been a long time.

"Have you presents? Who told you it was my birthday?" Torey was irrepressible in her excitement.

"So it's presents, is it?" Liam teased her. "Of course I brought presents, milady, my footman is bringing them." He crushed her to him and kissed her passionately. She had missed the feel of him in her bed.

"Let me look at you." He held her away from him, and nodded approvingly. "Now, mayhap you and your friend can show me the dance you were doing when I came in."

"Aye, my lord, Anne just taught me!" Torey called Anne to join them, and the two women demonstrated the moves. Torey danced with her new sword, and Liam allowed Anne to use his. With one hand, Torey made sure the sword was balanced on her head, the other hand clasped Anne's hand. They mirrored each other in the graceful moves of the unusual, sensual dance, moved together in perfect rhythm to the tune Anne had asked the musicians to play. Everyone made room for them and watched with admiration.

Liam's eyes shone with appreciation and desire for the two beautiful women as they undulated and swayed before him. At the end of the dance, they bowed before him and everyone in the tavern applauded.

Liam lifted his mug and proclaimed in a bawdy voice, "another round of ale for everyone!"

Then he gazed at Torey. He did not try to hide how much he appreciated her loveliness.

"And what would this dance be called, milady?" He asked with a husky voice.

Torey reddened, surprised at how difficult it was to tell him.

"The Dance of Defiance," she replied softly, dropping her eyes.

The handsome nobleman smiled, "Ah, Torey, my lovely lady," he scolded gently, "always tempting fate."

He ravaged both of them with his eyes as they stood before him, smiling, coy, and glistening from their arduous dance, but his gaze came to rest on Torey. He could suppress his desire no longer. He encircled Torey's waist, kissed her soundly, and smiled wickedly. "With your permission, little lady?"

Torey and Anne exchanged glances, blushed, and giggled.

Liam could not be more pleased as he escorted Torey up the stairs. "Aye, 'tis a lucky man, I am!"

Liam and Torey

Torey awoke ensconced in Liam's strong arms. The curtains were pulled around the big bed, shutting out the world, and it was cozy and deliciously warm. Her eyes fluttered open and she gazed into the deepest, bluest eyes she had ever seen. His eyes were like the depths of the ocean, mysterious and beautiful, she could never tell what he was thinking, but she never tired of trying. He smiled at her like the cat that ate the canary. She arched one eyebrow and smiled back.

"Why are you smiling at me like that?" she asked.

"Because I have a surprise for you, birthday girl." He replied, still wearing that wicked grin.

"More?" Torey exclaimed in disbelief. "You spoil me so! I will be spoiled more rotten than the most rotten princess in all the land!"

"We can't have that," he said in mock disdain, "I shall have to take my presents back."

"Don't you dare! I shall show my appreciation properly!" she said, as she kissed him soundly and slid her hand down to caress his manhood.

Liam laughed and grabbed her wandering hand, bringing her small fingers to his lips, covering them with kisses. "Your present isn't a thing you can unwrap, sweeting, I'm taking you away for a week on holiday. I've already talked to Leigh, and she is arranging for Anne's daughter to come and help while you're away." He waited for her reaction.

Torey was so happy she couldn't believe her ears. "You've never taken me away on holiday before." Torey was so excited she was practically bouncing on the bed. "Where shall we go, and when do we depart?"

Liam laughed with a mixture of relief and delight. He hadn't been sure Torey would go, for she had become quite attached to her adopted family and her life at the tavern. He knew she felt a strong sense of loyalty to Gregg and the Rebellion. Truth be known, he was trying to lure her away from that danger, if only for a little while.

"We leave right away, and I'm taking you to my manor by the sea." He was surprised that he felt as excited as she. "Come, get dressed, let us break our fast, and be on our way."

Soon they were saying their fond farewells to Torey's family, with Gregg giving Liam a stern warning to take good care of his cousin. Liam smiled to himself, waving to Gregg as the carriage pulled away from the tavern for Gregg had no idea how much Liam cared for Torey.

Torey was so excited she could not contain herself. What a wonderful birthday she was having. "I've never been to the sea before! Can we go swimming naked?" But then she thought for a moment. "How cold is the water? Are you going to teach me how to swim? Are there wild, man-eating creatures in the sea?"

Liam chuckled at her child-like delight, and then grew quiet just for a moment as he stroked the soft roundness of her cheek and gazed tenderly into her eyes; eyes that were filled with wonderment at this new adventure. There was so much she hadn't done and so much she hadn't seen, her life had been so consumed with just surviving that he wanted to show her how wonderful living could be. She put her nose to his like a child, with widened eyes and wrapped her arms around his neck and repeated in mock fear, "Are there wild man-eating creatures in the sea?"

"Only me!" he replied, laughing, and began to nibble her ear as she continued to volley him with questions in her excitement. "Say, are you going to be a chatterbox the whole way there?" he asked, smiling. "You will see!" and they laughed and bantered while the carriage driver sang bawdy Irish ballads.

After several stops at inns along the way to rest and feed and water the horses, and one night spent at an inn, Liam told her they were almost there. Both Liam and Torey watched out the carriage window as the carriage topped the next hill. The sight took Torey's breath away. From the crest of the hill the sea stretched as far as one could see, and right on the beach was the most sedate, grand manor Torey had ever seen.

As the carriage drew closer, Torey admired the architecture of the manor. It was built in Spanish style in white sandstone with a great white archway entrance. On either side of the archway were towers, one of them held a great bell. In the middle was a picturesque courtyard, and within it there was a well and a garden. Built around the courtyard were various buildings and living accommodations, all of white sandstone. All the roofs were made of red tile. The sandstone manor with its red tile roofs stood out in stunning contrast against the blue-green of the sea. The grounds were a lush green with flower and vegetable gardens breaking up the greenery here and there.

A priest in a black robe turned and waved at them as he entered the tower that housed the bell and soon the bell pealed several times. Torey was in awe, and said in a reverent whisper, "Oh, Liam, it's magnificent, what is it called?"

Liam smiled at her child-like reverence. "And I thought you only called me magnificent." he said, feigning hurt.

Torey blushed and returned his smile, realizing that he was teasing her for being awe-struck.

Liam put his arm around her. "It is called Calafia," he said with pride, "and is named after a Black Amazon warrior queen. The castle has been in my family for generations; it was passed down to me when my father died, and will be passed down to my son."

Torey grew quiet and continued to stare in awe at the beauty of the architecture and the crashing waves as far as the eye could see, and to consider Liam's explanation. She knew he was married, but like most arranged marriages of the time, it was loveless and perfunctory. His wife preferred the company of others; she had her life and Liam had his. Calafia belonged to Liam, and it would be passed down to the next male heir. Women rarely owned property unless there were no male heirs, or if a girl's father was wealthy enough to include property in a dowry if he wanted a good marriage for his daughter; and that rarely happened, either, unless a daughter was fortunate enough to be well-born.

"Why is there a priest here?" Torey wanted to know.

"Because my family is Catholic," was Liam's simple explanation. "Come, let me show you around." Liam helped Torey down from the carriage, and the driver carried in their trunks as Liam took Torey by the hand.

"I'll race you to the beach!" Torey challenged, letting go of his hand, and Liam laughed and sprinted after her.

They were soon running along the water's edge, laughing and splashing each other like children. "The water IS cold, and very salty!" Torey exclaimed. They soon stood still together and looked out over the vastness of the ocean. The sun would be setting soon. Torey was soaked and had begun shivering, and Liam was hungry.

"Come Torey, I'm sure our dinner is ready, and we need to get you into dry clothes." They walked slowly back up the beach hand-in-hand in quiet conversation, as lovers do.

When they reached Calafia, Liam took Torey to a grand bedchamber that had colorful tapestries that hung on the sandstone walls, lush carpets on the stone floors, and a blazing fireplace. The room was filled with candles that cast a soft, romantic glow upon the chamber. He helped her out of her wet things, and wrapped her in a warm blanket, then shed his own wet clothing. She watched him disrobe and caught his hand as he reached for dry trousers that were thrown across the back of a chair next to the large, four-poster bed. She pulled him close, letting the blanket fall away from her shoulders. He never tired of looking at her creamy white skin, and lovely, full bosoms, and she never tired of looking at his handsome, lean, muscular form.

"My lord, why make such haste? Is it not more fun to have dessert first?" She asked as she kissed him longingly, teasing him with her tongue. Leaning back on the bed she wrapped her bare, silky legs invitingly around his torso, and drew him to her. He kissed her hungrily, gently darting his eager tongue in her mouth. She wrapped the two of them in the blanket and said in a husky voice, "warm me." Liam took her as the fire blazed and crackled in the fireplace.

Torey awoke to the sound of Liam's stomach rumbling as he gazed into her sleepy eyes. She smiled up into his mesmerizing blue eyes and teased him, patting his stomach, "I think the man-eating sea creatures are in there!" He chuckled as Torey found his ticklish spot and held her hands captive in his, kissing her slender fingers. Torey's own stomach began grumbling loudly, so they disentangled themselves, yawned and stretched, and decided it was time to go to dinner.

They ate by candlelight with a bright fire burning in the great dining hall. Liam studied her over his glass of wine. She was enjoying the crunchy, buttery bread, strips of meat, sweet potatoes, and beans that were grown in Calafia's garden.

"Why are you staring at me like that?" she asked through a mouth full of sweet potatoes. "Do I have beans in my teeth?" She bared her teeth with a grin and a mouth full of food.

"That's disgusting!" he said, and they grinned at each other. "I have a special gift for you." He said cautiously.

His tone was serious. She eyed him as she sipped her wine. "You're not fattening me up so you can feed me to the man-eating sea creatures, are you?" She jested.

"I might," he said. Without returning her banter, he handed her a small, wooden jewelry box.

She opened it and gasped, covering her mouth and then her heart. The tiny box held a gold Irish Claddagh ring. The design featured two hands clasping a heart, surmounted by a crown, symbolizing love, friendship, and loyalty.

"Will you wear it?" He asked, his eyes reflecting the depth of his emotion. He longed for a place in her life and in her heart, and he knew she had lived her independent life at the tavern for only a short time, so he wasn't sure how she would react. He knew her life would continue as it had, but he promised himself he would be with her as often as possible.

"Aye, and gladly, my own sweet love!" She was ecstatically happy and could hardly speak.

Rising, he slid the ring on her finger, and kissed her hand. She rose and hugged him close to her.

"There's more." He said, in that same serious tone. "Slide your nail between the side and the bottom of the ring box, there's a false bottom in it."

Torey did so, and the false bottom flipped up, revealing a gold coin. Torey looked at him quizzically, and blushed as she remembered all the gold coins he had spent at the tavern to have her undivided attention, and all the gifts he had brought for her.

He realized what she was thinking and said, "It's not what you're thinking, Torey. You are not, I repeat not, a whore whose services I'm paying for. That gold coin will pay a messenger to bring me the ring should you ever get in trouble – the kind of trouble Gregg cannot help you out of." He paused and then continued with his instructions.

"You must tell Gregg to send a messenger to me with the ring and the promise of another gold coin should a messenger think of keeping the gold and the ring for himself. I pray that day never comes, but you are a runaway slave, Torey, and as I said before, if I found you, others might, too. And, much more seriously, you are involved with the Rebellion, which you know is punishable by death."

Liam continued with a hint of resignation. "I would fight to my last breath defending you, my sweeting, but you would have to get word to me that you needed help. I think this is the way to do it, since I cannot dissuade you from a fight you cannot win."

She sat on the floor at his feet and rested her head in his lap. "Thank you." She said in a quiet voice.

He stroked her hair for a moment, and then said in a bright voice, "I'm taking you to collect sea shells on the morrow, and we shall go out in a boat and make a day of it!"

Torey climbed into his lap and draped her arm around him and hugged him. She kissed him and then kissed the ring on her right hand. "I shall wear it always, and when you must be away on business, you will be in my heart and behind my eyes every moment."

Liam gazed into the depths of her eyes, and kissed her mouth wantonly; then he lifted her and carried her easily to their chamber.

Simon Tracks Torey

The pool of water in which Simon had sprinkled the crystals reflected Torey so clearly that it was like looking at her through an open window. Simon licked his lips and smiled to himself.

"You did well, Keena," Simon thought to himself, "I shall let you live."

He watched the birthday festivities reflected in the pool. So, she has a family, he observed. If she were very good, he would give them visiting privileges when he took her away. Maybe.

He rose from his position of repose and observation at the pool of water deep in the forest. Even though the forest was very cold, Simon removed his clothing and folded everything neatly, hiding his things under a bush. He stood with his arms loose at his sides, his head drooping as he went into the wizard's trance. Soon a falcon stretched its wings in the place where Simon had stood.

The falcon took flight beneath the cold winter moon toward the valley where Daniel's tavern was nestled. It flew at a leisurely pace while it scanned the landscape.

The commotion in the treetop at such a late hour gave Gertie such a rude startle she nearly fell off her perch. She crooned quietly to herself as she scrutinized the dark treetop. The wary goose sensed Wickedness was about, so she sat quietly, hoping it would show itself. Presently, there was a flitter and rustle of leaves. With a keen eye, she spotted it.

The falcon spotted her at the same time.

"Is that you?" the falcon asked in disbelief.

Gertie sat motionless, eyeing him intently and threateningly.

Delighted that his guess was correct, the falcon threw its head back and laughed, punctuating the still night with its evil cacophony. The falcon glided gracefully from the treetop, lit upon the ground, and suddenly transformed back into the evil wizard, trying to catch the goose off guard.

Gertie spread wide her wings, and in a lightning flash of brilliant, incandescent blue light, Danu was standing before Simon. She positioned herself between him and the back entrance of the tavern and prepared herself for battle.

"I can see you never learned discretion," the goddess observed.

"You can't stop me! Torey is rightfully mine and I have come for her!" Simon sputtered as he arrogantly strode by Danu. He was suddenly stopped in his tracks as arrows of blue flame shot right at him. He dove for the ground, rolled, and landed on his feet, barely dodging them.

Danu and Simon both stared intently in the direction from whence the flaming arrows came. The Tamlin, Danu's personal bodyguard, and Lugh Lamfada, Danu's champion, were standing on the roof of the barn, ready to defend their queen and her earth-bound child. The Silver Riders circled in the heavens above, their weapons ready. They all knew that Simon was an evil force to be reckoned with.

Wizards can only transform themselves into their birthright shapeshift form, but the gods can transform into whatever they want.

Simon cursed the immortal deities before transforming back into the falcon. Defeated for the moment, he quickly took flight into the night sky. Overhead, he circled the barnyard.

"This is not over! Mark my words! Torey is mine, and I will have her!" he declared, and then he flew into the darkness of the cold winter night.

The Tamlin transformed into a winged horse, and Lugh, a great eagle. The Tuatha de Dannan Champions took flight with the Silver Riders, back to their home, the enchanted Isle of Tir-na-nog.

But Danu continued her vigil over the tavern and her beloved daughter through the eyes of Gertie the goose.

Gregg's Decision

orey greeted the dawn in the barnyard, humming the tunes the musicians had played at her birthday party, swaying with the dance moves Anne had taught her. She literally glowed and her cheeks were pink remembering the ecstasy of Liam's arms, and the week spent at his manor.

She was still dancing as she began her chores when Gertie waddled across the barnyard to greet her.

"Good morrow, my sweet, bossy Gertie! How are you this fine morning? I hope your evening was as wonderful as mine!" Torey cooed to Gertie in a happy singsong voice. Surprised, Torey blinked her eyes as she stared at the goose. If she didn't know better, she would have sworn the goose bowed to her as though she understood every word.

Then the bossy, green-eyed goose flapped her wings and scolded especially expressively, so much so that Torey stopped in her tracks, knelt, and scratched Gertie's neck.

Looking deeply into the goose's green eyes Torey said, "My, but you're acting strangely, you are. Worry not, poppet, for Gregg and I will protect you!"

Gertie's eyes widened at those words, and she waddled away, honking to herself and shaking her head.

High above the barnyard, from his bedchamber window, Gregg watched Torey. He had an ominous feeling that the falcon was evil and that Torey was in grave danger. He was also just as sure that they had not seen the last of the falcon. He had to protect her. He had to find a way to stop the evil, and he knew he had to do it very soon, before his beloved cousin ran out of time.

Gregg Makes
A Journey

Gregg knew what he must do. He also knew he could not tell anyone. He used the excuse that he needed to do some bartering on his own for the tavern and that he would be back in a few days. He instructed Torey that she was not to go on any raids with the rebellion, no matter the urgency, until he returned.

She became highly suspicious and questioned him at great length. She wanted to go with him, but he was adamant about going alone. She was very upset with him, and they fought for the first time ever. Torey had burst into tears and would not come downstairs to see him off. This pained him greatly, but at least he knew she would be safe.

It was not quite dawn when he began his journey. He figured he would not be gone for more than four or five days. About five hours out he stopped, watered his horse, and ate, while keeping a close eye on the sky for falcons. Shortly before darkness fell, he made camp in a spot fairly secluded by the low-hanging boughs of a very large tree. He slept for only a few hours and broke camp before dawn.

He knew the general direction of the forest that he sought, and from the descriptions he had heard, he knew that he was drawing near. The forest had become dark and gloomy, even in the late afternoon when the winter sun usually still shone brightly. He didn't like the morose look of this forest, it was dense and the shadows were unnerving. The willow trees seemed to have eyes and arms of their own. He realized he had reached the Forbidden Forest.

The harsh cawing of a black crow high in the trees gave Gregg such a start after the eerie, heavy silence that he jumped in the saddle, and then laughed at himself for his own imagined fright. At least it wasn't a falcon, he thought. He soon came to a path, and he could tell it was not often traveled, for it was difficult to follow. He was also aware that the crow had become his traveling companion.

Gregg soon came to a gnarled little house that was set deep in the gloomy wood. He tethered his horse and rapped on the door. The door creaked open. He poked his head just inside.

"Hello, is anyone home?" he inquired cautiously.

"Come in, young fellow. It is not locked! Know you not when a witch has invited you into her abode?"

"Nay, milady, I have never visited a witch's home before."

Keena smiled. She liked him immediately. "I haven't been called milady in..." Keena rolled her eyes thoughtfully, trying to recall just when the last time she had been addressed in such a noble manner, then her attention came back to her visitor.

Gregg ducked as Uta flew in the door and settled upon his perch next to Keena's <u>Book of Spells</u>.

"He has a pure heart, he does." Uta remarked to Keena.

"Your crow talks," Gregg said in great surprise.

"Aye," Keena smiled again, eyeing Gregg as he stared at the crow. "His name is Uta. Long ago he was an arrogant nobleman who trifled with a temperamental goddess. I saved him when I offered to turn him into a crow rather than see her turn him into a pile of ash, now his eternal spirit resides here with me rather than in the Underworld." Keena watched Gregg as she talked and completed the spell she had been working on. She was impressed with his courage.

"You love her, don't you?" Keena met Gregg's surprised look. It was an observation, not a question.

"Not in the way that you think." Gregg blushed. "She is my kin."

Keena smiled again, this time knowingly. Gregg reddened and dropped his eyes, then turned his thoughts to the matter at hand.

"I have traveled a long way to ask for your help ..." Gregg began.

"I know what you seek," Keena gently interrupted him. "I am a witch," she stated matter-of-factly.

Gregg stood in respectful silence.

"Give me what you brought," she instructed him, and then added, "what you seek will not be cheap."

Gregg reached inside his coat for his leather bag, and laid the feathers, which he had collected from the forest floor the day Torey was attacked, and the gold upon Keena's table. The gold was for payment, and the feathers would be used to invoke the spell.

"If that is not enough gold, I can bring you more." He offered her his word, which she knew was of trustworthy mettle.

"Understand, sire, that I can cast a spell that will keep the wizard from transforming into his birthright form, but only for a season, and then the spell loses its strength. I cannot protect the girl from the wizard in his human form, but he will not approach your home in human form, for he would be as vulnerable to your sword as any mortal enemy would be."

"Who is this wizard who seeks her?"

"Simon the Brute," Keena began, "I'm surprised she did not tell you about him." Keena's brow furrowed with concern for Gregg. "Beware, young man, and take great caution, for he is a particularly nasty wizard. He is of the mind that Torey belongs to him, and he is determined to have her, even though she is protected by the gods, and his own mother, Isabella, Princess of the Underworld, has warned him to abandon his pursuit. But alas, he will not." She sighed and shook her head sadly.

Gregg studied her as he listened to her, his eyes narrowing.

"He came here, didn't he? And you helped him. Why?" Though he asked in surprise, his voice held no reproof.

"I value my life, as you value yours," Keena stated simply. Then she continued, "When you return, the spell will be cast, and you will not have to fear the transformation of the falcon, for a season. As I have said, I am sure he will not approach your home in his vulnerable human form." Then she added in a sad, prophetic voice, "Away with you now, young man. You haven't much time left with her."

Gregg stared at her in alarmed disbelief.

"Tell me true, milady, is my beloved cousin to die soon?" The muscles in his jaw hardened as he braced himself for the answer.

"The prophecy unfolds as it will." She gazed at him, compassion filling her sunken eyes. "Go to her now, good Sir, for she needs you, she does. Take your leave quickly for Father Time waits for no man."

He stared at the witch for a moment, then he turned and hastened away.

"Go Uta," she said to the crow, "guide him to the edge of my forest."

Gregg Hurries Home

Gregg rode hard and fast to reach home. The uneasiness in the pit of his stomach had been growing since the skirmish when Torey was wounded during the battle, and the incident of the soldiers stopping them on the road. His sense of apprehension had only grown stronger, and now the witch had confirmed his worst fears. How could he stop Simon? How could he protect Torey? He was not a wizard, only a simple man armed with determination and a sword, and his love for her.

Late the next day he finally reached the tavern. He had ridden non-stop, nearly riding his horse to death. Leigh met him at the door with a mug of ale and a tearful, worried expression.

"What troubles are about?" he asked anxiously, expecting the worst.

"Anne's farm was pillaged, the soldiers took Katy, her daughter. Anne heard them say they were planning on skirmishing in the clearing on the other side of the valley. We couldn't stop Torey from going with Anne to get Katy back." Leigh was beside herself, and she was crying so hard Gregg could hardly understand her.

Gregg knew Torey was as valiant as he, and that she loved Anne and her young daughter. He knew Torey would put herself at risk if it meant getting the girl back. He had to go after her.

TOREY RESCUES KATY

orey flattened herself against the ground, brushing twigs and leaves out of her line of vision as she stared intently into the encampment, searching for the tent that held Katy, Anne's child. There were few members in the raiding party this time since the purpose was not to pick off soldiers, but to rescue Katy. Torey had a plan. If all went well, they would get the girl back, and retreat with no losses.

With everyone at their stations, Torey called upon her goddess mother. Danu responded above and beyond Torey's expectations. Ember and Sparkle appeared in a burst of light at the opposite end of the encampment to create a diversion away from the group of tents where Torey was sure Katy was being held. Then the goddess sent Glow, who, like all Prisms, possessed the magical ability to subdue her bright butterfly colors to become nearly transparent.

In the state of near-transparency, Glow twirled above Torey, exuding magic dust on her, evoking the only magical gift Torey possessed within herself.

Torey could not know that Gregg had crept up and joined the rescue party and was not far behind her, but he could not call out to her for fear of giving them all away.

Gregg was astounded as he watched Torey transform into a small red fox with a bushy tail, for he did not know about her heritage.

He watched the fox make its way across the encampment as the soldiers dealt with the Prisms. The fox poked its nose into first one tent, then the next, until finally it came to the one that held the girl. In only moments, the girl and the fox emerged, making their way quickly to the other side of the camp. Everyone in the rescue party watched as the fox and the child disappeared into the forest on the other side, then each slowly crept away from the encampment and made their retreat.

Gregg climbed upon his horse and rode toward the place where he had seen the fox and the girl disappear, riding in a wide circle to avoid the soldiers. When he came upon them, Torey was herself again and she and the girl were running as best they could through the underbrush.

Torey looked up, startled and scared at the sound of an approaching horse. She smiled with great relief when she saw that it was Gregg. He slid off his horse, and picked up the girl and sat her in the saddle. He tried to help Torey up too, but she insisted on walking with him, so they made their way as quietly and quickly as possible back to the tavern.

As they neared home, Gregg stared in wonder at Torey. She knew what he was thinking, and smiled.

"I have a mortal father, but I am the daughter of Danu."

"So, you're not a witch?" Gregg posed the question more to tease her than for an answer. He knew she wasn't a witch. If she were, he felt he would have known that by now. But he was surprised to learn she was the daughter of a goddess. Evidently, Keena had not told him the whole story, but then again, he hadn't really asked. At the time he had thought it wiser not to risk annoying a witch with questions. In hindsight, maybe he should have.

"Are you immortal like her?" Gregg asked, wondering about Keena's prophecy.

"Nay, I shall die someday." Torey smiled, and then added reassuringly, "but I shall love life, and live it passionately until then."

She didn't like the serious, melancholy tone in his voice, so she smiled warmly and boxed his arm affectionately.

"I am a magical creature, I possess the gifts of a muse to encourage and inspire. For my protection, I can call upon my immortal mother to transform me into a fox, and I can call upon the Prisms who also help me."

Gregg smiled and hugged her tight. But can you stop a mad wizard? He wondered.

A Different Strategy

Gregg didn't worry about Torey quite as much after learning that she was magical. He should have felt reassured that the falcon could not track her for a time, but this new information seemed to contradict Keena's prophecy, and the contradiction tugged at his mind insistently because all the pieces didn't fit together.

Though it had made him crazy with worry, he was rather proud of her for pulling off the rescue. He had taught her well, and she had been astute, earning his confidence.

It was almost dawn, and for this raid, he had positioned the rebel party a little differently, spacing his archers farther apart to cover the full perimeter of the encampment.

The rebels could not know that a valiant warrior had separated himself from worldly distraction and sought the reverent counsel and wisdom of the gods before the battle.

CHANCE ENCOUNTER

The warrior stood among the trees in the half-shadows of early dawn. He looked westward to the gods of Tir-na-nog and meditated, asking for their help and blessings for the victory in the battle that would soon begin. He liked this time of day, for magical things sometimes happened when the two worlds of night and day converged upon each other.

Suddenly, a movement behind a cluster of trees distracted his meditation. What was that? He had barely caught a glimpse of it. It was too small to be an enemy soldier, and too large to be a squirrel. He crept with stealth in the direction of the trees, dressed in the typical soldier's undergarments of a plain tunic, breeches, and boots made of soft leather.

The warrior reached the trees without being detected. With a mighty lunge, he tackled the slight figure behind the trees. A quiver of arrows and a bow were sent spilling to the forest floor during the commotion, as the warrior pinned his prey.

Fully expecting to have captured a scout soldier, he was forceful in the tackle. Instead of the broad shoulders and thick torso of a man, the warrior was quite surprised to find that he straddled a shapely, slight figure.

He flipped his captive over easily, straddling the captured scout, easily braceleting the captive's wrists with his hands.

He nearly let go in surprise when his search for other weapons discovered, instead, full breasts and rounded hips under a soldier's tunic. The warrior tore off the head-covering the captive scout wore, and lovely red hair cascaded over his hands and forearms. He was greeted by the enticing fragrance of lavender. The warrior could not have been more shocked.

"You're not a soldier, or a scout! You're a woman!" he accused in utter surprise.

Torey was beside herself. This had never happened before; she had never been apprehended. She had been one of several archers in the peasants' uprising against the land barons, skulking around the edge of a battle, picking off as many soldiers with her arrows as she could. It had been easy because she was an exceptional archer and she was small and fast, and dressed like a peasant man in a tunic, breeches, and boots. She wore a head-covering to hide her identity.

Torey twisted and squirmed hard and tried to bring her knee up to deliver a blow to her captor's groin, but it was no use; he held her fast.

She watched his eyes move from her to the spilled quiver of arrows that had landed nearby and then back to her again. He was, up to now, rather pleasantly surprised. His countenance became slightly serious but still amused as he looked deeply into her eyes.

Torey's life as a castle slave flashed in her memory. Fully expecting this strong warrior who had overpowered her to take her, she clenched her eyes shut and turned her face away. A whimper that was almost a plea escaped her. The warrior, suddenly realizing what she was thinking, immediately protested.

"Worry not, lass! I have never taken a woman by force, especially one that fancies herself a man!"

At this comment, Torey's temper flared and she found her courage and her tongue.

"'Tis true I am an archer. I defend the peasants against soldiers like you who plunder villages, take what they want, and leave women without their men, and children without food!"

"You are sadly mistaken, little wench." The warrior, looking down at Torey, spoke with authority mingled with amusement, even though his objection was quite serious.

His intense gaze both caressed and searched Torey's face, appreciating her loveliness. He probed deeper still, full, furrowed brows handsomely framing deep brown eyes that scrutinized her character, her mettle. Torey returned his deep, searching gaze, not realizing that she was returning the hint of a smile that had, at first, curved the corners of his sensuous mouth. She returned his gaze, intent for intent, defiant, and unafraid.

A loud male voice called for the warrior from the distance. Torey became terrified at the sound of the approaching voice, "Please, milord, please! I beg you, release me!" She sent a silent prayer to her goddess mother to transform her.

He looked up in the direction of the beckoning voice. In the instant he was distracted, she bit him, hard. He yelped and drew back, sitting on his haunches. Torey stole her moment; she rolled, sprang up, and ran. The warrior almost gave chase as he watched her disappear behind a dense clump of trees and brush.

Much to his surprise, a small, red fox with a full, bushy tail, bounded from behind the trees and dashed across the open meadow, closing the distance to the other side with remarkable speed. It disappeared behind a clump of trees on the outer edge of the distant side of the meadow. He blinked in astonishment and rubbed his eyes to make sure he wasn't imagining things. This fox was unlike any he had ever seen.

The warrior shaded his eyes against the glint of the rising sun, peering at a figure he could barely see. The fox was no longer there. Instead, a petite figure of a woman dressed like a peasant man stood, tentatively peering back at him with fear and curiosity.

From a safe distance, she gazed at him. Their eyes locked for just a moment. She thought him handsome, strong, and commanding, the kind of warrior ladies at court swooned over.

But there was more than that. What had so captured her attention as he lay atop her on the forest floor?

What had she seen deep in his rapt gaze that had made her reluctant to run from him, even as she fled telling herself she would be crazy not to?

Unlike any warrior, or any king she had ever encountered, she'd been confronted with something foreign to her of men of their ilk:

Respect.

Torey Is Apprehended

Gregg had decided that he and Torey would not lead the rebels in any more raids for a time. He could not ignore the growing feeling of apprehension that gnawed at his gut increasingly every day.

But it was Saturday night and he was determined to enjoy the festivities. Torey was certainly not worried. He enjoyed her sunny spirit as she waited on customers and served ale, drinking and dancing with the gentlemen when invited to do so.

As the evening wore on, Gregg noticed that several patrons had come in and posted themselves by the front and back doors. They were attired in shabby peasant clothes, and he couldn't tell if they were just weary travelers or if there were something that he should be concerned about, so he kept a watchful eye.

The tavern hummed with an exceptionally festive mood. He watched Torey beam with delight as she served stew to Anne and her daughter. He knew she was pleased about the difference all of them felt the rebels were making. Try as he might to relax and enjoy Torey's reverie, though, worry tugged at him like a demanding child. He knew she had become overconfident; her overconfidence had made her complacent; and, as a result, she had grown careless.

He took some comfort in watching her dance with Anne and Leigh. These ladies were all goddesses in their own right. Any gentleman in the place would have given his last gold coin to have even one hour with any one of them. As far as Gregg could tell, things were going well, so he tried to dismiss his feelings of apprehension.

Suddenly, one of the men who had seemed out of place to Gregg reached for Torey and grabbed her by the wrist, holding her fast, insisting on her undivided attention. Gregg tensed and prepared himself to defend her. He watched her closely as she struggled to discourage the gentleman's attention, and loosen his grip. Without thinking, Gregg's hand rested lightly on the hilt of his sword, ready to intervene.

As Torey tried to free her wrist from the grip of the stranger, he rose, withdrew a parchment from his vest, and in a loud voice proclaimed, "By order of the king, you are under arrest!"

Torey stood motionless, too surprised to say anything. The musicians stopped playing. Everyone stopped dancing and talking. Anne, Leigh, and Teresa came and stood by Torey. The others whom Gregg had felt were suspicious stood and drew their swords.

Gregg and the other patrons immediately drew their swords, as well.

The soldiers took a defensive stance, and announced with authority, "anyone who interferes with the apprehension of a criminal will be judged treasonous and will be arrested and executed."

"By what legal right do you arrest this woman?" Gregg demanded in an even voice.

The soldier in peasant clothes read his decree against Torey. "The charges are theft, affiliation with rebels, and treason. The accused will appear before his majesty for judgment and sentencing." He snapped the parchment closed, still holding tight to Torey's wrist.

The soldier continued, "The accused has been identified as one of the rebels with the raiding parties. We are to bring her to justice."

Torey acknowledged the charges to the soldier, and begged to have a moment with Gregg. The soldier granted her request.

She looked bravely into her beloved cousin's eyes. Then, with her hand upon his on the hilt of his sword, she gently tried to guide it back into its scabbard, but he resisted.

"Please, I beg you, my beloved cousin," she beseeched softly, "let there be no bloodshed on my behalf this night. I will go peacefully."

Gregg stood tense and motionless, his heart pounding in his chest, every fiber of his being wanted to cut the soldiers down.

"Please, I beg you," she whispered tearfully.

With her hand on his, he allowed her to slide his sword back into its scabbard. She slid Liam's ring off her finger, slipped the gold coin from the tiny pocket she had sewn in her corset, and placed them in his hand, closing his fingers around them. Without saying a word, their eyes met, and Gregg understood.

He closed his eyes against the pain that tore at his heart and against the chain of events that were beyond his control.

"Where are you taking her?" His voice quaked with emotion, his gaze challenging the soldier that held Torey.

"I am not obliged to answer to you," the soldier retorted rudely and spat at Gregg's boots.

Gregg drew his dagger from his belt and placed the point of it against the soldier's throat.

"She is my kin! I have a right to know where you take her, or you die this night, Sir!"

The soldier swallowed hard.

"We are taking her to King Byron. It is in his majesty's province that she is accused of committing her crimes."

Gregg breathed a small sigh of relief. At least it was not back to King Alexander's castle and the new Regent who ruled there in Simon's province.

Torey fought the fear that threatened to overwhelm her. She was determined to be brave so that those who must continue to fight would have the courage to do so. She hugged Gregg fiercely, holding back her tears. He hugged her so hard she feared for her ribs.

"I'll come for you, Torey," he whispered in her ear.

She looked intently, first at Leigh, then Daniel, Anne, Teresa, and everyone else who had become her family, bidding them each a silent, wrenching farewell, holding her chin up high as the soldiers marched her out the door.

Once outside in the barnyard, Gertie scolded and honked and flapped her wings in great protest, nipping savagely at the soldiers' ankles. The soldier who imprisoned Torey kicked at Gertie, knocking her over in the dirt. She recovered and kept her distance from the soldiers' boots, but continued to honk in great protest. Torey screamed when she saw Gertie being mistreated by the soldier on whose horse she sat, and struck at him with her small fists. He easily held fast her fists in his large, meaty hand.

"You will be still and you will be quiet, or you will be a dead rebel."

Torey's protests caught in her throat. As the soldiers pulled away from the tavern, she looked back. Through her nearly blinding tears, she saw Gregg standing in the doorway with his fists clenched; one hand held the hilt of his sword in a white-knuckled grip as he watched the soldiers take her away. Leigh and Daniel, and Anne and Terry stood behind him, tears streaming down their faces.

Torey glanced up into the night sky and realized the treetops were filled with Prisms, singing their song of agony for her.

It was a dark day, indeed, for Queen Danu, the Tamlin, the de Dannans, and all of the inhabitants of the enchanted emerald isle of Tir-na-nog.

KING BYRON

Captured and Arrested

orey was marched into the great throne room, flanked by the king's soldiers. She had finally been captured and arrested and was being brought before the king to be judged and hear her fate.

"On your knees before the king, wench!" the soldier leading Torey demanded.

Torey was shoved hard from behind and fell to her knees before King Byron's throne. The soldiers and guards had not bound her with leather straps or chains like a common criminal, as women were so rarely arrested and were not perceived as a threat.

Not binding her was their mistake. As soon as Torey was on her knees and out of reach of the soldiers, she sprang to her feet in a lightning-quick move, nimbly drew a hidden dagger from her waist belt, and faced her captors.

A gasp of horror rose from those gathered in the assembly. Everyone in the royal assembly stepped back, except the king's guards and soldiers. Torey meant to defend herself, to the death, if necessary.

The Tamlin, Queen Danu's bodyguard, stood beside the king's throne, as she had many times before, at the queen's request. Although Queen Danu's champions, the Tuatha de Dannan, rarely interfered in mortal affairs, there were times the deity of Ireland saw fit to do so. This was one of those times. Danu's daughter, sired by a dashing Irishman, was being brought before King Byron for judgment, and the queen mother intended to keep a very close eye on the proceedings. She sent the Tamlin to King Byron once again. Danu watched through the Pool of Mortals in the garden on the isle of Tir-na-nog.

The Tamlin's orders were not easy. She was to safeguard the king while in the great room of judgment, but she had also vowed to her queen when Torey was born that she would protect the earth-bound child. Tam took a deep breath to prepare herself for whatever might happen, never taking her eyes off of Torey.

Torey's wild gaze rested on the king. She caught her breath at the compassion, justice, and authority that seemed to emanate from him. His entire court was humbled by his regal and imposing presence as he stood before them attired in the robes of justice. Close fitting stockings and breeches displayed his muscular legs, a waistcoat of ermine was worn over a purple tunic made wide at the shoulders and flared at the sleeves for his well developed arms that allowed to better wield his sword should the need arise. His royal attire was bedecked by a glowing green jewel that hung from a massive gold chain around his thick neck. On his head he wore a jeweled crown, also of gold. Even in this dire circumstance, Torey could not help but notice that this king was godly handsome. He sat on his throne, in a relaxed repose, with one muscular leg crossed over the other.

The king seemed amused by the scene unfolding before him. This girl, whom everyone in his kingdom believed to be a man, was either courageous or foolhardy.

A soldier lunged for Torey. The Tamlin took a step forward and raised her spear. The king raised his hand to stay the soldier, never taking his eyes off the petite, defiant captive. The Tamlin held her combat-ready stance.

Torey brandished the dagger with as much menace as she could muster. She pointed it threateningly at the king himself. This was a serious move, for it was treasonous, punishable by death, if the king judged it so, but she was trapped and she was desperate. There was nowhere left to run. She had run out of hiding places, she had run out of luck, and now she had run out of time. Torey summoned her courage.

"Tell them to keep their distance," she warned as she wielded her knife deftly from the king to his soldiers, then back to the king again, "or we shall both die!" She realized the odds were against her, but tried mightily to sound menacing.

The king said nothing. He sat stoically, her every move captive under his hawk-like gaze, studying her all the while. Reason, compassion, justice, and his sovereignty snapped and sparkled, doing their dance of the judgment of life or death in the depths of his eyes.

She had been stealing food, and silver coins from the king's guards and soldiers, as well as the noblemen and land barons in the countryside. She was known for stealing horses, cows, and small livestock and giving them to the widows in the countryside, especially those with children.

King Byron and Torey had heard much about each other. The king knew Torey was not the usual criminal, greedy or vicious, but she was a thief and an archer, who had killed his soldiers, and had, therefore, broken the law.

His law.

Still, he knew from what he had heard of her, and from what he had seen of her that day on the battlefield, and from what he could see of her as she stood before him now, that she had a good heart. He was a flawless judge of these things for the gods themselves, seeing him to be an exceptional mortal ruler of men, had gifted him with the ability to see men's hearts and measure their character. He continued to study her.

She was very frightened but very courageous. Torey's heart pounded in her chest, sweat beaded on her forehead, as she stood on slightly bent, muscular legs firmly planted on the stone floor, ready for battle. Her eyes darted from the king, to his soldiers, and back again, but the dagger she kept trained on the king. Terror coursed through her veins, racing through her heart as she eyed the captain of the soldiers, who seemed all too anxious to use his sword. The image of the chopping block she had seen as she was being marched in, on its platform in the castle square, flashed in her mind.

One of the king's younger, less experienced soldiers was uneasy at having a wild, dagger-brandishing female doing a dance of death so close to the king, even with Danu's champion, the Tamlin, at the king's side. The soldier disobeyed the Sovereign's order and lunged for Torey with his short sword in hand. He underestimated her experience in self-defense, and she saw it coming.

He was smaller in stature than most of the soldiers, but he was still stout, thick, and powerfully built compared to Torey. She sidestepped him, letting his own weight send him crashing to the floor, but not before Torey deftly delivered a flesh wound, spilling the soldier's blood on the stone floor. The soldier cried out, but more in embarrassed surprise than in pain. He sprang to his feet and lunged again. Torey twirled around and dealt a swift kick to his side. The blow was true and rewarded her with the sound of cracked ribs. The soldier yelped and doubled up in real pain this time, cursing her.

Another guard charged her, sounding a battle cry. A third soldier hovered, wanting his chance to overpower the prisoner.

At that moment Torey cried out to her goddess mother.

"Mother Danu, I beseech thee to help thy daughter in my hour of need!" She mouthed the words barely above a whisper. Her stomach wrenched painfully with the sudden rush of adrenalin. She stood at the ready, her heart was beating a war drum in her chest; sweat was beading on her brow, her bosom heaved as her lungs compelled her on to battle stance.

A ball of blinding, bright blue light appeared in mid-air above the fallen soldier and began growing in size. Soon a Prism appeared. The creature whirled above the soldier, exuding a very fine black dust that dissipated before it touched the floor, but settled in a fine layer on the fallen, armed soldier.

A great gust of wind swept through the great throne room, billowing up cloaks, ladies' skirts, and blowing parchments around. The air encircled the soldier, completely engulfing him in black dust until there was nothing on the stone floor but a heap of dust in the shape of a man on the spot where Torey had felled the soldier. After a few moments, the small cyclone of air carried the dust away with it and out an open window, the magnificent winged Prism disappearing with it in the same manner in which it had appeared.

At that moment Torey had become as annoying as a horsefly, buzzing about the king's head, trying furiously yet ineffectually, to bite him. He sprang to his feet; his hand gripped the hilt of his sword. Irritation glowered in his eyes.

The king was irked.

"ENOUGH!" The king's voice thundered through the throne room. The thunderous command brought immediate silence, fear, and submission.

The soldier who had been hovering instantly dropped to one knee and slapped a fist to his heart in salute, bowing his head in submission to the king's order.

The king sprang to his feet and stood before his throne, his feet apart, with one hand on the hilt of his sword. The gesture did not escape Torey's attention, but only served to strengthen her resolve, her dagger still poised directly at him.

"You are like an annoying horsefly that buzzes around my head thinking to have my blood but gets squashed instead!" he admonished her, fanning and then swatting the air about his face, clapping his hands together and then dusting them off, as though swatting and killing a fly in mid-air, in an exaggerated demonstration of his sovereign anger.

Torey was close to tears, in an impassioned plea that was as much accusation as supplication, "Aye! Pleased I am that I annoy you like a horsefly! Then you shall not soon forget me after my execution, for I am the one who steals on behalf of the women in your countryside for they starve and are without their men because of kings like you! Kings like you, who must have their whores, their wars, and their sieges!"

He considered her as he paced to and fro before his throne, hands clasped behind his back, as he often did to think and ponder. He glanced at the Tamlin, she was attentive, but expressionless. The judgment was his, and his alone to make.

"So you are the one who has been terrorizing my kingdom and frustrating my noblemen," King Byron said with one handsome eyebrow cocked and irrepressible amusement dancing in his eyes, as his anger abated. It was a rhetorical statement, for he was certain of what he knew, but he was baiting her in his quest for confirmation. Her courage and resourcefulness impressed him.

It amused him that she actually thought there was a chance she could be victorious against a battalion of soldiers in the very heart of the seat of power. A hint of a smile turned up the corners of his sensuous mouth.

Torey found his being amused bedevilingly annoying – nay - downright disconcerting. She had hoped to appear threatening. Ha! The king was far from threatened. In truth, he completely ignored the fact that she still held her dagger, as though it were of little consequence to him.

His voice held power, resonating in the large room of judgment, and was strangely calming to her. She felt fairly certain his soldiers and guards would not molest her unless he gave an order to do so. She relaxed, ever so slightly, the dagger, nonetheless, still poised.

The king, still studying her every move, noticed the almost imperceptible ease in her posture, and an almost imperceptible amusement crossed his handsome features and danced in the depths of his sensuous, dark brown eyes that were framed by full, expressive brows.

Now it was her turn to study him. She had heard that he was a just and wise king, preferring education and rehabilitation for lawbreakers rather than long prison terms or putting them to death.

She had heard that this king, unlike other kings, trained and fenced with his sword and lance, wielding both in practice regularly with his soldiers so as not to go soft in the event that he needed to lead a siege.

She saw that he was handsome, and muscular, with deep intense brown eyes in which a woman could get lost. She had also heard that he was an accomplished and tender lover. Torey could tell by his muscular build, and his eagle-like observation of her, even beneath the royal robes and crown he wore, that at least the former was true. He was, indeed, desirable. She wondered if the latter were also true.

But this most unexpected meeting was not about the conversations Torey had had with the peasant women who had befriended her in the countryside during her days with the Rebellion. They had given her respite, shelter, and companionship. They would oft share a bottle of wine with her while lying in fresh hay, staring at the stars through the slats and holes in the ceiling, and talk about the king, his concubines and mistresses, and his rumored trysts.

Nay, this most unexpected meeting was an assessment, a summing-up, a measuring of the mettle with which one was made, each sizing up the other.

The king knew Torey could send the dagger flying at any time, but he sensed that she would not.

Torey knew that the king, with a mere wave of his hand, could give the order to have her imprisoned or executed, but she sensed that he would not.

Finally, after a long hesitation and confused thoughts, losing the battle between her head and her heart, Torey exclaimed with sudden recognition, "You were the warrior on the battlefield!" Torey remembered now, and she was incredulous, but he had known that it was she as soon as she was marched in.

"Aye, lass, and you bit me!" King Byron was now more amused than annoyed.

"I beg your forgiveness, my lord," Her tone rang with sincerity, but her demeanor was still defiant.

A hush fell upon the room at Torey's request and what it implied caused all attention to turn to the king and the task at hand: his judgment. The air was thick with anticipation. Torey sensed that her life hung in the balance, and she was suddenly filled with great apprehension.

King Byron's gaze held her as surely as a vise grip. There was no amusement dancing in his eyes - now they were the eyes of a judge, of a sovereign king about to make a life or death decision. His expression became frighteningly somber, filling Torey with an icy fear that crept up from the pit of her stomach, climbing up her spine, to the back of her neck, making all the little hairs stand on end.

He must now cast judgment, and he must be fair. If he were too lenient, his people and his men would think him soft, if his judgment were too harsh, he would be accused of barbaric rule, of letting his stubborn temper drive him.

He stood before his throne, pulled a deep breath, and drew himself up to his full, muscular height. His gaze locked on Torey. He turned once, twice, her eyes following his every move, as he finally seated himself upon his throne. He considered Torey as he lightly stroked the whiskers on his chin with his thumb. No one in the throne room so much as coughed.

Finally, he made a decision. His raptor-gaze relaxed, he leaned forward, extending his hand out to her, indicating that she was to surrender the dagger to him.

Torey hesitated, her heart pounding in her chest. She had learned through harsh experience not to trust - and especially, not to trust - a king. She maintained her combat stance, unsure of what to do.

King Byron's intent gaze held her in reprimand, like a child caught in thievery. All eyes in the great room of judgment were on her, Torey bit her lower lip; her arms trembled from the strain of indecision.

The Tamlin held her breath. Queen Danu sat motionless as she peered through the Pool of Mortals with her hand extended, reaching for her beloved child.

For an eternal moment, Torey grappled with indecision. She parted dry lips, flicking her tongue across them, and blew back strands of damp red hair from her face. She blinked back the sweat that was burning her eyes.

"Young woman!" he reasoned with her fear, "Do you wish to die this day?" His handsome, full brows knit together over knowing, deep brown eyes that asked, "are you mad?" He paused. "In case you hadn't noticed," he added gently with a small smile, his head tilted to one side, and one eyebrow cocked at her, "You are sadly out-numbered."

In that moment, her rationale told her that obeying the king's request was the wisest thing to do. If she were to be executed, there was naught to be done about it. If he spared her, she would bide her time to escape.

Torey expertly flipped the dagger around in her hand so that the hilt, not the blade, pointed outward, then she slowly approached the throne.

This made the king's guards uneasy and they stepped forward to protect their Sovereign. Once again, King Byron held up his hand, staying them, and then addressed the Captain of the guards with cutting sarcasm.

"Perhaps you should intensify the training of your men, Captain Henry. It took you a long time to capture this dangerous, blood-thirsty female."

Everyone in the throne room had a good laugh at the Captain's expense. The Captain, however, was not amused. He could hear his men snickering and making jokes, and the lovely courtesans who usually vied for his attention were now laughing at him. Humiliated before his men and the royal assembly, Captain Henry glowered angrily at Torey, who now stood before the throne. He vowed to repay this humiliation another time.

Torey slowly and carefully handed the dagger to the Sovereign and stepped back. This pleased King Byron immensely. Good, he thought, as he continued to study her.

As if hearing his thoughts, Torey looked up into his handsome face. Contemplative, furrowed brows framed his deep, intense brown eyes as he studied her. She returned his intent gaze unwaveringly. She was still studying him, too.

Nay, my lord, not so quickly, she thought to herself. I've been captive too many times. I will yield if I must, to have my life spared, but I'll not do it willingly, and I'll not trust thee.

His stubborn, rapt gaze held her, steadfastly, though she stood in her defiance.

The Judgment

Torey still stood before King Byron's throne, flanked by soldiers, when the king finally spoke.

"Kneel before me, young woman." King Byron's voice left no room for doubt that it was an order, not a request.

Torey knelt on one knee as she had seen the soldier kneel.

"On both knees!" he demanded, wiggling his finger at the floor for emphasis. "You are now my prisoner. You are not a soldier. You have not the privileges of an oath sworn to me. To bow to me on one knee is a posture of loyalty."

He paced slowly to and fro, with his hands clasped behind him, as he sentenced her. "You will be placed under guard and confined to the castle. You will work in the castle with the other slaves and servants. Starting at dawn of every day you will labor in the kitchen with the scullery maids, cooking and cleaning, milking the cows, tending the garden, and so forth. You will attend to my horses. You will polish silver, chain mail, armor, spears, and swords." He stood before her and looked down into her eyes as he proclaimed the final part of the sentence. "You will attend to chamber pots."

At this, Torey protested passionately, interrupting the king, "I will not!" She fairly snorted her indignation, her nostrils flaring, her eyes snapping. It was one thing to pound laundry, muck out stables, and empty chamber pots for those who were her family, in the place she considered home, but she would not do this vile chore for strangers, even if she were a prisoner.

She had never been asked to do this, not even as a slave at King Alexander's castle before she had become one of his many concubines.

"Nay?" King Byron met her defiant scowl with a scowl of stubborn, determined admonition, and then waved a hand in the air. "Guards, take her to the dungeon beneath the castle, perhaps she will like the company of rats better." He smiled to himself at the cleverness of his ploy.

The guards came forward quickly, each grabbing an arm, and began dragging her away.

"My lord!" Torey wailed. There was no way around this, and Torey resigned herself to this despicable sentence for now.

Without releasing her, the guards paused, looking at the king for confirmation of this rather contrary and drastic order.

The king met their gaze with one cocked brow and an amused nod in Torey's direction, and then said to them as though it was a private joke she couldn't hear, "NOW 'tis 'my lord'." Then he looked at her, waiting for her to speak.

She knew his sarcasm was meant for her. "I," she sucked in a quick breath, "I submit!" she said, dropping her gaze, finally breaking eye contact with the king.

King Byron glanced at both guards and motioned for them to release her, and she knelt before the king.

He continued, "You will attend to me in whatever capacity I require of you. If that is not enough work to keep you busy, I am sure I can find other things for you to do to keep you out of trouble. You shall live under my protection. Any man who molests you will answer to me."

He paused as he gazed around the great room, this warning was meant for those gathered in the great throne room. He made eye contact with his soldiers and guards until they briefly dropped their gaze. He was satisfied that his men and subjects understood his meaning. King Byron knew that by the time his guards locked Torey in the chamber where he intended to keep her, his judgment and warning would have spread throughout the castle by way of court gossip. This was one time he was glad that particular medium of communication, which he normally disdained, worked the way it did.

Torey stared at the king incredulously. She wasn't certain she had heard correctly. She was to be his prisoner and servant, sentenced to a life of labor in the castle, yet he was pledging his protection.

"You are my prisoner. I own you. You belong to me, and you are commanded to hold your passion true to me, as your king. Whether you are summoned to my chamber is at my discretion."

"There 'tis," Torey thought to herself, "another King Alexander; I can handle him, no problem."

He paused, staring intently at Torey's face, gauging her reaction, and watching her body language. He was pleased that she was wise enough to kneel and listen quietly to his sovereign authority.

King Byron continued. "If you misbehave, I will order you flogged, and confined to the prison below the castle. It is dark there and vermin scurry about, they nibble on the fingers and toes of those held in chains. The prisoners' screams can be heard in the dark of night. Sometimes the guards forget to feed the prisoners or give them their ration of water. I hope this is all the motivation you will need for you to determine to behave yourself. If you are accused again, I will give you one chance to prove your innocence. If guilt is proven, instead, I will order your execution. Do you understand?" His brow arched to emphasize the question.

Torey's posture was proud even in her kneeling position; her shoulders were back, with her bosom thrust forward, visibly straining against her tunic. Her muscles flexed and her stomach sucked in as she listened to her judgment. She tossed her red mane off her shoulders and stared intently at him, her green eyes burning into him.

"What say you, woman? I must have your answer."

She dropped her eyes, her body drooped with resignation. "Aye," she said quietly.

He was not pleased that he had to drag it out of her. He rose and walked over to her. Standing before her, he reached down to lift her chin. For the briefest moment, she flinched, as though to avoid being struck, the way an abused dog flinches. For the briefest moment King Byron closed his eyes and shook his head in compassion and admiration of the undaunted, incorrigible creature that, even as she knelt before him, was stubborn in her defiance of his authority. He gently stroked the side of her face, tilting her chin up, making her look up into his eyes.

"Aaaayeee, what?" He insisted, drawing the word out in exaggerated fashion, leaning in close to her, his other hand motioning for her to finish the answer he sought of her, his gaze piercing her.

"Aye, my lord," she replied softly, looking into his eyes as he gently, but firmly, held her chin in his hand.

"That's better," he said.

"But, your majesty, she's guilty of treason!" Captain Henry's voice protested angrily in the great throne room. "And you reward her? This is an outrage!" The captain was so beside himself at what he felt was a travesty of justice that his face had become bright red, the veins popping out at his temples. He simply could not contain himself.

"King Byron," the Captain's plaintive appeal held the familiar tone of a trusted, frustrated advisor who was trying desperately to reason with what he believed to be an unbelievably bad judgment. His impatient, disapproving glare was now fixed on the king as he appealed to him, trying to gain control of his rage and incredulity.

"The decree of this province states that treason is punishable by death! As a member of your royal advisory court, how dare you offer this manipulating female criminal a position close to your person as though she were a trustworthy citizen!" Captain Henry was beside himself.

King Byron's eyes flashed hot with anger, and he strode toward the captain. The king was now himself incredulous, in disbelief that his captain would question his sovereign judgment at all, much less in open court. Standing before him, the king struck the captain hard in his chest. The captain went down on one knee to regain his balance.

"It is unwise, Captain Henry," the king's voice was ominous, "to forget to whom you speak!"

The king turned so that everyone in the room could hear him.

"I AM the Law!" The king's voice shook the room like a thunderclap, making everyone jump.

Those in the royal assembly stood by, breathlessly watching. It was difficult to tell which they thought was the more offensive crime, Torey's or Captain Henry's.

King Byron's eyebrows were drawn furiously downward, his deep brown eyes snapped with righteous anger. He was definitely a man not to be trifled with.

"Am I not still king, Captain Henry?" The king growled. "Perhaps you would care for a chance to see whom is the better swordsman?" The king cocked one brow, his hand on the hilt of his sword as he challenged his highest in command of the royal Army. The king's closest guards stepped forward, as did the Tamlin.

Torey watched the tug-of-war for power go on between the two men. Captain Henry realized he had gone too far. Now subdued, he dropped to one knee before his king, fist to chest in fealty salute, to beg forgiveness, and to have his life spared.

"Nay, my king," his voice barely above a whisper, his head was down, sweat dripping from his brow, "I bow to you, my liege, you may have my life if you require it."

King Byron, satisfied with his rebellious subject's humility to him, leaned his head back, and rolled his eyes heavenward. He pulled a deep breath, and with his hand on the man's shoulder, quietly answered as though it was just he and his captain, alone in the room.

"Nay, Captain Henry, not today. King Byron shook his head, and gripped the fellow's shoulder in a fatherly manner, "I decree that you should live, and live to become a wiser man."

King Byron looked at Torey, shook his head, and said under his breath, "All this trouble over a woman." Then he dismissed Captain Henry from the assembly with a displeased frown and a wave of his hand.

Before Captain Henry retreated, grateful to have his head intact, he glared at Torey, the promise of vengeance in his eyes, sending ominous chills through her heart.

Her gaze followed him as he took his leave. She knew she had made a dangerous enemy.

LIAM JOURNEYS

Liam's horse plodded along slowly, matching his rider's dark mood and heavy heart. There was no need for great haste now. Liam kept turning the chain of events over and over in his mind, wondering if there was anything he could have done differently.

He remembered having several members of nobility and royalty in his study. They were busy going over business issues, trying to make decisions, trying to quash the unrest among the peasants, and making plans. His houseman had come to him in the great study to tell him there was a messenger with urgent business who must see him right away. Liam met with him privately, and the messenger had handed him a small leather pouch. Upon seeing it, Liam's heart plummeted for he knew what it was. He opened it anyway; the Claddagh ring fell into his hand, and he grasped it to his chest. Torey was in the kind of trouble he had prayed would never happen.

Liam had ordered a horse prepared immediately for the journey to the castle where Torey was under arrest. He had ridden so hard his horse nearly collapsed under him. After he arrived at the castle, he had been kept waiting for several agonizing hours. And then he had been turned away, without ever getting to see Torey.

He played it over again in his mind as his tired horse lumbered along toward home. King Byron was compassionate and understanding of Liam's ardor for her, but the king could not release her to him, or make any promises. The people demanded justice for Torey's crimes, and the king's own counsel of advisors favored putting her to death. King Byron was steadfast in his decision. When Liam asked if he might see her, talk to her for just a moment, King Byron denied the audience. He felt it would only upset Torey and make it harder for her to serve out her sentence. King Byron would not even tell Torey that Liam had tried to see her, nor return to her the ring that Liam had given her long ago.

King Byron had ended the meeting by saying, "keep the ring for her, she may yet be able to claim it again, someday."

That was little consolation to Liam. He was devastated, but made his departure from King Byron without incident.

Torey Adjusts

orey had never been slothful. Even though her heart sorely missed Liam, Gregg and her family, and her life at the tavern, she labored from sunup every day to complete her assigned duties. She knew she was guilty of at least some of the charges, regardless of the motivation, and that her sentence was lenient considering that treason was punishable by death. Torey was well aware that King Byron had been most generous in his judgment, which wasn't at all like the sovereignty Torey had known before. She was also aware that the king's advisors were in favor of the punishment of death for treason.

In the weeks that followed, Torey labored to fulfill the terms of her imprisonment. She thought that by doing so, the king's advisors would be less likely to petition the king for the harsher punishment of death.

As Torey went about her duties in the castle, she kept expecting King Byron to summon her, or to slide his hands under her skirts when he found her working in a room alone, or to explore the contours of her bosom, like all the kings and noblemen before him. But this one, puzzlement of all puzzlements, was as aloof as he was handsome and commanding. She found she could go about her duties without expecting to have to submit to him at any moment. She even spent a little time now and then appreciating the garden, losing herself in her thoughts and enjoying the warmth of the sun, confident that he would not take her.

When he did come across her, he smiled his most disarming smile and asked how she was doing, and really seemed to mean it, waiting for her reply. She was so stunned her mouth gaped open, and he had grinned, good-naturedly, at her surprise.

Late one afternoon while Torey was attending to the particularly deplorable task of emptying chamber pots, a messenger came to her.

"I have a message from King Byron. A visitor has requested to see you and the king has granted the request. You may see your visitor now," the messenger stated.

Torey was so beside herself with delight that she did not even think to ask the messenger who the visitor was. She looked beyond the open doorway from whence the messenger had come and saw King Byron, himself, observing her reaction. He seemed pleased to see her smile. He nodded to her, turned, and strode away. Olaf, the guard, who was Torey's constant companion, did something she had never seen him do: he smiled at her joy.

The guards and soldiers posted within the castle walls liked Torey because she labored as though she were a citizen, she never complained, and she maintained a good sense of humor. Sometimes she bantered with them. They liked her because she had a sunny disposition despite her circumstances, and, even though they were not permitted to banter in kind; sometimes she made them smile despite themselves.

Olaf escorted Torey into a receiving room near the main throne room. When Torey saw Leigh she cried out in exulted greeting and gave her such an excited hug that it nearly knocked Leigh over.

After they exchanged greetings and heartfelt sentiments, they stood in awkward silence. Torey desperately wanted to know how Gregg fared, and the progress of the Rebellion, but Olaf could hear everything. Torey was sure King Byron had ordered it so. All Leigh could tell her was that everyone was well and missed her fiercely, and to take care and be well. The guard soon announced they were out of time; Torey and Leigh hugged and cried and said their painful farewells, and the guard led Torey back to her duties.

Torey's adjustment to her new life proved difficult and heart wrenching. Many of the servants and slaves were less than kind to her, but there was one in particular. The old wench, who was the head of domestic staff, overseeing the duties of the kitchen, laundry, and other household tasks, was quite nasty to Torey. Her name was Agnes. Torey, undaunted, affectionately called her Agnes the Grouch; and sometimes, not so affectionately, Agnes the Witch.

Agnes was short and stout, of dark skin, and tied her coarse, silver hair in a knot at the back of her head so tight that it made her black, beady eyes appear even more snake-like than they already were. Agnes constantly whined and complained about her lot in life, and, no matter how well a task was completed, she never had a kind word for any of the slaves or servants.

At first Torey worked desperately hard to win this woman's approval, but it soon became apparent that was not going to happen. So Torey contented herself with doing her tasks well and avoiding the sour old wench as much as possible. Torey could not understand why his majesty was so tolerant of the bossy, disagreeable, old woman, especially those times when her tone with the Sovereign bordered on insolence.

On the other hand, Torey did not understand why King Byron had given her a chance, either, considering her misdeeds and her reputation as an archer, a rebel, and a woman of the tavern.

Late one afternoon as Torey was completing her tasks and looking forward to the evening meal, the king's messenger came to her again. "By order of the king, Olaf will escort you to the back of the main throne room early tomorrow morning." The guard spoke gently but firmly. "You will wear these." He handed her garments of a simple peasant woman, but to Torey it was like the gown of a noblewoman compared to the clothes of a scullery maid she had been wearing.

"May I speak?" Torey asked the guard.

"Briefly," the guard answered cautiously, not sure who might be listening.

"Why has his majesty summoned me? Am I to die this day?" Torey asked, keeping her eyes down to show her respect.

"Nay, woman. It is his majesty's wish, for reasons unknown to the rest of us, that you are to kneel, quietly, in the back of the throne room, and observe the Sovereign rule."

Torey was so surprised that she glanced up into the guard's face. He was looking down at her with an expression of sympathy and bewilderment, wondering why the king was mindful of this lowly, baseborn prisoner, and a woman, at that.

Torey rose earlier than usual to wash and dress and was ready when Olaf unlocked her door to escort her to the throne room. There were already petitioners waiting in line before the king was even seated upon his throne to hear them and to attend to matters of state. She had not realized that his day began so very early. Olaf quietly indicated where she was to kneel, and took his post next to her, his sword on his hip, and his spear at attention as did all the guards in the throne room and throughout the castle.

Soon the entourage that always preceded the king strode into the throne room and took their positions in proximity to the throne according to rank and service. The trumpeters blasted their trumpets announcing the entrance of the king. When King Byron strode in, flanked by bodyguards, Torey sucked in a quick breath of admiration and surprise. He was regal and commanding in his robes. His deep brown eyes and full furrowed brows held the solemnity of the office of King, his ornate crown set sedately upon his head, the green jewel about his neck glowing as though alive.

He stood before his throne, glancing around the room at his cabinet in their places, at the citizen's common area behind the velvet ropes. Finally his glance came to rest, ever so briefly, on Torey. A hint of approval that everything and everyone was in its place ghosted across the serious face. Everyone knelt until the king was seated on his throne.

The scribe came forward and announced in a loud voice to the quiet, filled room, "The business of state shall begin. The first petitioner, Lady Valerie, argues that upon her husband's death, the lands that she and her children are living upon are hers and not the baron's."

The king responded, "Does Lady Valerie continue to show a profit? If so, then she may keep the farmland. If not, she may continue to live there until her death, but the baron will hold the deed. Tell her to bring me an expense report at the end of harvest season next year. The judgment will be deferred until then."

Torey could not see the petitioners well from her kneeling position, but she could hear the exchange, and she had an unimpaired view of the king.

The woman objected, "But, your majesty," King Byron looked up from the parchments before him, his piercing look, alone, silencing her. Torey heard the woman thank the king for his very generous judgment as she knelt before him in gratitude. The woman was dismissed and the scribe announced the next petitioner and the next, and so it went for hours.

Torey watched the king listen intently to each petition, to each plea, until the line of petitioners was almost empty. Then the scribe approached the throne and whispered something to the king. The king waved his hand in the air as he answered, also in a whisper. The king looked up and announced, "That will be all the petitions I have time for today." There were groans from the few left in line that had stood for hours waiting to bring their case before their Sovereign.

Captain Henry stepped forward, angry with the petitioners for complaining. "Silence, insolent curs! You are fortunate, indeed, that your king listens to your petty problems. Go quietly before you are judged treasonous and lose your ungrateful tongue along with your head!"

This brought immediate obedience to the command of silence, however, King Byron looked sharply at his Captain who had been testy since Torey's incarceration.

"That is not necessary, Captain. It is my decision to judge what is treasonous and what is not." King Byron knew that having Torey at the back of the room did not set well with his Captain. "Scribe, tell the citizens they may come back tomorrow and wait their turn, if they wish, until their cases are heard."

Olaf nudged Torey, indicating that she was to follow him out of the throne room. Torey's legs had fallen asleep, she had been kneeling and listening for so long, so Olaf helped her up onto her feet. She glanced back as they left the room. Torey asked, "When does the king take his midday meal? It is already well past midday."

The guard was surprised that Torey was concerned about the king. After all, she was a prisoner and of little consequence to the castle, much less matters of sovereignty. Torey was surprised at herself. She had never seen a sovereign rule, much less one who did so with such empathy tempered with justice, and her observations stirred within her unexpected emotions.

King Alexander had been lazy, he had been much more interested in cricket, the fox hunt, and the flirtatious courtesans, and the many balls, than he was in matters of state. He only attended to matters that he absolutely had to, leaving the other matters to those he had appointed. Despite Torey's life-long, scalding hatred of kings and nobility, she couldn't help but be impressed by King Byron's rulership.

"Be not concerned, lass," Olaf said, still eyeing her with surprise, "the king has personal attendants that he takes his midday meal with, then he will finish the day's business at court. He often works well into the night, much to the displeasure of his queen and his attendants, who feel that he works too hard. Alas, they are often right."

Olaf escorted Torey back to her duties, telling her she would not be returning to the throne room that day, but that the king wanted her to come and observe once a week.

This news surprised Torey, so she asked him why. The guard shrugged his shoulders and said, "I know not, lass, but you must obey, and you must not neglect your duties."

Every week Olaf escorted Torey to the back of the throne room where she silently knelt and observed King Byron rule. Every week the king made his rounds in the castle and the grounds, checking on the progress of this or that, taking a personal interest in the concerns of those who lived under his rule. The first time Torey had looked up from her tasks to see King Byron, accompanied by his guards, observing her work, she immediately fell to her knees before him. He had waved the formality away.

Torey soon learned that the king had certain expectations of how things should be done. When Torey completed a task in haste, or it was poorly done, she fully expected the king to berate her, or beat her, but, much to her surprise, he didn't. Instead, he looked at her, then the task, and back again, his full, expressive brows knit together, downward, expressing his disappointment, and then he turned, and walked away, without saying a word.

Torey tried to tell herself she didn't care, that he was still a king, not to be trusted, and that it didn't matter whether she did a good job. But her heart ached, and she felt a torrent of emotions because it did matter to her.

From the back of the great throne room she watched him rule, and began to understand why his subjects were so loyal to him. Despite herself and her long-held, justified hatred of kings, she found herself putting forth greater effort to do things well to earn his praise.

Conversation on the Veranda

The clear, nighttime sky held its starry vigil over the castle. Since the king had given Torey more freedom around the castle, she often came out on the veranda and gazed up at the wintry nighttime sky. She longed to know how fared her family, how Gregg was managing without her, and if he remembered to give Gertie her clover treats.

Liam was a constant and sure thread in her thoughts and reflections, and her steadfast rock against despair. But on this night, that thread bore the unbearable weight of loneliness upon her; she longed for him so. Oh, to nestle in the hollow of his shoulder, safely ensconced under warm blankets with the curtains drawn around the bed shutting out the world so they two were all that existed. She wondered had he gotten her plea, would he come for her, or did the messenger make away with the gold and the ring.

Gregg was on her mind, too, this night, and she feared for him. In fact, she had a great feeling of fear and terrible apprehension, and she'd had a frightening dream. When they had executed the skirmishes together, he had had a courageous boldness, a demeanor of victorious energy. His newly found purpose was to protect her, and bring about some mite of justice to the common folk and the merchants.

When she was arrested, she feared he had lost his purpose, and consequently, his caution and care. She knew the Rebellion and the skirmishes would resume in the spring, which wasn't far away, as winter slowly relinquished its frigid grip.

Despite the trust that was growing between her and the king, and his kindness of giving her more freedom around the castle to accomplish her tasks, she was feeling melancholy. It didn't help that Agnes was consumed with spiteful jealousy as Torey earned favor, and struck out at her at every opportunity, wearing on Torey like a shoe against an ulcerated blister.

Torey was sitting atop the stone guard that encircled the length of the veranda at the highest pinnacle of the castle with her arms wrapped around her legs, her chin resting upon her knees, dressed in her nightshirt with a blanket wrapped around her. Her hair was loose, cascading over her shoulders with a night bonnet atop her head for warmth.

She dropped one leg over the side, calculating, though not seriously, how difficult it would be for her to descend the wall and land on the rocks and dirt below, to freedom, without breaking anything.

A noise behind her startled her out of her dark, private brooding.

"Tis a long way down," said King Byron gently, "even for one as athletic and accomplished as you are."

She suddenly realized he had kicked a stone on purpose to make his presence known.

He had seen her desperation, as of late, and had seen the contemplation written on her face as she dangled her leg over the side.

Silence followed.

He tried again, "I often seek solitude to meditate and confer with the gods to seek their wisdom and counsel."

Torey remembered her first encounter with him on that early morn on the battlefield long ago. He had been conferring with the gods then. As he pinned her to the forest floor, his gaze had mesmerized and held her, judged and measured her. She had been in frustrated awe of him ever since. At hearing his reference to the gods, Torey felt tears sting her eyes, but she fought for control, not wanting them to spill over. She dearly missed her goddess mother, and longed to be with her on the magical isle.

King Byron knew she was distraught. Still standing behind her he asked, "What troubles thee, Torey?"

A flash of anger gave Torey her voice. She turned to look at him, "Why did you send my gentlemen callers away?" A torrent of emotion choked her voice.

King Byron sighed deeply in his exasperation. Despite his efforts, she was still defensive and angry, and more rebellious than he would like to see.

"Did my messenger not tell you my express wishes?" He asked solicitously.

Torey sniffled, a tear slid unchecked down her cheek. "Nay, my lord, only that Gregg and then the nobleman, Liam, had been turned away.

"Do you not recall the terms of my judgment?" He knew she was vulnerable just now, so he made his voice resolute, but gentle, maintaining control over his own annoyance. If he was ever going to make her understand, now was not the time to admonish her angrily. He knew full well who her male visitors were, but found it very effective, indeed, to frame his instruction in questions, especially with her.

Torey sniffled again, tears choked her voice, "Aye, my lord, I do recall. But I'm lonely, I miss Liam and Gregg so much, and I have no one here," and then, losing control of her tears, she wailed, "and you puzzle me."

His eyes widened in surprise, and again silence followed, for he didn't know how to respond to that.

Then she asked, in the most imploring, heartfelt way, "Is this how the rest of my life is going to be?"

She had the most unexpected, endearing way of catching him by surprise with her candor. He wasn't always sure whether he was addressing the woman or the child when he responded to this woman-child.

"That is largely up to you." He answered gently.

Dian had gifted King Byron with the power of a wizard. His majesty's power allowed him to look upon a man's heart and read true intent; therefore, his judgments were infallible. He could tell she didn't understand his answer, and he knew she was too mired in her melancholy to delve into it.

So, he tried a different approach in an effort to make her think and help her reason through her emotions, which he felt were understandable, but he could not say that to her just now, as it would not help her to be strong. "Was Gregg a lover?" He asked gently, though he already knew the answer.

"Nay, my lord, he is my cousin, my long-lost family," she sniffled, "lost to me once again." There was a hint of defensive accusation in her voice. "He..."

Torey stopped, realizing that anything she might tell the king could get Gregg arrested.

The Sovereign caught her hesitation and finished her thought for her, "Gregg protected you in the Rebellion, he was there with you during all the skirmishes, and he was probably responsible for killing some of my soldiers."

Torey was stunned. She stared at King Byron in disbelief, fearing the worst.

He immediately set her fears at ease, "Torey, you were seen and identified on several occasions, and your cousin was not. I had no choice but to send soldiers for your arrest." The king hesitated a moment, then continued, "Was Liam your lover?" He was surprised at himself at how difficult it was to ask the question.

Torey turned her face away, reddened, and then said in a small voice, "aye, my lord."

The king was surprised at how much he didn't like hearing that, but he would rather she tell him the truth, especially when he already knew the truth, than have her lie to him.

"Do you love him?" His brows furrowed as he braced himself for the answer.

Torey was surprised at how much the king sounded like a betrayed lover, himself, rather than the absolute sovereign power that he was. She was also surprised at how embarrassed she felt by the question, even though the king had not summoned her to his bed.

"Aye, my lord, deeply" came her soft reply, "he taught me much about myself, my body, and about love, but he is of noble blood." Then she smiled wryly through her tears and added, "I should have asked him to marry me, I know he desires an annulment of his arranged marriage, and mayhap I would be the lady of a manor now, instead of an imprisoned rebel."

King Byron was not expecting an answer like that, and, not wishing to pursue the conversation any further, said simply, "Come, it is to your chamber with you, the morrow comes quickly with all its duty."

She slid off her perch on the stone guard, and he indicated for her to walk ahead of him, across the veranda, to the door. He followed behind her and took her by the arm for just a moment.

"I do appreciate your honesty," he said softly. She could feel his warm breath on her neck, he leaned his head against hers ever so briefly, his lips brushing her ear.

Surprised at such a statement coming from this king, she turned to face him. A powerful wave of emotions washed over her, but different ones this time. She looked up at him, and was surprised to find his eyes filled with tenderness.

He was sharply aware that she stood, attired in nothing but a night-shirt and a blanket, scantily clad, and vulnerable before him. Her lovely red tresses were fragrant with lavender. She looked up into his deep brown eyes and saw that his soul was engaged in a struggle.

"And I, yours." She replied. He returned her gaze for just a moment, his eyes never wavering, and then his expression suddenly became the ruling Sovereign's face again. He turned her around, firmly, as though she were an errant child he was being tolerant of, and escorted her to her room.

Olaf was at her door, standing guard, as he always was. The king opened the door for Torey and said to Olaf, "You are relieved of your guard duty at this station, I do not think it will be necessary anymore. I believe Torey knows her way around the castle now, and knows where she needs to be in the course of her duties."

Olaf looked as surprised as Torey. He slapped a fist to his heart and said, "As you wish, my king."

Torey smiled and scooted into her room as King Byron closed the door behind her. Torey listened for the key to turn in the lock, locking her in, when she didn't hear the sound of metal turning metal, she realized with heartfelt gratitude that she would never hear it again.

She dropped to one knee, with her fist to her heart, "My Sovereign, my Sir." She reverently whispered her private oath of loyalty to her dark, empty chamber as she heard the king's and Olaf's boot steps fade down the hall.

When she first encountered him, a lone warrior praying on the bat-tlefield at dawn, he had taught her Respect.

Now he taught her something just as foreign of his ilk.

Trust.

KING SERRELL PROPOSES A DEAL

king Byron snapped the parchment closed with great annoyance. The document had informed him that a messenger from King Serrell's kingdom would be arriving soon with an important business proposal. King Byron had a feeling he knew what the neighboring king wanted. King Serrell was shrewd and calculating, he should have been a tax collector or an accountant instead of a king. If there were a deal to be made, or gain to be had, with little or no effort, you could be sure King Serrell would want a part of it. He had no problem using exploitation to get what he wanted. King Serrell was the type of man King Byron particularly disliked.

The kingdoms of King Serrell, King Francis, and King John II were neighboring monarchies, and though they were far enough removed geographically from King Byron's kingdom, they still created problems for him. The jousting contests that were held in spring were an effective way to release the tension that always seemed to be just below the surface between the soldiers and knights of each kingdom. Alas, over the years there were still times tempers flared, and they declared war on each other; King Byron would intervene with negotiation, and once again, peace would reign, until the next time.

Early the next morning while King Byron was seated on his throne, patiently listening to the cases of his subjects as they stood in line and waited their turn to be heard, the scribe whispered discreetly in his ear. King Byron's full brows furrowed downward, his deep brown eyes snapped with annoyance, and his mouth set in a frown. King Serrell's messenger had arrived and begged a private audience with him.

"Tell him his request is granted," said King Byron to the scribe, "and take him to the receiving room, offer him wine, I will meet with him there in an hour. Tell Olaf to stand guard, I do not wish to meet with this man alone." The scribe nodded his agreement and hurried off to make the preparations.

Presently, King Byron entered the receiving room. He smiled to himself as he noticed Olaf at attention, and a serving woman pouring the wine for the messenger. Ordinarily, protocol did not require such hospitality for a mere messenger, but King Byron felt it was easier to maintain good will if he did so for King Serrell's runner. Everyone bowed as King Byron strode into the room. He seated himself and indicated to the messenger to be seated.

"What is this urgent, important message that you bring me?" He asked.

The messenger was nervous. "My master, King Serrell, has heard that you have a bothersome female prisoner who is purported to be a tavern woman and to have participated in the Rebellion."

King Byron said nothing. The messenger continued, even more nervously.

"King Serrell would be willing to take her off your hands and teach her to mind her betters, uh, the greater points of subservience, as he put it." The man was so nervous that beads of sweat formed on his brow, and he kept licking his lips.

"Does he, indeed?" King Byron was not amused, his eyes snapped angrily, and the messenger became fearful that the king might strike him. It was as King Byron had suspected. King Serrell thought he could get a slave to do his bidding, and have her to warm his bed. He loathed to think of what would become of Torey in such circumstances, although the thought of how she would drive him to distraction for any liberties he might take with her amused him.

The messenger continued, "My master thinks to capitalize on the girl's, shall we say, ah, talents, and split the profits with you. It could be a prosperous venture, indeed." The messenger rubbed his sweaty palms together, and smiled, displaying crooked teeth.

This sweaty, greedy, little ferret of a man, and his proposal, repulsed King Byron.

King Byron stood up and strode about the room, his fists clenching and unclenching. All thoughts of civility or protocol were forgotten.

Queen Danu peered through the Pool of Mortals and seethed as she thought, how dare he!

This was an odious proposal, even for King Serrell. Finally, the king stood before the small man, with his face very close to the man's face and said, in an ominously threatening voice, "Get out of my court before I have you beaten for the dog that you are. Never darken my door again!"

The man stammered and sputtered, grabbed his cloak, plopped his hat upon his head, and made haste out the door.

Without missing a beat, King Byron said, "Come, Olaf, we have work to do."

Queen Danu sat back in her own throne chuckling and applauding King Byron.

A Good Man
Is Felled

orey sang to herself as she went about her duties. She looked up to see Olaf who filled the doorway of the room she was working in. "Good mornin' to 'ya, Olaf!" Torey greeted him cheerfully. When he stood motionless, staring at her, Torey stopped, and looked at him. He held a parchment in his hands, his eyes held sorrow and sympathy. Torey was suddenly filled with apprehension.

"What news have you, Olaf?" She dared to ask.

He had come to be very fond of her and hated that King Byron had asked him to bear this most grievous news, for the king himself could not break away from his court duties when the news had arrived. The king would make a point to come see about Torey later.

Olaf dropped his eyes to the parchment, took a deep breath, and reluctantly announced, "Your kinfolk, Gregg, was felled by a soldier's arrow during a skirmish. He died quickly."

Torey dropped the bowls that she held in her hands; they clattered, unheeded, on the floor. Her face drained of its color and she turned ashen, her brows furrowed as though she was in pain, and she blinked her eyes as though that would help her understand what he had just said.

"Nay! Nay! That cannot be!" She cried out in disbelief, as though her denial would make it not so.

"My cousin is accomplished at weaponry, he knows the woods. I told him to be careful!"

She crossed the room to stand before Olaf and started shoving him. "This is not funny, Olaf! This is not even a poor Irish jest." Now she was angry, raising her voice, pounding on his massive chest with her small fists. "Tis one thing to banter with the servants, but this is cruel."

He grabbed her fists and held her to him in a restraining, but gentle hug, pressing her hands to his lips, kissing them, as though to kiss away her hurt. "I would not jest about your kin, lass, I would not hurt you like that." The big man had seen more killing and death than he cared to think about, and he knew what it was to lose one's family. He had spent months guarding this little lass and had grown protective of her. His voice became strong and resolute. "He is gone, lass, and there is naught to be done about it."

She pressed her face into his chest, slumping against him, whimpering, "I never got to say goodbye." She wailed into his chest. He held her for a long moment, and then she gathered herself together and turned away from him.

"Lass," he tried to comfort her, but she held up her hand to silence him. He finally turned and left the room, leaving her alone.

That night King Byron came to see her on the veranda where he normally found her, but this night, she was staring out at nothing. He kicked a stone, but she didn't turn around. "I'm so sorry for your loss," he said, emotion straining his voice, for his heart ached for her. But she still did not respond. After a long moment, he said, "Torey, would you like to go home and bid him farewell properly?"

Torey was so overcome that she sprang from her perch on the stone wall and threw herself at his feet, "Oh, please, your majesty, may I?" Her tears slid down her nose and splashed upon his boots.

King Byron wasn't at all sure this was a wise decision, but he couldn't have his servant grieving herself to death. "I will arrange for you to leave in the morning, Olaf and another guard will accompany you, but it is not because I don't trust you will return, Torey, please understand, it is for your safety. The civil unrest still goes on."

Torey hugged and kissed his feet, her tears still splashing on his boots.

The regal Queen Danu melted with immeasurable gratitude as she peered through the Pool of Mortals. Queen Danu made a silent vow to herself and to King Byron that she would show him great favor for his kindness to her beloved child.

"Come Torey," gently he drew her up off her knees. "Get your rest, 'tis a long ride. You may stay one night only; then you must return with Olaf."

TOREY GRIEVES

hen Torey returned with Olaf she was a ghost of her former self. King Byron looked at Olaf, who quietly shook his head, indicating that Torey was taking Gregg's death very hard.

Torey rose every morning to perform her duties, but often retired to her room, too mournful to finish her tasks or take her evening meal. King Byron would look for her on the veranda, but would find her, instead, lying across her bed, either crying, or worse, just staring. One night, after finding her like that, he sat on the edge of her bed, gently stroked her hair, and said, "Torey, if you want to talk, you may come to my chamber anytime you wish." She only looked up at him, a tear sliding unchecked across the bridge of her nose. He got up and left her room.

Danu's own tears spilled over into the Pool of Mortals; so grieved was she for her daughter's broken heart.

King Byron often worked into the night in his study, sometimes sleeping there so as not to disturb the queen by coming in so late. He was awakened this night by Torey's mournful presence, kneeling next to his bed, weeping, her head inclined near his.

When she realized she had awakened him she said through her tears, "I miss him so, my lord, that I cannot bear it."

"Aye, lass, I know you do." The king pulled her into bed with him, so that she was lying on top of the quilt that he lay under. He was sharply aware that she was clad in only a nightshirt and felt it best to keep the coverlet between them. He reached down for the blanket that was folded at the foot of the small bed and covered her with it. He rolled over onto his side so that he cradled her in the crook of his arm.

"Tis my fault he is dead. He lost his purpose and his caution because I was careless." She said between gasping sobs and wept so bitterly that her shoulders shook with her sobs as the king held her.

"Nay, 'tis not true, lass. He was a brave man, and he believed in what he was doing." But Torey would not be comforted. At long last she fell asleep cradled in his arms, but she quaked with grief even as she slept.

Torey was bereft.

The king was deeply concerned that he was losing her in the throes of inconsolable grief. He believed that all of Torey's life's events that led to her being here with him, and now Gregg's death, had finally broken her spirit, and she had not the courage, nor the desire to go on.

Before he finally drifted off to sleep himself, he thought of a plan that he hoped would bring her out of her mire of sorrow.

CRUST AND COMPASSION GROW

Torey had worked very hard since her arrest and had proven herself to be industrious, resourceful, and trustworthy. King Byron felt he could encourage her toward continued improved citizenry, and dispel the veil of grief that shrouded her in one fell swoop. He had an idea.

Torey awoke in the king's bed in his study feeling somewhat embarrassed when she recalled her Sovereign holding her until she cried herself to sleep, but it had been incredibly comforting to her wounded spirit.

She could not help but have great feelings of admiration and respect, and, yes, affection for such a king as he. That he was handsome and strong and commanded her well didn't escape Torey's attention, either. He was disciplined with her, taking care not to encourage the angry rebellious child that often knelt before him, and he handled her life's wounds with such compassion that Torey was in awe of him.

She had watched him perform his duties with such fervor that he often forgot that she was observing him. She had learned from watching him that it was difficult, indeed, to rule a kingdom as a truly sovereign, just king. He often had to say "Nay," when he would have liked to say "Aye." And he often deferred simple personal pleasures that are a given for others, in order to fulfill his sovereign duties.

Even though she missed Liam, and Gregg, and the tavern; and some of the servants here, like Agnes, were less than kind, his majesty gave Torey a sense of belonging, to him, and to his life at the castle. He greeted her as though she were a noblewoman. She found his smile so disarming, and the way his eyes sparkled at her every time he came upon her, that she worked hard to earn those sparkly smiles.

"Rise and be well," said the kitchen maid, as she entered the king's study. "The king has plans for you today. You must break your fast quickly and don this riding gear." The maid set a tray of food on the table and laid clothes and boots on the bed. Torey squealed in delight when she realized the riding gear was her own. The king must have sent for her belongings from the tavern. Torey quickly jumped out of bed, and ate and dressed, and was ready for the king when he came for her.

Torey bowed deeply when his majesty came in, but he waved aside the formality, ushering her to the door. "We must leave immediately if we are to hunt choice game!" He gave her a broad grin, and handed her the bow and leather quiver, full of arrows, that Gregg had made for her. Torey was beside herself with delight and could only grin back at him. He took her to the stables where Patch was waiting for her. She was so overcome to see Patch, all ready to go and waiting for her, that she leaned her head against the saddle and welled with tears.

"Ah, now, lass, come, come, we have a hunt to attend to." King Byron urged her on, good-naturedly.

Torey shouldered the quiver of arrows and the bow, straddled Patch, and followed his majesty's horse, with the hunting dogs and the royal hunting party, over the drawbridge, and out into the countryside.

She breathed deeply of the brisk, refreshing morning air. King Byron was a striking figure riding ahead of her. He sat tall in the saddle, his muscular legs firmly commanding his horse beneath him. For the briefest of a moment, Torey imagined him to be the most passionate, commanding lover. She could feel her face redden. Oh, my, she had been confined in the castle far too long.

Soon the king held up his hand, they dismounted and tethered the horses, and then quietly walked a short distance before coming upon pheasant in the underbrush. Torey motioned for them to duck down. She lay on her belly, with the king right next to her. She nocked an arrow, and neither of them breathed as Torey took careful aim.

The king admired her singular concentration. Danu again guided her aim, and with a flick of her fingers, Torey let her arrow fly. With Danu's help, it was true to its mark, as it had always been. The pheasant was felled, and the dogs retrieved it and brought it to the king. Smiling coyly, the king could not resist teasing her. "My soldiers never stood a chance against you, did they?"

Torey's gaze fell on the king, his candid banter catching her by surprise. He was wearing that endearing, disarming smile, and his eyes were sparkling at her. Torey melted and admitted, "Nay, my lord, they did not."

"Torey," the king began, ready to spring his plan, "I have some new tasks for you to do."

She eyed him warily.

He said slyly, "I need you to take documents and messages for me to other provinces, to guard my door, and assist me in my personal needs." He glanced at her furtively while he adjusted Bolt's saddle.

"But isn't that what your castle guard does? What about my other duties?" She asked with great surprise, for this was too good to be true.

"Aye, but the domestic servants can take over your work." He reasoned.

She looked a little fearful. "What about Captain Henry? He hates that I even kneel in the back of the throne room to observe, much less be in a position of castle guard to the king." And Agnes will hate me even more and become even more spiteful, Torey thought glumly.

The king had anticipated her reservations. "Is your fear of one of my subjects greater than your obedience to your king?"

"Nay, my lord!" Torey immediately fell to one knee, kneeling to him to rebuke his doubt.

He pulled her up on her feet to face him. He was aware of her petite stature, her bosom pressed against him, her fragrant hair so close to his face. But this was important, and he must make her understand. "Then I will inform the counsel in my court tomorrow morning, and you shall be named my castle guard. They cannot argue, for you have earned it."

Torey looked into his eyes, kissed his hands, and then knelt deeply before him. "My Sovereign, my Sir, I will strive to prove myself worthy."

Queen Danu Encourages Torey

That night as Torey sat on the veranda watching the stars and thinking about her hunting excursion with the king, she smiled to herself.

But soon Liam, Gregg, and the tavern slipped into her thoughts, and she floated away on a wave of melancholy loneliness, for they were there and she could be with them, if only for a little while. She remembered the way Gregg bowed jesterly, sweeping his hat in an arc, calling her 'Lady Torey.' She remembered when he helped her draw her bath and promised to teach her survival skills, and all the lessons that followed.

She remembered her birthday party and the handsome sword he had presented to her, and the Dance of Defiance that Anne had performed for her. She remembered every single time he had called her a long-eared galoot when he was affectionately annoyed with her. She remembered how he always worried about her.

Torey thought of Liam, her own sweet nobleman, their time at Calafia, and the rhythm of their bodies when they came together as one. She thought of his laughing blue eyes, the heat of his skin, and the wonderment he brought to her life. Torey sat on the veranda, her head resting on her knees, and wondered if this grief would ever lift from her heart as tears slid across her nose.

A familiar whoosh filled the warm night air around her. Torey looked up into the dark nighttime sky and smiled as Sparkle, the Prism, appeared out of the darkness and hovered just overhead, her wings buffeting the still air. Then all the Prisms appeared to Torey, their rainbow of color and beating wings filling the sky.

Sparkle bowed gracefully and announced, "My lady, I give you the goddess, Queen Danu." In a magical twinkling, Gertie appeared on the stone guard next to Torey, honking, making her smile at her goddess mother's sense of humor. Then, in a bright flash of blue iridescent light, the goose transformed, and Queen Danu was sitting next to her.

"Oh, Mother!" Torey cried out and threw her arms around her.

Queen Danu smiled and brushed the tears off her daughter's cheeks. "What is this sadness I see in your heart, my Child?"

Torey dropped her head somewhat shamefully, and listened to her mother.

"King Byron is a powerful and just king. Because he is the king prophecy spoke of, Dian empowered him as a wizard, but he is still a mortal man of flesh and blood, inclined to illness and the needs and temptations of all mortal men."

Danu gently stroked her daughter's cheek, and then lifted her chin so she could look into her eyes, and continued. "He needs you to be strong. You must guard him and care for him as I have instructed you in all your past lives. He has named you his castle guard. This is an honor, and a trusted position of intimate proximity to his majesty." Queen Danu gently brushed wisps of red hair away from Torey's face, and waited for her to respond.

"Aye, Mother, you are right." Torey bit her lip, held her tears in check, and then pressed the goddess' palm to her lips, kissing it, and then tenderly held the back of her beloved mother's hand to her cheek.

Queen Danu stroked Torey's hair and hugged her tight, kissed her forehead, and then motioned to all the winged Prisms as she ascended into their midst.

All of the beautiful glowing Prisms whirled in the air above Torey, exuding a fine multi-hued mist that settled on her. It was cold, but refreshing, lifting the veil of grief from Torey's spirit.

Queen Danu blew her kisses and bade her farewell. The goddess' silky voice echoed softly all around Torey as she and the Prisms flew away into the night sky, "Grieve no more, my child, grieve no more."

The Dragon

Torey was lying quite still on the forest floor with her bow at the ready. She had a turkey in her sights. The forest suddenly shook and she heard shrieking on the other side of the clearing. The turkey gobbled fiercely and bolted out of the clearing. Torey lay as flat as she could, shielded her eyes from the sun, and peered hard into the forest on the other side of the clearing. She could hear the villagers, afar off as they were, running and screaming, for they were terrified.

There, through the trees, she could see it. It was the dragon! There would be no turkey meat on the table tonight. Torey squeezed her eyes shut and concentrated hard, "Fear not, fear not!" She said to herself, for the dragon could smell fear. The dragon's sense of smell was phenomenal. It could smell everything; smoke and fire from a hearth, the blood of an injured workman or soldier, the evening meal cooking over an open fire. But mostly, it could smell fear. So Torey lay very still and willed herself not to fear. She could hear the branches breaking and the leaves crackling on the forest floor as it walked slowly closer to her hiding place, throwing its ugly head back to throw shots of fire out of its mouth.

Torey's heart was pounding so hard she could hear the roar of blood in her ears. And now she could smell the dragon as it neared her. That old, hideously ugly dragon smelled of putrid eggs left in the sun to rot. Torey could hear the dragon walking away. She had nearly given herself away retching from the smell. Now she thought she would die from relief. She slowly inched her way backward on her hands and knees until she was far enough away that she could run.

Torey was sure that King Byron's soldiers would be here within a few hours, the townspeople whose village the dragon had attacked would surely send a speedy messenger to the king for help. Even though she herself was a servant of the king, she did not want to be anywhere around when the soldiers arrived, lest anyone think there was any connection between her and the dragon. There were those who would dearly love to see her fall from favor in the king's eyes.

An Unexpected Demand

Spring was well under way and the promise of life renewed could be felt everywhere. Torey was kneeling at the back of the throne room at her point of observation. She was pleased that the king had long since relieved Olaf of his duty to guard her everywhere she went.

Spring was in the air and Torey found it difficult to focus on the Scribe as he read each petition and waited for King Byron's judgment of each, for her mind kept wandering into her daydreams. She would love to go for a ride on Patch. Leigh had brought Patch to Torey on one of her visits, and King Byron had stabled the horse to give Torey encouragement and hope, and to motivate her to abide by his wishes.

The king felt that she could be incorrigible and stubborn, but for the most part she had pleased him with her obedience. He was growing more confident that she would not try to run away, especially since he had named her his castle guard. He had feared that she might when she was so melancholy, and in so doing would have made it necessary for him to carry out the sentence of death. He knew that if she bolted his advisors would give him no choice.

Torey was about to leave the great throne room for the midday meal and her duties when a royal messenger from another province approached the throne.

"What is your petition?" King Byron's scribe asked in his monotone, businesslike manner.

"I represent the ruling regent and the counsel of advisors from the deposed King Alexander's province," the messenger stated with exaggerated authority.

Upon hearing her former master's name, Torey froze in her tracks, her stomach lurched with fear, and the hairs at the back of her neck stood on end.

"The ruling regent has received word that the deposed king's slave is being held in King Byron's prison. The regent demands the return of the slave that rightfully belongs to him. What say you, uh, your majesty?"

King Byron's stated title was a weak, perfunctory effort at diplomatic courtesy. The royal messenger was arrogant and surly, the kind King Byron particularly disliked. That alone would have tempted the king to be curt with the messenger and have him escorted, no, ejected, from his courtroom.

Torey's eyes were wide with terror as she stood silently, watching King Byron's face, waiting for his answer. Indeed, the whole court had grown quiet waiting for their Sovereign's response. King Byron could see Torey and the fear in her eyes from where he sat upon his throne, even though he never took his eyes off the arrogant, surly messenger. His majesty never even flinched. If it were possible for a piercing gaze to literally impale a man to a wall, this man would be.

Torey expected the king to be angry, but he said simply, "Nay. You are dismissed." And then, looking past the messenger as though he were no longer standing there, the king said, "Next."

The messenger became furious and started sputtering and making inane statements to the king, which only caused the king's bodyguards and soldiers to step forward very threateningly, brandishing their swords and spears. Even the Tam, who was normally expressionless, was annoyed at this insolent outburst, and brought her spear up in throw-ready stance.

"Are you deaf, man?" King Byron asked irritably, his full brows knit together in an angry frown at the messenger's persistence. The king wanted to add, 'or are you a fool?' but he didn't.

The messenger sputtered and stammered as though he had suffered a great offense, "By what authority do you hold property that belongs to another king?"

This sounded so ridiculous to King Byron that he used his clever method of framing a question to gain reason, "By what authority do you uphold the authority of a deposed king?"

The messenger again sputtered and stammered angrily, but was clearly not leaving. King Byron, wishing to be rid of this nuisance, but not wishing to stir what could potentially be a witch's cauldron of trouble, offered an explanation. "The servant to whom you are referring was arrested for crimes committed against my sovereignty in my kingdom and is currently carrying out her sentence, and is held accountable to me, personally."

The messenger snapped his parchment closed. "You have not heard the last of this matter, Sir." With the veins in his temples looking as though they might burst, and his eyes fairly popping from their sockets, he strode angrily from the throne room.

Torey nearly collapsed with relief. Everyone gathered in the room turned and looked at her as she walked to the edge of the thick red carpet and knelt deeply to the Sovereign. King Byron knew she was asking permission to approach the throne, with a flick of his hand, he granted it. She threw herself at the foot of his throne, tearfully kissing his feet with gratitude.

Sensing that she needed to be near him he urged her up on her feet. "Come, come, now, Torey, I think today you shall take your midday meal with me and my attendants."

As the king, his entourage, and Torey were leaving the throne room he asked her in a teasing, confident voice, "surely you didn't think I was going to let him take you away?" He folded her hand under his arm, smiled at her, and escorted her and his entourage from the room. "We shall eat and then repose in the castle bath."

Torey beamed up at him through her blur of tears.

Captain Henry and Simon Scheme

Simon became enraged when the tracking crystals he sprinkled in the pool of water revealed that Torey had been arrested and was being held at King Byron's castle. He couldn't believe this unfair twist of fate when he had been so close to claiming his prize.

King Byron walked slowly along the top of his castle, past each arrow slit, and scanned the sky with his soldiers. All eyes were on the menacing falcon as it flew in circles above their heads. Several of his best archers had already sent their arrows flying, only to miss the target. The king used his power to judge intent, and sensed that the falcon was evil. Captain Henry sensed it too, and suspected it might have something to do with Torey.

Captain Henry often left the castle to go into town to drink and brawl and get a wench for the night. This night he bought rounds of ale for everyone. With each round he became louder and more obnoxious, and complained about Torey and how he felt the king was going easy on her, giving her preferential treatment. She had caused him to be publicly humiliated and he had long since vowed vengeance. He was drunk, angry, and resentful.

A tall, powerful looking man approached his table, "May I join you? My name is Simon. I think we have something in common."

Captain Henry looked up with bloodshot eyes, "Sit yourself down, my friend, and tell me your story."

"I heard you lamenting over a wench named Torey."

"Aye, aye, That wench! She is like a flea on a dog's arse. She has been a thorn in my side since she was brought to the castle. I would give anything to be rid of her."

Simon's predatory eyes narrowed as he leaned close to the captain and said, "And I would give anything to have her back. She rightfully belongs to me." There was no mistaking his determination or his menace should anyone get in his way.

All of a sudden Captain Henry wasn't so drunk. He licked his lips as he eyed Simon. "It would have to be done carefully," he said conspiratorially, rubbing his hands together. "Planned out," then he added with obvious jealous resentment, "She's protected by the king, you know."

Simon didn't mention that Torey was also protected by the gods. Why include details that would only hinder his getting what he wanted? "Have you a plan?" Simon asked.

"Possibly. We would have to make it look like she betrayed the king, he would then have to order the death sentence be carried out, and I could spirit her away and give her to you before she was executed!" Captain Henry schemed. "But it would have to be convincing, King Byron is very clever, very smart."

"Work on it!" Simon urged "I had appealed to the reigning Regent in the castle of the deposed King Alexander to send a messenger to demand her return, but the messenger was turned away from King Byron's court, empty-handed." Simon grated in frustration.

"'Tis a deal," Captain Henry raised his mug to Simon, and they drank on it.

Keena Tests Simon

ta cawed murderously as he danced first on one clawed foot, then the other, beating the musty air in the witch's house with his wings. The black crow, once a foolish wizard himself, was very distraught.

Keena busied herself stirring the potion in the small black cauldron that sat on the rough wooden table before her. It was summer now, but the fireplace, spelled by the witch, burned night and day, and cast foreboding, misshapen shadows across her dark abode.

"Why do I find you at my door once again, foolish wizard?" Keena asked, glancing up only momentarily from her work. She was annoyed by Simon's lack of courtesy, and a little apprehensive. Simon had, once again, rudely burst into her home, unannounced and uninvited.

"You would do well to watch your tongue," threatened Simon. Then, shaking a finger at her, "I want a masking spell. I want to be able to slip into King Byron's ranks without being detected, so that not even the girl will recognize me."

"Nay. I will not help you this time," Keena's voice crackled.

Simon heard the finality in her tone and became furious.

"Name your price!" he demanded.

"There is no price to be named." Keena replied unwaveringly, "I told you, the gods protect the wench you pursue, and I will not bring the wrath of the gods upon my head. Now go." She peered at him over the top of the pot that she stirred, hoping that was discouragement enough.

He angrily pushed the table and chairs over, spilling the cauldron and its contents on the floor, and took a step toward Keena. She threw her hands up, and the moment Simon made a grab for her, a protective shield, like a lightning bolt, sent him flying backward, crashing against a crude chair that sat by the fireplace, spraying the room with pieces of wood and splinters.

As he pulled himself up and shook it off, Keena warned in her raspy voice, "If you try to bring harm to me, Danu herself will strike you dead." Her straw-like hair cast strange shadows behind her making her look even older and more mystical than she was. She shook a stirring spoon at him, "Now go, and never darken my door again."

"Very well, then. I take my leave, but think you not that your feeble attempt to stop me will keep me from having her, for I have another plan."

"Fools always do," she mumbled to herself as he strode out of her home.

Uta cawed plaintively from his perch on her shoulder. "Sorry, Uta, it wasn't meant personally. But I don't need to remind you that you wouldn't be a crow if you hadn't behaved most ungentlemanly and most foolishly." She stroked the crow's head to soothe his offended feelings.

Breaking Bread

I t was time for the evening meal in King Byron's castle. A celebratory mood prevailed throughout the household, in the servants' quarters, and the royal court. The king's army had had many victories in the recent skirmishes and had taken few losses. The farmland in the countryside of the kingdom was fluorishing, the weather had been kind, and prosperity afforded civilian, royal, and servant alike a time of festivity.

Though Torey was not a free citizen, but still an owned prisoner, she enjoyed an unusual position of trust and close proximity to the king. He had decreed that she would be his castle guard, for which she had given him her sworn oath. If she ever broke it, or tried to run away, she knew he must order her death. Torey suspected, however, that he had decreed this to satisfy the bloodthirsty members of his assembly when she was captured and brought before him for judgment.

Torey lounged on her couch in the great dining hall of the castle watching the many steaming dishes being brought in from the kitchen. She was seated across from the royal table and had an unencumbered view of the king and his queen, who had attired herself in flattering robes for the occasion; the neckline dipped invitingly low, as was the fashion, and the skirts showed off her shapely calves and dainty ankles in her reclined repose.

Unbeknownst to anyone, earlier that day, King Byron had discreetly invited Torey to have the midday meal alone with him. An invitation such as this occurred so rarely and was such an honor that it was coveted by all the ladies at court. A bond of trust and friendship had grown between them; they were less than lovers, but greater than Sovereign and subject.

The midday repast had been splendid. King Byron was many faceted. He was debonair and handsome, relaxed and confident, sharing tidbits of culinary facts and history with her, as they ate, as a friend would, and, at the same time, bantering and teasing with her, as a lover would. The midday repast had ended perfectly, as well. Her lord had yielded to her impassioned request that she be allowed to feed him the first bite of dessert. It had been spontaneous, an innocent but intimate gesture, and he had shared it with her.

Everyone in the great dining hall was seated and the servers were serving the most wonderful dishes, one course at a time. Everything smelled delicious, and the guests' plates were heaped full as trays of food were passed around. Conversation and laughter filled the great hall, as the feast got under way. Torey gazed at the royal table. The king and queen were an attractive couple. He with his dark, brooding, sensuous eyes framed by full, arched brows, with a smile that immediately set people at ease; and she, with her lovely blue-gray almond shaped eyes set over perfectly curved cheek bones, and a hint of dimples when she smiled. King Byron was tan with perfect olive skin, his queen, Katherine, was a blonde of ethereal beauty. The contrast was striking. Torey had suggested that King Byron hire an artist to paint the royal couple's portrait, and the queen had been pleased with the idea.

Torey was, just now, gazing with studied interest at the queen. Queen Katherine's gown was made of blue satin, cut low, showing off her luscious curves and creamy skin. Torey would have liked to kiss the queen's full lips and stroke her perfect creamy skin.

The king's stare, after a moment, made its intended connection and distracted Torey's gaze. She hadn't realized he had noticed that her rapt attention was fixed on the queen. He had seen the way Torey was looking at his queen. He arched one brow at Torey and gave her a look of amused disapproval. The question conveyed to Torey from the Sovereign hung resolutely in the arch of his brow. Her lord presented such a commanding presence that, oft times, all that was needed to accomplish his purpose was a look, a nod, a smile, or a scowl. Just now he was somewhere between an amused smirk and a mildly disapproving scowl. The arched brow asked, what are you doing, and is there something in that rapt gaze I need to worry about? Torey was a never-ending source of disconcerting amusement to him. His visual connection with her became intense as he mouthed, "NAY," to her and shook his head slightly in emphasis.

She knew he expected her to drop her gaze and stop staring at Queen Katherine. Torey complied, but not before giving him an incorrigible grin, and sticking her tongue out at him before returning her attention to her dinner.

When next Torey glanced at the royal table, the king was still smirking to himself over his victory. Torey stole another glance, although brief, at his ethereally beautiful queen.

CAPTAIN HENRY DECEIVES TOREY

It was very early in the morn, and the king had not yet made his official entrance into the main throne room. Captain Henry summoned Torey into a side room off the main throne room. "I have a job for you to do." He said in a surly tone.

Torey did not kneel. "I take no orders from you." She retorted with heated disdain.

The Captain snapped a parchment in her face. "This is an official document, signed by King Byron. You are to take this document and a treasury bag to King Serrell's castle. The bag carries farmland deeds as well as taxes gathered from the citizens."

Her uncertain reaction was what he had hoped for. "It is of great importance. The king will not have to be pulled away from urgent duties here at court if you take this to King Serrell for him."

Torey took the parchment of orders from the Captain, and scrutinized them. They seemed authentic enough, with the king's wax seal, and his initials on the outside. "I will carry out this task, but I am not doing this for you, I serve only my king."

"Well enough." Captain Henry's lips twitched into an evil smile.

The trap was set.

Torey Is Ambushed

Torey donned her riding gear, tucking her dagger, the one King Byron himself had given her, inside her tunic, and shouldered her bow and quiver of arrows, adjusting the quiver comfortably on her back. She met Captain Henry in the king's treasury room, and without conversation, signed for the bag and took the document from him.

Torey was King Byron's castle guard now, so taking a message or pouch to another castle was one of her many duties, and not at all unusual. She knew the Sovereign and Captain Henry had their differences, and she disagreed at times with the way the king handled them, but she refrained from telling him how to run his affairs. After all, she was not a wizard king gifted with the ability to read men's hearts and intentions. But she worried about him and the way he always extended the benefit of the doubt, just the same.

Patch was saddled and ready for her when she reached the stables. The sun was just rising. Torey secured the leather bag to the pommel of the saddle, and rode out, over the drawbridge and onto the main road with haste.

The sooner she completed this task, the better. Maybe she could even be back in time for the evening meal. With this thought she decided to turn off the main road and take a shortcut through the wood. Tugging hard on the reins Torey tried to guide Patch off the road, but he resisted.

"What troubles you, Patch? Do you not want to get back home in time for your favorite treats?" She tried crooning to Patch in a persuasive voice. He finally obeyed her tug on the reins, and they disappeared off the road into the woods. Torey could not see the falcon that circled far overhead.

She had not ridden far when a net dropped onto her from the trees above. Patch reared up in his surprise, pawing the air wildly with his front hooves, bawling loudly and thrashing his head from side to side, losing his petite rider in the process. Torey screamed and landed with a painful thud on the forest floor, clawing at the net, trying to gain her freedom from it.

The last thing she saw was Simon the Wizard standing nude before her, surrounded by a cadre of soldiers from the Underworld. The scene pulled away into blackness as the mad wizard blasted her with a small fireball, knocking her out and disintegrating the net that bound her.

Patch took off at a full gallop, the leather treasury bag still attached to the pommel of his saddle, bolting back in the direction of the castle.

Simon cared not that Patch galloped away, for he finally and at long last had snatched his elusive prize. He would reward Captain Henry most handsomely for his assistance. For now, however, he hovered over Torey, moving his hands in a circular motion, chanting, transforming her into her fox form. He lifted the small fox and placed it in a cage that was spelled by evil magic. He ordered the soldiers to place the cage in the back of a wagon that had been hidden nearby, and then he took the driver's seat. The macabre soldiers mounted their horses and readied themselves to follow Simon.

His eyes gleamed, and he flicked his tongue across his lips. He could feel his manhood stir as he whipped the horses into a frenzied gallop. Once they reached the estate, her lessons would begin.

Simon the Brute was so filled with evil delight to be carrying his coveted prize back to the castle he had purchased from King Alexander that his ominous laughter echoed through the wood. The Forest of the Eire shuddered as the terrible message of a victorious mad wizard and a captured, doomed fox blew on the wings of the wind, making its way to the listening ears of those on the emerald isle of Tir-na-nog.

Captain Henry Accuses Torey

The day, with all its official duty and tasks, passed quickly. King Byron noticed that he had not seen Torey all day, and, even though this was unusual, he felt he needed to trust that she was tending to her duties. He would look for her on the veranda later.

As was often the case, duty imposed itself on King Byron's evening, and it was very late when the last of the books were closed and the last of the scribes and advisors took their leave from his study. He missed Torey at the evening meal, but since he had not summoned her to the castle bath to serve him and refresh him, along with his other personal attendants, he figured he would see her in the morning. He retired to his chambers with his queen, and slept fitfully.

He rose earlier than usual. After his royal valets prepared him for his morning at court, he made his appearance in the throne room, fully expecting Torey to either be at her post in the throne room, or guarding his castle door. He grew annoyed when she was not there, neither had anyone seen her. He sent out a discreet, displeased message that she was to come directly to his throne as soon as she returned.

Court had been in session for several hours when Captain Henry pushed open the great, massive doors of the chamber of the royal courtroom. Court was in process, the scribe was reading petitions, and there was a long line of citizens and petitioners waiting patiently for their turn to be heard by the king. The Sovereign's entire cabinet of advisors and magistrates were seated in their appointed chairs. Captain Henry stalked into the room and rudely interrupted the king. This was unheard of.

"Your majesty! Might I have a word?" He blundered on.

King Byron was extremely vexed, and his furrowed brows and snapping brown eyes spiked their displeasure at his Captain, but the Captain ignored the piercing admonition.

The Sovereign waved away those in immediate attendance of him, and glared at the Captain. "This displeases me greatly, Captain Henry, this had better be an urgent matter of state."

Captain Henry's mouth twitched into an evil grin. "Aye, my lord, I think you will decree it so when you have heard the circumstances." His eyes gleamed wickedly, enjoying recounting the details that he was sure would be Torey's death sentence.

After a volley of questions, the king thanked Captain Henry for bringing the news to him, and dismissed him. King Byron was devastated.

He didn't want to believe that, after all this time, Torey might have betrayed him, stolen from him, and bolted.

He didn't want to believe that, after giving her amnesty for her crimes, and elevating her to a position close to him, that she would play him for a fool before his cabinet, and run away with the state's treasury.

He could not believe that his gift of wizardry from the gods would have failed him, that he would not know the intent of Captain Henry's heart. Nay, something was wrong. The king felt a great need to confer with the gods, so deeply troubled was he that he sequestered himself away to meditate and turn his voice to Tir-na-nog.

He sat on the veranda where he had spent many hours talking with Torey after the night he had stood behind her watching as she dangled her leg over the side, his heart aching for her wounded spirit. They had sat under the velvety night sky with Queen Danu looking on, as he explained why the balance of power stood as it does in the world. He had ruled her with his gentle and fair, but firm and absolute sovereignty.

He had listened to the sorrows of her life, about King Alexander, and Simon, and of her flight to the tavern. He had appealed to the gods when Gregg's death nearly overwhelmed her with grief. He had pressed her hands to his lips and emanated healing to her, a gift all wizards possess, but most especially those that rule.

He gazed out at the night sky that was perforated with blinking stars and recalled how he had shown her that he could look upon her loveliness, and refrain from taking her, even though he greatly desired to, without making her feel rejected. He had demonstrated to her many times that she was worthy of his defense, and so, had become her Champion.

A tear slid down his nose. He wiped it away angrily and admonished himself for going soft, like a woman. He closed his eyes to shut out his sorrow.

Suddenly a searing, bright blue iridescent light burst across the sky and a whirring noise filled the night air. King Byron squinted into the bright blue orb and suddenly Queen Danu hovered before him, accompanied by several of the beautiful winged Prisms.

King Byron knelt to her, "Goddess, I am honored."

"Your majesty, the honor is mine, for you have protected my daughter." The goddess knelt in return, "You must accompany me to Tir-na-nog."

"Command me as you will, lovely goddess." King Byron kissed her hand. Queen Danu was pleased indeed that this king was the gentle yet deadly champion that her daughter had been destined to serve.

The goddess motioned to Ember to exude the dust of flight over the king, and soon they were flying, arm in arm, to the home of the gods.

Together, they set down lightly on the earthen floor of Tir-na-nog. Dian greeted them, and Queen Danu led King Byron into a great garden.

"Come, your majesty, and gaze into the Pool of Mortals."

King Byron seated himself next to Queen Danu and peered into the Pool. He was horrified by what he saw. "By the gods!" he exclaimed in disbelief.

"Aye, but not the gods of Tir-na-nog, your majesty." Dian said to the king.

The Sovereign gave Dian a questioning look with furrowed brows. Dian continued, "Captain Henry became inflamed with offended pride when Torey was brought to you. When he learned Simon wanted her, he appealed to the Underworld for a masking spell so he could plot to be rid of her, and you would not see the intent of his heart."

Queen Danu interjected, "You must rescue Torey, your majesty, or she will surely die by Simon's hand."

King Byron was greatly relieved that Torey had not done what he almost believed she had. He was suddenly filled with the most passionate righteous anger that he had ever experienced in his time as wizard king. "Take me home, goddess. I have business to attend to and a castle guard to rescue."

In a whirl and a whoosh King Byron was once again standing on the veranda. He strode through the door and into the great corridor shouting orders. "Guards, arrest Captain Henry immediately! Saddle my fastest horse, Bolt, get my armor, and gather a cadre of my best warriors, and prepare to siege!"

King Byron Declares War on Simon

As the king's men donned their chain mail and helmets, and readied their spears and swords, a stable hand came running out of the stables to the Sovereign. "Patch was found in the outer courtyard near the watering trough in a spooked and agitated state with the leather treasury bag still attached to the saddle. Andrew tracked the way Patch had come from, and found Torey's weapons in the wood a short distance from where she left the road. Her clothing was also found there, your majesty, and there are wagon tracks."

King Byron had never felt such righteous rage stir in his breast as he did this moment. He dropped to his knees in the dirt and lifted his fists heavenward and shouted in anguish toward the magical isle. "Queen Danu, goddess of the Tuatha, make my sword true this day! I WILL have the blood of Simon the Brute!" He pledged this oath to the gods, and to Simon, he promised, "May the Underworld have mercy on your soul, Simon, for I will have none as I send you there this day, you son of a whore!"

The stable boys made haste to help King Byron don his armor and mount his horse, Bolt, when a messenger galloped up to the king. "We have word from Simon the Brute. He says the wench belongs to him, and he will not release her. If you try to take her from him, he will take her life, then he will take great pleasure in killing the great wizard king."

King Byron's lips curled and his eyes flashed with righteous anger, "Onward!" he commanded.

Churned-up dust and the deafening thunder of what seemed like a thousand war horses filled the air as King Byron led his men into battle to lay siege upon Simon's castle.

Simon's Castle

Simon summoned Carole Ness, the town's apothecary, and ordered her to care for Torey's wounds just enough to keep her from dying. Carole was an only child and had grown up learning from her father. He was gone now and she had taken her rightful place as his only heir. Simon had been a customer in the apothecary shop in the past and had purchased rare items that Carole knew were used in dark magic. When Simon darkened her door, Carole, who was now a widow, shielded her young son, Alex, sending him to the back of the shop, not allowing him to run errands or deliver packages for this customer of questionable repute. It was rumored that Simon was a formidable wizard, and from the tales she had heard about him, true or not, she knew she would do well to avoid him.

Simon had warned Carole not to give the captive any water until she agreed to obey him, but Carole feared that Torey would die without it. Simon used his dark magic to cast a spell on the cage so that it held Torey bound in her fox form until he released her out of the cage for her lessons, but she was still under his spell even then. He would not even let her go to the privy, so she lay in her own waste in the cage. Carole took pity on the poor girl, and when she was sure neither Simon nor his soldiers would notice, she gave Torey sips of water, but she knew if she got caught, her own life could be in danger.

Simon had taken Torey out of the cage once again and held her in a cruel embrace, his fingers wrapped in her hair and her bruised, naked body pressed against him as he hissed in her face, "my lovely little whore, you can put an end to all of this, just submit to me."

Her eyes rolled back, and a barely audible response escaped her lips, "Nay."

His hot breath whispered in her ear, "that is okay, my stubborn little one," and his mouth traveled down her neck and nipped roughly at her bosom, "we have time for you to learn." Simon motioned for two of his men to take her back to the cage.

Carole hovered in the corner of the small, musty chamber, pretending to be busy preparing an apothecary order, waiting and watching until Simon's macabre soldiers threw Torey back into the cage. When the otherworldly soldiers took their leave and she could hear them guffawing with Simon in the chamber down the hall, Carole quickly gave the semi-conscious captive a few more sips of water.

Dian Is Enraged

Queen Danu, and her lover, Dian, the physician of the Tautha de Danaan, watched in the Pool of Mortals as Simon tortured Torey. Dian rose to prepare his lightning bolts of death-fire, for he could not bear to watch any longer.

Queen Danu held up her hand to stay him. "Nay, Dian, King Byron must be the one to save her. As it is written in the prophecy, only he can finally dispel the veil of shame that has haunted her through each of her lives, and make her dignity whole again, and in turn, his faith in mankind will be restored. Prophecy will be fulfilled when this valiant king becomes her Champion against the evil wizard. The king and his men are riding hard; they will arrive soon."

Dian refrained from striking Simon down, but the god's undisciplined rage sent lightning bolts flashing through the sky, striking the domain of mortal men. The fiery panorama heightened King Byron's attack.

King Byron to the Rescue

Oian and Queen Danu watched in the Pool of Mortals as King Byron and his soldiers crashed through the massive solid wooden gates of Simon's castle with their battering ram. Once the gates crashed open, the king's men poured into the courtyard of the castle, crashing in doorways and setting buildings on fire as they went. Anyone who resisted them got their skull smashed in.

Black smoke curled into the sky and greeted the dawn of a new day with the promise of death. King Byron rode into the courtyard, his eyes searching everywhere for Torey until he spotted a woman, Carole, waving the hem of her skirt at him. He rode toward her, and led his soldiers into the castle's inner courtyard.

There, on the steps of the castle's keep that housed royalty and noblemen, stood Simon, next to a cage that held the very still, lifeless form of a fox. Simon stood with his hand held over the cage sending a blue, electric line of light that connected him to the fox, keeping Torey trapped and unconscious in that form.

King Byron raised his hand indicating to his soldiers to stay back while he brought his horse closer to the cage.

"Stay back or I will kill her," Simon warned.

"Release her," King Byron demanded.

"Nay! She is mine, she is mine," Simon repeated over and over again.

"You are defeated, Simon. It is over. Release her," the king repeated.

But Simon could no longer be reasoned with.

At that moment an arrow pierced Simon's arm through, the impact throwing him back onto the stone steps. The connection between Simon and the fox was broken, but the animal did not transform. The fox still lay motionless.

Simon gathered himself, drew his sword with his good hand and took a stand, stumbling, to defend himself.

Another arrow flew, piercing Simon's leg. He went down with an agonized scream.

King Byron pulled his horse around to the front of the cage. Lifting his sword heavenward, he shouted, "by the gods!" and brought his sword around in a perfect arc.

At that moment, Dian, who could no longer control his own rage, sent a deadly lightning bolt through King Byron's sword. When the king delivered the blow to the cage, the supernaturally charged blade splintered it, disintegrating it completely, leaving only the iron lock on the stone step.

Two of the king's soldiers came to the fox's side. They pulled full skins of water from their shoulders, dripping water on the furry forehead.

Two more of the king's men rushed forward to finish off the demented wizard. Even with an arrow through his arm, and one through his leg, he was an able swordsman, but in his weakened state, he could not take on two men, and took the worst of the sword fight until King Byron commanded, "Enough! His blood is mine!"

The fox pulled a deep breath, disappeared into a warm red glow, and, at long last, shapeshifted.

The world appeared to Torcy as a painful, disorienting blur. King Byron ordered his men to wrap her in a blanket and gently hand her up to him, atop his horse.

The Vanquished Wizard

With a barely conscious Torey now cradled safely in his arms, King Byron sat victoriously atop his horse, looking down with disgust at the defeated wizard writhing painfully and pathetically, in the dirt, on the ground before him.

"Why do you besiege my castle for a lowly slave?" The wizard demanded. "You can buy servants every day in the market place!" The tirade-come-to-life that now lay dying continued to petition the king, in a voice that trembled with confusion and disbelief, for understanding as to why a monarch as powerful as he would concern himself with a mere servant.

King Byron gently brushed Torey's filthy, matted hair out of her eyes. There was dried blood on her legs, and she reeked of sweat and urine. His eyes tried to search hers in an effort to know how badly she was hurt, but she kept drifting in and out. He moistened his thumb and gently wiped the dirt from Torey's dry, cracked lips.

He felt his fury rise, his eyes snapped with rage at finding his servant in this condition. Finding Torey like this was the insult to the injury of having her, his possession, stolen from him.

King Byron looked down at the defeated wizard who was shielding his eyes from the hot, midday sun with one hand and keeping himself upright in the dirt with the other, the arrows still lodged in his arm and leg, dripping his life's blood in the dirt. The king's majestic chestnut war-horse, Bolt, snorted impatiently and stamped the dirt, anxious to be homeward bound.

King Byron answered the mad wizard's question in a low, ominous voice.

"Because she is MY slave."

"But she is a servant." The wizard further protested; his questioning eyes were now devoid of any depth of intelligence or reasoning.

"She is MY servant." King Byron's voice held the steel edge of warning that was lost on Simon. The Sovereign's raptor gaze shifted from the pathetic man groveling in the dirt, to the burning buildings belching black smoke all around him, and the cries that could still be heard across the razed castle.

War was not King Byron's favorite tack. In fact, it was his last resort, but when he declared it, he meant to win. King Byron had been further enraged when his messengers returned with the reply that Simon refused to relinquish Torey and bring her back to him. That was a foolish mistake that would cost the rogue his life.

Simon, still grappling with the significance of stealing from the king, continued to protest the reasons for the siege of his castle.

"But she is nothing but a woman! Horses and livestock are worth more!"

"She is MY woman." King Byron spoke with the finality of victory, with only one act left to finish it.

Simon dropped his head, and he looked around himself. The buildings were still burning, and cries could still be heard throughout the courtyard and beyond as King Byron's army continued to put down any resistance. Humiliation fanned Simon's anger over the loss of what he thought was his. Simon glared up into the face of his victor, shielding his eyes against the hot sun, his anger giving him a fool's courage.

"And she is a whore!" He shouted at King Byron and spat the ugly word out as though his declaration would condemn her and cause him to appear righteous, and therefore free of guilt.

"Then she is MY whore." King Byron's rage edged dangerously toward the point of no return. His left arm cradled Torey firmly, while his right hand twitched on the hilt of his sword.

Simon sneered up at King Byron. "I gave my best men a turn at her when I was done." Knowing that he was going to die bolstered his arrogance.

"I was disappointed," he rambled, his words careening him toward his collision with death. "She is not as good a whore as was rumored, King Byron, though she fought well, like a vixen. My men subdued her easily, and she was good entertainment even after she passed out."

That sealed Simon's fate, as if it weren't already.

King Byron's eyes snapped as he allowed his rage to possess him. In one graceful, fluid motion, his heels commanded Bolt, he drew his sword; the pronouncement of death came as the ring of steel filled the air. Bolt's hooves pawed the sky, dipping the king low enough in the saddle to bring his sword around in one powerful, deft arc.

King Byron beheaded Simon in one fell swoop. Simon's head hit the hot, dusty ground with a thud that was followed by the sound of blood spurting from his severed neck. In that frozen moment in time the only sound to be heard was the evil wizard's blood spilling onto the ground.

King Byron and his immediate accompaniment watched as the blood of the vanquished mad wizard stained the ground crimson. The king's soldiers cheered. The men slapped each other's backs and jabbed the air with their swords as they celebrated their victory and their sovereign's decision to siege.

Dian magically filled the sky with thunder and lightning bolts and the winged Prisms' songs filled the heavenlies above the army as they celebrated the king's victory.

The guard closest to King Byron looked down at Torey. The guard knew Torey was in a bad way, but not so bad that time and care couldn't heal. "We should get you and your servant home." The guard addressed his king with a slight smile that spoke of his compassion for Torey, his respect for his Sovereign's feelings for her, and his curiosity of just what those feelings were.

King Byron sheathed his bloody sword back into its scabbard, and slid a skin of water off his shoulder. He returned his guard's direct gaze, and smiled, but did not respond. He opened the leather skin and dripped water on Torey's face. The water formed inky rivulets as it dripped down her dirty, bruised face.

He was relieved to see her eyes flutter as she brought her hand up to guide the water skin to her mouth. Torey couldn't remember ever being this thirsty. She tried to gulp the water, but her mouth was dry and her throat was swollen; she choked, spewing water all over herself.

"Easy there now, slow down, small sips," She clung to him as his gentle voice brought healing and comfort to her. He smiled down at her with that small special smile that was just for her, as he held her in the crook of his arm atop his horse. She could see the concern and relief in his eyes as he put his hand over hers and held the skin to her mouth to help her drink.

King Byron was giddy at his victory. It wasn't so much that he had killed Simon the Brute and reclaimed what was his, although that had been gratifying enough, but he knew the tale would be told far and wide, and that it would be embellished with the telling, not that it needed to be. This victory would serve as a warning across the land that King Byron was a man not to be trifled with. He ordered Simon's head be put in a basket so it could be carried back to the castle and placed on a pike in front of the castle gates as a warning to the king's enemies.

He would not, just now, think about the unrest growing in surrounding kingdoms, or the troublesome dragon terrorizing countryside villages, or having to behead the once-trusted Captain Henry.

For now he would relish this victory and take his servant home to heal.

Torey Heals

King Byron stood observing, unnoticed, in the archway of the inner chambers where his personal attendants lived. He had come to see how Torey was doing, and to check on the healing of her wounds. It had been several days since King Byron and his men besieged Simon's castle and rescued her. The Sovereign had arranged for a temporary communal chamber for his ladies so they would be close at hand to care for Torey's needs until she healed. He watched as Jane finished brushing Torey's hair, and put ointment on her bruised face and cracked lips.

It was midday and his ladies always prepared the midday meal for him. They still had not noticed his quiet observation of them from his vantage point in the archway. He had made a shushing motion to his guard outside in the great hall, pressing a forefinger to his lips to indicate silence so he could do just what he was doing. He enjoyed watching his ladies in their repose. They were chatting amongst themselves, munching on the sweetmeats, bread, and wine that were on the low table in the center of the room. The chatter was sprinkled, now and then, with amused laughter. It pleased the king that those he ruled were happy.

Torey was shaking her head in earnest agreement at some tidbit that had just been shared. There was a momentary flurry of excited comments before the conversation ebbed and attention was turned to munching once again.

His ladies enjoyed different kinds of fruit, cheese, and bread, and a variety of vegetables from the royal garden that were served on a platter, and sweet meats from the last hunt. Torey was reclined on a chaise. Jane plopped a grape in Torey's mouth, with a smile, and brushed Torey's hair out of her eyes, then she tore off a large piece of bread and touched a smaller piece of it to Torey's bottom lip, indicating to Torey to open her mouth for the bread.

"I'm not helpless!" Torey declared with an impish grin as she chewed the bread. The meal and the companionship were nurturing and lent well to Torey's healing, and she was truly grateful to be so well cared for. Jane smiled at Torey, dropping a sisterly kiss to the top of her head, and mutual understanding passed between them. They both knew it would be a little while before Torey was strong enough to resume her duties. In the meantime, the ladies were enjoying this time together.

Sometimes King Byron's queen joined them, but usually she was away attending to the matters of her station that were expected of her, such as gathering food for the widows, and placing orphaned children. The queen would join her king later for the evening's activities, and they would then retire to their chamber together.

The midday meal, when King Byron was at the castle to enjoy it and not off seeing to matters of state himself, was one of his favorite pasttimes.

The king chose not to have mistresses or concubines, but he did have his ladies, his personal attendants that saw to his intimate needs. They did many things for him; such as maintain his field gear, his royal wardrobe, and the royal living quarters. They saw to his meals, completed numerous other domestic tasks in the castle, and sometimes assisted with the entertainment of visitors.

Unlike other kings, and viewed as most unusual by other rulers, King Byron refrained from exercising his sovereign right to summon the women he owned to his private chambers. He allowed them to choose with whom they would lay. He felt he would not want anyone dictating to him with whom he must share his bed.

The only exception to this was Torey. When she had been arrested, long ago, and brought before him, her notorious history made it necessary for him to require her to pledge not only her loyalty to him, but her passionate nature as well.

He had given her a choice: obedience to him, or life in the king's prison. Even though he hadn't summoned her to his chambers, he figured he didn't need more problems within the castle, so he had placed that restriction on her that was not placed on his other personal servants.

His personal servants, however, were as close to concubines as King Byron would ever have, especially his personal bathers. The king would not ask his men to do anything he would not do himself. Sometimes that required him to swing an axe, pick up a shovel, or don his chain mail, sword, and armor, to lead his men. It was the king's philosophy to set an example for those who followed him, looked up to him, and lived under his rulership. In so doing, however, the king would sometimes return after days or weeks on the move with his men, covered in sweat, dust, dirt, mud, or blood, and smelling of the trail and his horse. He gladly allowed his bathers to tend to him, disrobing him of the layers of field gear, dust, and dirt, and bathing him with sponges, pumice, and lavender water in the castle bath and soothing away his fatigue and his cares.

Today, though, he was most concerned about his castle guard, Torey. He had spared her life against terrible odds, and the death sentence his advisors favored when she had long ago been brought before him for judgment.

When she stood before him, awaiting his judgment, he had seen the fear, anger, and rebelliousness in her eyes. They had studied each other with a hawk-like appraisal, measuring, testing, sizing up, he from his throne, surrounded by the royal court and advisors; she from her fighting stance, her dagger drawn, surrounded by his soldiers who stood at the ready.

He knew she had been sure she was going to die that day. He had taken a risk, based on his confidence of his judgment of character as a wizard, and made her his castle guard, giving her close, intimate access to him. His risk had proven accurate and worthwhile, and his faith in mankind had been restored.

At first she had been aloof and suspicious of his kindness, she tested him and pushed him, expecting harsh consequences. Instead, to her surprise, she got furrowed down eyebrows and a look of disappointment mingled with mild anger, but even then he had not abused her or exploited her. He hadn't even raised his voice. She was surprised that his disappointment in her could cause her such grief. She tried to apologize, but he would not have it, making her determined to do better. Over time, she came to understand that a duty well done earned his warm smiles. He gave her duties she enjoyed doing, and sometimes, even the rare honor of his company.

King Byron stood in the archway and cleared his throat, finally making his presence known. The activity and conversation ceased and all bowed, pressing their foreheads to the stone floor. A small, pleased smile turned up the corners of his sensuous heart-shaped mouth as he strode into the room.

"Rise, my lovely ladies, let us sup together." He waved a hand indicating for them to rise and join him for the midday repast. Each of them immediately filled a plate with his favorite morsels, each wanting him to eat from the plate they made for him. He wisely ate one piece of food from each plate, thanking them with great appreciation for preparing it for him.

When the excitement of his arrival subsided, he rose and went over to Torey. He sat on the edge of her couch so he could check her injuries. She smiled into the depths of his intense, dark brown eyes.

"Lie back, Torey," he instructed gently, "I want to see to your wounds."

She reclined, lifting her arms above her head. She dropped her eyes and tried unsuccessfully to suppress a small smile. He pretended not to notice. He slid his fingers gently along her small ribs, feeling for the integrity of their healing.

When his hand was even with her bosom, she leaned her body slightly to one side so that the side of her round firm breast brushed the palm of his hand. He was secretly pleased that she was lovely, that she was spirited, and that she cared for him, but he could never let her know. The gods be warned, he knew better than to encourage her! He very subtly moved his hand away from the round fullness of her breast and continued checking all of her ribs, as though nothing had happened.

It irked Torey sometimes, but also amused her that her lord ignored her antics. She thought she could steal a quick glance at his face to see if he had noticed, but alas, she wasn't fast enough! She knew he saw her look at him, and knew that he knew why. She thought he must surely be chuckling to himself knowing that not only did he win this round of their game of bantering, which, with Torey was challenging enough, with him trying to maintain just the right amount of tension on the reins of her spirit without distancing her too much and wounding her heart, but he also knew she couldn't read him, and he knew it drove her to distraction. This amused him greatly.

King Byron could see that she was still purplish-blue in some places, but most of the bruising was fading to yellow, hastening healing. He was loath to see the bruises, though fading now, on her small, lovely face. His fingers continued their search and inspection down the length of each of her small ribs. Torey winced slightly at one point as his fingers traced a sore rib. She hoped he had not sensed her pain, but his sharp intuition noted it.

Torey was definitely on the mend, and he was filled with relief for that, but his heart still grieved for what she had gone through. He looked away as his mind flashed back; if he hadn't gotten there ... in his mind he slammed the door shut to that dark room of her near-death.

His focus came back to her. He looked down at her, and stroked the side of her face tenderly and smiled that small smile that was just for her.

King Byron was relieved and pleased to see that the playful sparkle had returned to her eyes and she was, once again, up to her antics of teasing him. Even though the healing process was slow and painful, he could see that she could hardly contain her delight that he had come to see about her. He finished examining her ribs and sat on the side of her couch, gazing fondly at her. King Byron didn't want her to think that this visit was nothing more than an official duty as her king. He cared for Torey, but needed to maintain discipline with her.

"You're healing well, Torey, I am hopeful that you will be able to return to your duties soon." He meant that he missed her, but he could not say that.

Her smile faded. Feeling hurt, she dropped her eyes and answered with a small nod of her head. To ease the implication of his question, which had the opposite effect he had intended, he took an apple from the basket, and put it firmly to her mouth, saying nothing.

Caught by surprise, Torey gazed into his face, seeing the invitation to banter with him snapping in his deep brown eyes, and his sensuous heart-shaped mouth giving her his special small smile. She bit into the apple he held to her mouth, the juice dripping on her chin. He dabbed at the juice on her mouth and chin with his fingers. Accepting his challenge to banter, she drew his fingers into her mouth and sucked the juice on them. This time King Byron could not suppress an amused, affectionate chuckle for this woman-child that he owned.

He indulged her for a moment, then, leaning forward, he gently withdrew his fingers from her warm mouth, cupped her face with both hands, and dropped a sedate, sovereign kiss on her forehead.

An Evil Dragon

Torey had long since returned to her duties, and was in the forest hunting when she was confronted by the dragon again.

The dragon was two inches from Torey's face. She flattened herself as much as she could against the face of the rock on the side of the mountain. She squeezed her eyes shut and tried to hold still and not breathe. Her legs fairly trembled, but she tried to calm her fear. The dragon was bellowing and breathing its hot angry breath in her face, and stomping the forest floor in its rage. Torey broke out in a terrified sweat.

This was the second time in a fortnight Torey had crossed paths with the creature. Why the dragon didn't roast her alive and then eat her burnt flesh was beyond her, for this was the second time it could have, and didn't. Torey dared to open her eyes, and upon doing so, she found herself staring straight into the dragon's face.

There was something about the dragon's eyes that sent chills up Torey's spine. It was as though she'd looked into those eyes before, but that wasn't possible; this was the closest anyone had ever gotten to the dragon, and lived.

"You think you're so brave and wonderful. We'll see who slays whom," the dragon spoke low and menacingly to her.

Torey was so shocked her mouth dropped open and her eyes widened in disbelief.

The dragon stood up straight to its full height of 12 feet, threw its head back, and laughed an evil laugh as it slowly backed away from Torey and lumbered into the forest. Torey sank to her knees in the soft dirt of the forest floor in great relief that she was still a whole, unroasted castle guard. Why had she not reached for her dagger? It had all happened so quickly.

Torey would not tell the king she had been such an unworthy warrior today. She gathered herself and decided to track the dragon. She followed the large tracks for a short distance, and then they suddenly stopped before a large rock face as though the dragon had passed through solid rock. But that wasn't possible, was it? This day had been strange enough, and Torey was anxious to begin her journey back to the castle. She could not see the ugly smiling face, and the angry, black eyes as they bore into her retreating back, staring intently from the dimension it had stepped into.

King Byron's castle had been Torey's home for a while now, and, except for an old, mean servant woman, Torey had accepted her life as it was. She had learned to adjust following her arrest, observing the king's sovereignty, and coming to like and respect him, despite herself. She had worked very hard for his smiles of approval, and a bond of trust and affection had grown between them. After Gregg's death, the king had even made her his castle guard.

During the day the drawbridge was down. Torey walked into the courtyard, delighted to find the king, with members of his trusted army, fencing and practicing their skills. A smile spread across her face and her breath caught. "My champion," she murmured to herself.

Servants and slaves never have champions. They are captured, or bought and sold to one lord or another; they would never have worthiness notable enough to have need of a champion, for what virtue have they that their virtue would have need of defending? But he was her champion, just the same.

Torey watched the king lunge and parry, lunge and parry, with his opponent. The opponent was good, but the king was better, and better looking, too. The king was muscular and strong, and formidable, with singular focus and concentration. She knew he fought battles on horseback, captured villages, and brought those captured or arrested here. She knew because she was one of them. She watched his muscular frame take stance and then snap back with each lunge and parry. The movement was poetic, fluid, and disciplined. When he saw her, she grinned, beaming at him, making his face turn red.

"Agnes searches for you. Go now, see to your duties." His tone was firm, but his look of jest gave him away. She hurried to the castle, just the same, for it was best not to anger Agnes.

Agnes had been one of King Byron's servants for a very long time. He was the only one she had any respect for, and even then, she spoke her mind about how she saw things. Because she was old, King Byron was kind, or tried to be, but sometimes she made it very difficult for him. Agnes felt respect of age should be held above respect of rank, never mind that being King was the highest rank in the country, and held the power of life and death. And never mind how very fortunate she was that King Byron would listen to her whining and show her compassion. And still she would try him. Torey would scratch her head, dumbfounded, when she heard Agnes fuss with the Sovereign. Then Torey would become angry, especially after this woman had abused her. She was determined that no one should disrespect the king.

"Torey!" Agnes' angry, impatient tone made Torey jump as she hurried into the kitchen. Agnes glared at Torey. She had a squat, stout build and a sour disposition to match. "There is much work to be done, Torey, where have you been?" and, without missing a beat, "Do you expect me to do it all by myself? I should think not!" she said with derision. "Or maybe you think because the king likes you, you don't have to work hard!" Agnes boxed Torey's ears, grabbed a hand full of red hair, and pushed her toward the vegetable table.

Torey bit her lip to hold back an angry retort. At times like this Torey missed her life at the tavern, and would have liked to have Agnes's friendship, have girl talks and such, but that wasn't going to happen, and Torey knew it. In fact, Torey knew that if this old woman could be rid of her, she would. They finished the preparations for the evening feast, and started serving the trays of food.

This was not the usual dinner with wives, children, and members of office gathered around drinking wine, eating meat, and merrily discussing the day's activities and victories. The king had ordered that he and members of his army be served in the royal receiving chamber. Evidently, there was trouble in the countryside and local provinces. There was a dragon terrorizing and destroying villages. The lords from local provinces and kingdoms had requested an audience with the king to come up with a plan to conquer the dragon.

Once everyone had been seated and the wine had been served, conversation buzzed around the room.

"Where did the dragon come from?" asked one.

"Were there more where that one came from?" asked another.

"How could they conquer it?" asked yet another.

And worse was the loss of livestock the villagers, farmers, and peasants had suffered. It burned everything in its path. Now the villagers and peasants bore the burden of trying to rebuild their homes, barns, and places of business, all the while the dragon was still loose somewhere in the countryside. King Byron's brow furrowed. This was a serious problem.

Torey came through the door with a serving tray filled with fresh bread and bowls of meat. The king watched her, not in admiration, but wondering where she had been and what she may have seen. He would question her later. He could also see Agnes standing just on the other side of the open door, watching Torey with a scornful look upon her face. He would also talk to Agnes later about kindness to slaves and servants.

AGNES

"hy must I be the one to carry out Agnes's tasks while she recovers from her illness at the convent?" Torey whined as she knelt before the king's throne, obviously unhappy with her Sovereign's newest request.

"Among all my servants, you have worked most closely with her, Torey, you know what must be done. I know the two of you have had your differences, but you are not doing this for her, you are doing this for me." King Byron particularly disliked it when Torey whined, which, thankfully, was not very often.

The civil unrest had grown worse, as of late, and the king had been meeting with the neighboring Kings, King Serrell among them, and their council to resolve the many conflicts, not the least of which included the dragon. The Sovereign governed his people as he felt a good monarch ought, he worried about their safety, his kingdom's economy, and the ever-present threat of being conquered as the balance of powers shifted around him.

His troubled concern could be seen in his brows, knit together in a frown. He tended to be moody when he was greatly worried, and was uncharacteristically short with his subjects.

Torey could see her sovereign's worry, and tried not to take his dark mood personally, but there were times it was difficult not to. Torey had picked a bad time to be whiny. King Byron reigned as a disciplined ruler and felt the need to admonish Torey and remind her that he expected obedience.

"Would you prefer *I* carry out her tasks in her absence?" The question was laced with light sarcasm and heavy annoyance.

Torey felt the sting of the question, which was the king's intent. "Nay, my lord, please forgive my insolence," she knelt deeply before him, glancing up only momentarily into down eyebrows, his deep brown eyes flashing his annoyance. "I am pleased to do thy bidding."

"And Torey," he added, with exasperation, "please stay out of trouble."

Why must he always say that? Torey wondered to herself, a bit perplexed. She sighed deeply and shrugged her shoulders. "Aye, my lord."

"You had best take your leave now, and get started. You have much to do." He said, impatiently urging her to be on her way.

"Aye, my lord." Torey replied softly. Usually, Torey loved to be in the company of the king, today, however; she preferred to take her leave. He was contemplative, and needed solitude to think. Perhaps he wouldn't be so moody when next they met.

Over the next two weeks, while Agnes recuperated in the nuns' care, Torey worked hard to mind her own duties, and those of the head domestic mistress'. She took it upon herself to do some rearranging of Agnes's chores and workroom, she knew the older woman would fuss about it, but didn't think it would be of major consequence, and the new arrangement was much more efficient.

Olaf helped Torey stable the horses at the end of each day. Some of the saddles were rather worn, so she decided to treat them with oil. When she treated Agnes's saddle she decided to do a thorough job and clean out the saddlebag. She slid her fingers into the depths of the pocket, and withdrew a small pouch that had been hidden away.

Torey loosened the string and peered into the pouch. She gasped with great surprise, nearly dropping it. "Bloody hell!" she exclaimed to herself aloud. "Bloody hell!" she exclaimed again. "Well, it sure explains a lot!" She stuffed her find into her own leather pouch she wore on her waist belt.

Olaf poked his head into the livery. "The king summons you, Torey!" Olaf's voice startled her. "And I wouldn't keep him waiting if I were you, or you'll be a lot jumpier when he's done with you!" Olaf warned.

"Oh, Hell's bells!" Torey thought irritably to herself. She hurried past the sentries and decided to take a detour through the garden. She plucked an apple from one of the many fruit trees, and picked a handful of gardenias to give to the king. Torey often left the sweet white flowers on his desk, for she knew he enjoyed their fragrance as he pored over the many documents and parchments strewn before him.

First she looked for him in the throne room, and then the royal library, and not finding him there, either, she went to his study. She nodded at the sentry and knocked on the door, a guard opened it from the inside. Torey was surprised to find Olaf standing nearby, at attention, staring at the ceiling, and looking very sheepish. She gave him an inquisitive look, but he wouldn't look at her.

Torey stepped forward, placing the fragrant gardenias on the king's desk. He didn't look up. His quill pen continued to move across the parchment that sprawled across his desk. She stood before him in uncomfortable, awkward silence for a very long moment, not knowing whether she should remain standing or kneel, casting sidelong glances at Olaf, who continued to stare at the ceiling.

"Torey!" His admonishing voice broke the silence, making Torey jump and Olaf grimace. The annoyed king looked up at her with down eyebrows set over deep brown eyes that were definitely not amused at the moment. He set his quill pen down, leaned forward with both arms on the desk, laced his fingers together, and looked up at her with great displeasure.

"Olaf tells me you've rearranged Agnes's chores and workroom. Why did you do that? You know she's going to complain when she comes back!" He was displeased. Even though Torey knew it was the other concerns that were driving the king's dark mood as of late, that didn't make his displeasure any easier for Torey to bear.

It took a moment for Torey to realize that it wasn't a rhetorical question. He was waiting for an answer.

"Well?" he implored her.

"I felt the changes made things more efficient." Her voice lilted making her answer sound more like a question. It had seemed like such a good idea at the time, she thought to herself, as she shot Olaf a sidelong glare. He was still staring at the ceiling. You big coward, Torey thought sullenly to herself. She cast her eyes to the floor. She couldn't bear to look into the Sovereign's deep brown eyes when he was displeased with her, for it was too hurtful.

"And you wonder why I always ask you to stay out of trouble," he stated emphatically.

She looked at him, her eyes wide in astonishment. How did he know she thought that?

"How would you like it if she did that to you while you were away?" King Byron scolded, his handsome full brows frowning. She hated it when he gave her down eyebrows, for it meant he was greatly displeased with her, and she was in trouble.

"She never treats me kindly! She's always mean and spiteful, even though I always treat her with at least common courtesy, and you know it!" Torey felt hot, angry tears sting the back of her eyes. "Why do you always defend her when she's such a witch to everyone?" Torey wailed at the king.

One cocked eyebrow and an admonitive look told Torey she needed to change her tone and lower her voice. She immediately knelt before him. "Forgive my insolence, my king." She couldn't hold back a tear and sniffled as it slid down her cheek. She angrily wiped it away.

He knew he had been hard on her, but he had other, more pressing things on his mind right now that were demanding his attention. He would look for her on the veranda later in the evening, but right now, he needed to get back to work.

One of the king's messengers came to the door. "Your majesty, you are needed in the throne room."

King Byron nodded to him, and then said to Torey in a more kindly tone, "Finish your tasks, lass, we shall talk later."

Torey squeezed the apple that was still in her pocket. She had so wanted to offer it to him. Disappointed, she replied softly, "Aye, my lord," and rose, and went back to her duties, glaring at Olaf as she took her leave.

King Byron took his evening repast with his queen in their private chambers. The hour was late when he finally sought Torey on the veranda. His heart was saddened to find her crying softly to herself, hugging her knees to her chest, the evening breeze softly blowing her long red hair.

The long-suffering king drew a deep breath and looked heavenward, sending a prayer to the goddess Danu for patience. He found Torey to be a paradox, endearing and infuriating, she was bawdy, and yet, elegant. She was naïve even though she was intelligent; she could be coy, and then surprise him with her candor. Like it or not, she was his woman-child. He smiled wryly to himself, for most of the time he liked it.

He brushed a stray wisp of hair from her face, and caressed her cheek with the fragrant white petals of the gardenia that she had left on his desk, leaving the sweet flower to rest on her knees. She gave him a small smile.

"What is that you hold in your hand?" He asked.

She handed him the pouch. "Look within, you will be as surprised as I."

He shook the contents of the pouch into his hand, and out rolled a talisman, a tiny vial, and a small scroll that held instructions that read like an incantation.

"I found it in Agnes's saddlebag when Olaf and I were tending to the stables," Torey explained as she pouted, "when I said she was a witch to everyone, I didn't know she really was a witch."

"I must admit I am quite surprised." His handsome brows arched, framing disbelief in his deep brown eyes. "She has served in the castle for many years. I have never detected evil intent in her heart with my wizard's gift, but then, I have not scrutinized her mettle for a very long time. I did not find it necessary."

Torey gazed up at him, still perched atop the stone balcony on the veranda, her eyes still tearful.

"Even though this is very incriminating evidence, Torey, I want to be sure before I confront her." He knew even before he spoke that Torey wouldn't like what he said, she attested to that by rolling her eyes and making a face.

"Torey, lass, where would you be today if I had believed the rumors, or listened to the damning advice of my advisors when you were brought before me?" he tried to reason with her.

Torey looked downcast. "Why are you always defending her? She's mean-spirited and I hate her!" then added softly, her voice quavering, "I thought you cared for me, yet you defend my enemy." Torey was hurt and tearful.

The king took Torey's hand in his and tenderly kissed her fingers and the back of her hand. "I do care for you, lass. I care for all of my subjects. I defend her because she is old and set in her ways, even she does not know how much she is in need of kindness and respect."

With a firmer tone he added, "I don't expect my subjects to agree with my judgments - but I do expect their respect. I am the king." His full brows arched in admonishment.

She knew he was gently scolding her for her outburst in the study.

"Aye, my Sovereign." Torey answered softly, and slid from her perch to kneel before him, pressing his hand to her lips, her cheeks still wet with tears, and added in a subdued tone, "Your servant begs her Sovereign's forgiveness."

The Sovereign drew her to her feet and, wishing to banish the quarrelsome mood between them, embraced her warmly, and kissed the top of her head. "Not to worry, lass, I know your heart."

He took her by the hand, leading her off the veranda and down the stairs to her chamber. "I have a plan." He said in a low voice, looking around furtively, checking for curious ears. "Put the pouch back in her saddlebag. When she returns and goes for a ride into the forest to gather herbs, follow her, and report back to me."

"Aye, my lord."

"Now it's off to bed with you."

"Aye, my lord." Torey turned, stood on tiptoe, and kissed his cheek, then quickly scooted into her room before he could scold her.

He shook his head, blushing. He strode quickly down the hall. There was one more thing he must do before he headed for his own royal chambers and his sleeping queen.

The Evil
Spell is Broken

Olaf kept a discreet distance behind, as he followed Torey on horseback. King Byron had asked him to keep an eye on her and to follow her when she left to follow Agnes. The king, concerned for Torey's safety, sent Olaf to look out for her. Olaf was to fetch the king as quickly as possible should anything unusual or dangerous develop.

Torey felt that if she trailed Agnes on horseback, the chance of being spotted or heard was too great, so she followed her on foot, keeping a good distance behind Agnes, who was on horseback. Agnes rode quite a distance. Torey needed to rest and take a drink of water, but she dared not lose sight of her.

Torey suddenly recognized the woods around her, and realized where Agnes was headed. Agnes stopped, and tied her horse to a tree that was next to the same rock face in the clearing where Gregg had taken her that day long ago when he had wanted to show her new hunting ground.

Torey lay on her belly in the dense underbrush, watching Agnes, making sure she stayed well out of sight. Torey watched as Agnes removed the pouch from the saddlebag and emptied its contents into her hand. She sprinkled seven drops from the vial onto the face of the rock, murmured the incantation, and tapped the rock with the talisman. The silver-flecked, smooth rock rippled briefly like water, and then became smooth as glass.

Agnes reached out to test the rock, and her hand passed through it, and then she stepped forward and disappeared into another dimension.

Torey could not believe her eyes, she started to scoot backwards to take her leave and run to get the king when an angry, roaring, fire-breathing, foul-smelling black dragon stepped out into the clearing from the rock, filling the forest with its evil laughter.

Torey nearly cried out in terror and surprise. She covered her mouth with her hand to keep herself from screaming. It all made sense now. Why hadn't she seen it sooner? When the dragon had her pinned against the mountainside she knew she had seen those beady black eyes before. Why, the smell alone should have made Torey make the connection. Agnes always had a peculiar odor about her, and so did the dragon that day.

Torey was not the only one who was in disbelief. Fearing that Torey's life may be in danger, Olaf was already riding hard back to the castle to get the king.

Torey wasn't sure how long she lay there, but she dared not move. She had no idea when the dragon would return, but she was very sure she didn't want a formal introduction. If Torey hadn't already been lying on the ground, she would have collapsed with relief when Olaf and the king crawled up next to her in the brush. She leaned her head against his in thanks, he smiled at her and then pressed his finger to his lips to indicate quiet, and she nodded her understanding.

It was close to sundown when they heard a great rustling and the ground shuddered as the dragon returned to the rock. The three huddled figures watched as the dragon stepped back through the door into the Underworld.

King Byron and Olaf sprang up from their hiding place, and ran across the clearing. The king drew his sword as he ran, with Olaf right behind him.

"Great Dian, empower my sword!" the sovereign shouted. The deadly sword rang as it became one with the lightning bolt Dian sent. King Byron struck the rock, disintegrating it. For just a moment, the surprised dragon stood before them. The heavens around them resounded with thunder and lit up with lightning, and the ground quaked.

In moments, old Agnes stood before them, naked, bewildered, and surprised. Realizing her nakedness, she covered herself with her clothing that lay nearby. When she realized it was the Sovereign whom she stood before, she groveled on the ground, weeping, and hugging her garments to her body.

King Byron Judges Agnes

"hy?" King Byron's question broke the shocked silence in the wood that was punctuated by the only other sound: Agnes's weeping. The question was uttered in such sincere surprise that Torey wanted to hug the betrayed little boy that the king was in that moment. Then she wanted to kill Agnes in the most agonizing way possible.

Olaf lifted his spear to plunge it into the weeping, groveling woman that lay prostrate before them.

The king held up his hand and stayed Olaf's spear. "Nay, Olaf, I truly want an answer."

Then the Sovereign's voice became the Judge's voice. "You have but one chance to speak your truth. Be warned, I shall know whether you speak truth or deceit." The wizard king used the power that Dian had gifted him with and scrutinized the wizened old servant's mettle as he listened to her confession.

"I know I am old and bitter and angry, but at least I was the center of attention until you decided to treat Torey like a personal servant instead of like the criminal she is! She bewitches everyone when she's nothing but the castle whore." Agnes wept and sputtered as her tears splashed into the dirt, not because she was trying to win the sympathy of the king, but because she was truly a pathetic human being. "Tis Torey's fault no one likes me. That's why I went to see Keena the Witch and paid her to give me a spell that would give me access to the Underworld. I wanted to punish you for being so kind to that dirty little wench, so I took the form of a dragon and wreaked havoc upon the land." Agnes wept bitterly, but finally drew a deep breath. "That is my truth. Recompense is upon me. Judge me as you will." She dried her tears and lay quietly on the forest floor, waiting.

King Byron watched Torey's face as he listened to the conquered Agnes's confession. He wanted to see how Torey would react. Would she request of him that he punish Agnes? He hoped not. Would she be forgiving and look to him to be fair and just in his judgment? He hoped she would, for this is what he must do, regardless of Torey's feelings about it. But King Byron didn't want any more casualties; he was counting on Torey's trust in him as the Sovereign power that he was, and that his judgment would be fair.

He looked heavenward, knowing that Danu was looking down at them, waiting to see how he would judge.

Olaf gazed intently at the king, as he also waited to hear the judgment.

King Byron touched his sword to the top of Agnes's head and said gravely, "Because you have done this grievous thing I sentence you to one year of service in the Underworld. You shall carry water to all the tortured souls in the Underworld, especially those you are responsible for. If you still live at the end of one year, you are then sentenced to live out your natural days in service at King Serrell's castle, doing whatever he commands you."

Thunder and lightning rolled in the sky, the ground shook beneath them, and Agnes screamed in terror as the ground beneath her opened. Hands came out of the earth, pulling her down onto stairs that spiraled into the dark, foul abyss of the Underworld. Within moments, the earth closed its opening, and the forest was quiet again.

King Byron's sovereign gaze of absolute rule and absolute power fell upon Torey. She sank to her knees before him, pressing her forehead to the ground. Olaf sank to one knee with his fist clasped to his heart in oath and honor to his king.

In one fell swoop King Byron had rid his kingdom of the dragon, and taught Torey infallible justice, mercy, and compassion. He was pleased that she was humbled.

The King's Birthday

The night slumbered in velvet darkness, when the stars wink and twinkle, and the fairies feel safe to come out to play. The window had been thrown open by the evening chambermaid to cool the king's bedchamber, for it was very warm at summer's end. The nighttime breeze wafted gently through the open window and touched the sleeping king through the netting, forming the canopy above his large four-poster bed. The room, magnificently furnished, befitted a king of his status.

Torey loved to sneak in here when no one was around. She buried her face in the tapestries that hung on the wall, and breathed deeply of their ancient beauty and history. She liked the sound her sandals made on the stone floor, solid and light; at the same time, it gave her reassurance that this stone floor would still be here on the morrow and still be governed by the Sovereign and all would continue to be well. But most of all, every now and then, when she was feeling very brave, she very much liked to lie on the king's bed where he lay now. Those stolen moments banished her loneliness for a little while.

This night was different, though, because Torey asked special favor of her goddess mother, to travel in the dream state as though she were physically there, and then, upon arrival, become flesh again. She requested to appear as a transparent ghost anywhere her conscious state wanted to be while her physical form lay in her own bed chamber still sleeping. No one would be able to see her unless she wished it so. Tonight she wished it. Torey had come this night to her Sovereign's chambers to give him a very special gift, for it was his birthday. She beckoned to him softly, "Awaken, my Sovereign, come with me. There is much to show you while the night sky is still deep, velvety, and mystical." Her king stirred not.

"Help me, Danu, to rouse my king." The most brilliant star in the sky shone brighter still and filled the chamber with an amber glow as Danu's presence filled the room. "Rise, O powerful king, thy servant beckons to thee." Her beautiful voice echoed through the chamber, touching and beckoning his spirit to rise.

King Byron sat up, blinking and yawning sleepily and was startled to look down to see his own still sleeping form.

Torey bowed deeply in the presence of the sovereign and her magical goddess-mother, Danu, in the same room together, this was both humbling and exhilarating. To show her respect and humility Torey pressed her lips to the king's feet and waited for him to bid her to kneel before him.

"You may kneel." He enjoyed looking upon her, if the truth be known, but this was a little disconcerting for she appeared ghost-like, and he could see the furniture right through her.

"Please, my most respected Sovereign," she pleaded, extending her hand to him, "take my hand."

The moment he touched her hand, they were traveling together through patterns of stars in the velvety darkness. Soon they came to a very large stone structure with tall white columns. There was music and laughter coming from a hall. The king and Torey alighted there, and Torey called upon her magical heritage and turned herself, and King Byron, in physical form again.

They were immediately greeted by a strikingly beautiful woman in a white robe. "My lord, how lovely to see you again, I trust my beloved daughter is taking good care of you?"

The king knew intuitively that they were on the isle of Tir-na-nog, as if from a long-forgotten dream. Danu was, indeed, the most radiant creature he had ever seen. "Yes, she is an obedient and trustworthy servant."

Danu clapped her hands and servants instantly brought meat and wine, cheese, bread, and fruit. Danu turned to King Byron, "Please be our guest of honor in celebration of your birthday!" A beautiful winged nymph appeared from behind Dian's throne, she seated King Byron on a couch, and began feeding him.

He gazed around the great room. Musicians performing a magnificent symphony with harps, lutes, and oboes drew his attention. The room was filled with gods and goddesses dancing, laughing, chasing one another, and playing. Some were in different stages of undress as they danced, teased, and flirted, cavorting with one another. With the background of the nighttime sky and the sparkling stars, it was all very pleasant.

The lovely nymph who was feeding the king had slipped his sandals off and was coaxing him to become even more comfortable. Torey blushed and looked away. Her lord looked at her and grinned, taking boyish mischievous pleasure in making her blush. He smiled at the playful nymph, but decided not to let her remove his tunic. He gazed over at Torey, the desire in his eyes told Danu what he was thinking.

He summoned Torey to come sit at his feet, an honor to which she very happily complied. She sat on a pillow on the stone floor and watched, with her king, the festivities around her. Unaware that she was doing so, Torey leaned ever so slightly against the king's legs and ever so gently and absent-mindedly caressed his bare feet, as though she had done it a hundred times before. She felt his fingers playing with the loose tendrils of her red hair.

Torey perused the large ballroom. On one side of the room was a gigantic fountain that held mermaids and dolphins. The mermaids were delightful to watch as they frolicked together, kissing and caressing one another. Torey stole a discreet glance up at her sovereign to see if he was watching the mermaids, too. She was secretly delighted to see that he was a virile man who could appreciate beauty. She smiled to herself and quickly looked away.

Danu crossed the room amid the festivities to sit next to Torey at the king's feet. The beautiful goddess whispered to her daughter in a silky, pleased voice, "My child, you have learned much about the art of service and he is, indeed, a fine king. Not all of my daughters are blessed with a king such as this one, who slays dragons, challenges other kings, and wields his sword on your behalf, and protects you with his shield."

Danu smiled and put her arm around Torey. With a touch of sadness in her voice, she continued, "You must return soon for the sands of the hourglass that measure the night flow swiftly toward sunrise. You see?" she pointed to the hourglass that was suspended above the room, and then she pointed to the heavenlies, "He wishes to awaken with his queen." There was such urgency in Danu's voice that Torey felt compelled to obey.

Torey was reluctant to leave, but she bowed her head to Danu and kissed the back of the king's hand to evoke the magic that would take them back to the castle.

They were, at once, back in his royal bedchamber. The king sat up on the side of his bed, glanced at his own sleeping form, and then looked at his queen, who stirred not.

He held Torey's hand as she knelt before him, smiling up into his handsome face. "Will I remember this night, this enchanted night you took me to the Magical Isle?" He asked her.

Torey pressed the palm of his hand to her cheek and kissed it. She gazed deeply into the intense, dark brown eyes that were framed by full, dark brows. His eyes could stop her in her tracks, bring her to attention, or bring her to her knees with humility and the desire to please him. Even though the king had not required it of her, as other kings had that Torey had served, there were times she had wanted to give him the gift of the ancient art of Seduction, as taught to all the daughters of Danu, but she said, instead, "Yes, my lord, you will remember this most honored visit to Queen Danu." Then Torey rose and bid him to lie down and rest.

Smiling in wonderment, he watched her until she slowly faded from his chamber like a dream, saying softly, "Wondrous birthday, my Sir, wondrous birthday." He closed his eyes as sleep claimed him, the fragrance of her all around him.

The Castle Bath

Torey found peace here. The castle bath was so much better than the icy cold dips she took in the mountain streams when delivering a message or running an errand for the king to a neighboring kingdom, and the bath was a good place to repose and think. It was mid-to-late afternoon. The sun was still warm with just a hint of the light spring coolness the early evening would bring.

The castle bath was built with the architectural beauty of a Roman bath, to the king's specifications. It was located behind the king and his Queen's private chambers, but outside in the huge expanse of one of many large courtyards. It had been built here because the hot springs underground beneath the structure kept the water warm at all times of the year. The entire bath was surrounded by tall white columns, archways, and life-size statues, which provided some cover and privacy as well as artistic beauty. It had an open ceiling that lent a panoramic view of the blue sky and puffy white clouds in daylight hours, and the dark velvet magic of the nighttime sky.

Leaning back, she folded her hands behind her head, closed her eyes, and ever so slightly paddled the water with her toes. She listened to the sounds of the birds fussing and chirping and mating for it was spring and there was much for them to do. They brought the wonderful sounds of spring to her attentive ears.

She breathed deeply of the fragrances wafting across the courtyard, delighting her nose. There was jasmine, roses, and the sweetest of all, the gardenias.

Yes, that delicious aroma wafting across the courtyard was fresh bread being baked in the king's kitchen; how delicious that would be tonight!

A great variety of flowers and roses and brush had been planted near the bath for the royal family to enjoy. The wonderful fragrances caressed her nose. Sometimes she thought she could take a bath in nothing but flower petals. The thought made her smile.

This particular afternoon was quiet in the castle. The king was away attending to business of State, and the queen was overseeing the preparation of the feast and his entertainment for the evening.

The king and his queen were expecting a royal little one soon. The entire castle fairly trembled with excitement and anticipation and was a beehive of activity in preparation. Neither the king nor his queen had need of their castle guard's services so she was dismissed for the afternoon, but the castle was not without its armed sentries at their strategic posts.

She wondered what the urgency of the business was that furrowed the king's handsome brow. He was powerful but trusting, he could afford to be so, for he had won the respect and fear of all those around him. And only she knew, because she was the daughter of Danu, that the king consulted with Dian. He had won the favor of the gods and their wisdom of counsel. She, his watchful castle guard and ambassador, did not worry about his safety when dealing with known enemies. She worried about those who would veil their deception in the guise of friendship.

"My lord, have you your shield?" She would ask on his way out. That confident smile and the mischief that danced in his sparkly brown eyes made her worry more. You never knew when an arrow might find its mark. The roads between the townships and kingdoms were oft long and lonely. The thought made her shudder.

She opened her eyes and stared at the puffy white clouds to see what she could see. She pictured him on horseback, safe and sure, completing his duties, anxious for the ride home. She felt better.

The sun was warm on her upturned face and creamy white skin. She ran her hands along her muscular thighs to her flower. A flower is a beautiful thing, created to delight; she splashed the water about and washed herself. The sultry afternoon, the sky above her, the fragrances and comforting sounds of spring surrounding her were all very seductive.

She cupped water in her hands and let it drip down and form a pool at the top of her full breasts. Her thoughts drifted to her sweet memories of Liam. The celibate life was not for her, and she wondered if she would ever see him again. She also dared to wonder, for just a moment, if she would ever gain true freedom. She flipped herself over and pressed her cheek against the cool of the marble tile and splashed the water with her legs.

One of her duties, which she considered sacred, was to assist the royal bathers in their ritual in the castle bath to bathe the king before the evening's festivities and before he summoned his queen. The roads the king traveled with his entourage were long and hot and dusty. He would be travel-weary upon his return and his royal bathers would use pumice stones and jasmine oil and sponges to wash away his fatigue, and the dust and cares of the day.

He would order his flute player to play a soothing tune while the bathers filled their ceramic urns with jasmine-scented water, then she would tilt his head back against her lap and pour the water slowly through his thick black hair and over his brow, trickling it down his chest and shoulders, washing away all the tension.

Next, using an ancient technique, she would massage his scalp, working her fingers gently but firmly down the tense neck muscles in round, massaging strokes with her thumbs, to the shoulder muscles, on down to the biceps until all tension and cares of the day vanished. The other bathers would massage his feet with the pumice stones, rubbing away all the calluses caused from the leather sandals he wore.

The goddess Danu had taught the royal bathers how to locate and regenerate their lord's energy points, thereby nurturing and strengthening him after the duties and battles of the day. A servant brought the king a flask of wine to refresh himself while the bathers in the water with him climbed out to get the drying towels. They gently brushed his exotic dark skin with the thick soft towels to dry him.

Finally, they would dress him in the royal blue festive tunic he looked so handsome in, place his crown firmly upon his squeaky-clean head, and, with abashed smiles and thumbs-up, and deep, reverent bows, pronounce him ready for his queen!

The tile work in the royal bath was done in the most beautiful aquatic colors that caught the light and the movement of the water and reflected it back. No one but Torey was here on this unusually sultry spring afternoon. She could see a sentry across the courtyard. He was still, but watchful, giving reassurance that all was well.

Her thoughts floated like the puffy clouds above her. She watched the water and light reflecting around the bath and her thoughts went for a moment to the time when the king became her Champion and fought the evil wizard, making her an extremely fortunate servant, indeed.

A rude noise startled her repose, "Who goes there?" Her answer was a curious woodland creature with big eyes as startled as she. It was staring at her, its long, furry tail twitching its nervous discovery of her bath time.

"Silly creature," she murmured, "you gave me such a start! Run along, now, I'm not going to hurt you!" She splashed water in the direction of the creature, and with a twitch of his tail he fled.

The peal of the bells of the town hall where the townspeople held their meetings had begun to sound. The shopkeepers were closing their shops and readying themselves for home.

The king would be back soon, and her duties beckoned. She rose from her bath, dripping, sweet and fresh, and reached for her tunic, slipping it on over her head. She climbed into the breeches that were typical attire of her duty station.

She slipped the ornate dagger the king himself had given her firmly into its sheath, which hung from her waist belt; all those in the king's service had one, for one must always be ready to defend their lord. Next she donned her shield; it fit across her breast protecting her in the event of combat. It bore the beloved King's Coat of Arms insignia and she wore it proudly. She towel-dried her hair and slipped her sandals on.

There would be fresh bread, meat, and fruit, and wine tonight, and the music of the harp and lyre. But best of all would be the stories of the day's adventures of the king that he would tell 'round the table.

Though all servants and slaves longed to be freed men, and Torey was no exception, she had found acceptance in her circumstances.

The king's
Sovereignty

orey took great pride in her intimate but platonic relationship with the king. She had sworn her oath and had served him well for five years now. It was spring and preparations were being made for the celebration of Mayday. All around her marriage contracts were being negotiated, betrothal rings were proposed and accepted, and those already married were heavy with child. Even the king and his beloved queen had been blessed with a precocious, adorable princess.

Torey was twenty and three, passionate and spirited, and she grew restless as her own nesting urges grew stronger. At times the castle and her duties felt so confining that she grew discontented and became irritable. Her bed was cold and empty, and she lay awake nights longing for Liam.

Torey had requested an audience with the king at the end of his daily time at court, and King Byron had granted it, but was a little disconcerted when his servant would not state the purpose for the audience. Instead of insisting upon knowing beforehand, he indulged her and gave her the audience she sought. Torey had prepared herself properly for such an important audience. She wore the traditional long skirt and blouse, cinched by a corset.

It was now the end of the day and Torey waited patiently for the last of the business to be conducted and the last visitors to leave. She came forward to the foot of his throne and dropped humbly to her knees, waiting to be acknowledged.

"You may speak now, Torey." His voice was a no-nonsense sovereign's voice. The gentle thunder of it in the very large throne room caused Torey to start with surprise just a bit. She looked up into his face, from the foot of his throne. Her eyes were grave, and though she opened her mouth to speak, she could not, so overwhelmed was she with emotion. She stared imploringly into his intense brown eyes. The king's eyes were not sparkling and snapping in their lovely way, just now, for Torey's sadness concerned him greatly, his eyes grew deeper and even more intense with his concern. He dismissed the scribe, his advisors, and the rest of his cabinet, for he felt Torey needed a private audience.

"Come here to me, Torey." Torey's deeply sad expression melted into gratitude as she rose to go over to him. She sat down at his feet and was so overcome with emotion that she buried her face in his lap and silently wept. He caressed her head and let her cry for a moment. The king lifted her chin and searched her face and her eyes. He drew a heavy sigh at what he saw there. King Byron brushed the tears away from under both of her eyes with his thumbs, then pulled her up to him and sat her firmly in his lap facing him, her legs on either side. This was easy to do, as his servant was quite petite, and himself quite muscular. He held fast with his hands on her hips to steady her. There was nothing sensual or seductive in the way he seated her on his lap. The king was her sovereign, this was his kingdom and he ruled over it. He wanted her to calm down and realize that.

"Tell me what troubles thee, Torey." She stared back into the deepest, wisest eyes she had ever gazed into. She could feel his muscular legs easily supporting her weight. He sat motionless with his hands still on her hips holding her steady, and very still, unaffected by her weight or position on his lap.

"My king, I would petition his majesty for a boon. Mayday approaches, and, and . . . ." Torey could not finish.

He continued to stare into her eyes, motionless. He held his grip on her, his body felt strong and reassuring beneath her. He saw her need in the depths of her eyes. He hadn't considered that she might be lonely and want a mate and perhaps children of her own. He was somewhat abashed that this hadn't occurred to him. She was beautiful and young, and he knew she was wise in the ways of love, though they had never shared physical intimacy.

Torey could see the realization in his eyes. He sensed her growing needs and desires. She relaxed. His intense calm and realization had broken her tension.

"Good," the king thought to himself. He released the firm grip he had on her hips and put his arms around her shoulders. Torey rested her head against his chest and dared to hope.

Twilight at the Castle Bath

1t was on a sultry summer night that Olaf was sent to summon Torey. As she lay sleeping, with the cool night breeze bringing relief to her humid slumber, Olaf called her name. Thinking it a dream, she smiled to herself and said a prayer of benevolence to Queen Danu.

"Torey!" the voice sounded more urgent this time as it nudged her awake. Her eyes fluttered open as she realized that the voice was real, jarring her out of nestled slumber.

"What is it Olaf, and it had better be important!"

"The king summons you, Torey, he is refreshing himself at the royal bath, and there's no need to don your gear."

All the servants and slaves slept in nearly see-through gauze-like tunics to combat the oppressive summer heat. Torey wore that and nothing more this night, when duty called her to the king's bath.

As she walked the garden path to the royal bath, there was no breeze, and the still night air offered no relief.

She walked through the throne room that held the long-ago memory of squaring off with the king, when they measured each other, mettle for mettle, and the dance of sovereignty and compliance had begun.

She walked through the archway that led to the garden path, and beyond that, to the royal bath. This part of her journey was most pleasant. The stars twinkled at her; she could see Danu's smile in the velvety black night sky. Torey wondered curiously about Danu's nearness of presence this night. The perfume of the roses, jasmines, and gardenias, combined with her anticipation of being in the presence of the king, was exhilarating. She smiled to herself as she quickened her pace.

So lost in thought was she wondering about the purpose of this meeting that the guard on duty startled her most embarrassingly.

"Who goes there?" Came the demand, with his spear unmistakably pointed at Torey.

"Tis I, Torey, you big oaf!" Torey and the guard shared a handshake, a slap on the back, and a gruff, guard-type grin as they mutually acknowledged and dismissed an embarrassing moment.

The guard bid Torey a good evening, and turned back to his duty, urging Torey on to answer her lord's summons. She scurried up the remaining stairs. At the top, where the castle bath was seen in its architectural splendor, one's attention was always riveted to the throne at the center, where Torey's attention now came to rest, for King Byron was seated there. She stopped in her tracks.

"My lord, I am here, as you have summoned." Torey knelt before his throne where he sat, she could feel his contemplative gaze upon her.

He sat still in the moonlight, gazing upon her. They could both hear the gentle lap of water in the castle bath, the late night sounds of crickets, and the occasional hoot of the night owl as life stirred around them.

"Torey" he began, "I believe that shared experiences in which trust and respect have grown can create a relationship more intimate than even the most ardent lovers share."

Torey sat up straight and considered his words.

"I summoned you here that you might refresh yourself and sup with me." He rose, came over to her, and lifted her nightshirt over her arms, and tossed it over a nearby couch. With a playful grin, he tousled her hair, and jumped into the bath, splashing her.

Torey, always ready to banter, especially with him, said laughing, "Aye, my lord, but remember, 'twas your idea!" as she jumped in.

He swam to the other side and ducked each time she drew near and tried to splash him. He ducked underwater and came up laughing and taunting her playing keep-away. She finally out-witted him and splashed him full in the eyes when he came up for air.

"Ah, hahaha!" he laughed and exclaimed as the water stung his eyes.

"Aye, aye, that reminds me of what my face must have looked like when you scolded me for rearranging Agnes' work room!" Torey said good-naturedly.

"If truth be known, Torey, I liked what you did, but I could not tell you that at the time."

"I knew that," said Torey, as she brushed her wet hair out of her face, "and I knew your judgment of her at the rock face was just, but I didn't want to admit it at the time."

"I knew that, too," said he.

They talked for a long while of shared experiences, and truths and realizations that could not be spoken of before now, each gaining a deeper understanding of the other.

Presently, King Byron asked Torey what was important to her, what did she want most.

As soon as the question was posed, the sadness that King Byron had seen in her eyes, as of late, was there.

Torey's gaze drifted heavenward. "My mother can walk upon the earth and choose anyone with whom she wants to share her bed. She can lay with any of the gods whenever she chooses. Here am I, the daughter of the most sensual, desirable goddess, yet I am Earth-bound and so very lonely. I am not ungrateful to you, my lord, but I am a woman, with all the needs and passions of a woman."

King Byron felt he was her true friend as well as her king, and she his trusted confidante. Her skin glowed in the light of the candles around the bath. He drew near to her, ran his fingers into her red hair, pulling her face up to him, and kissed her tenderly.

Torey had been owned and taken by kings, their knights, and their land barons, but none had defended her honor or their ownership of her the way King Byron had.

"Come, we shall sup." They climbed out of the bath and wrapped themselves in towels. Torey poured wine and tore the bread that was on a tray that was set on a table nearby.

He stood before her. Muscular. Powerful. Absolute. This king, who was the sovereign ruler of all he could see, sole authority of life and death, the Champion of his kingdom, gazed at her. King Byron owned her, he protected her, and he avenged her honor. He slew her demons and her dragons, earning her oath. Taking her was his right, yet he did not.

"Look at me." He commanded her. He lifted her chin to gaze into her eyes. He was the symbol of justice and balance to her, for he was of Dian's ilk. She understood that there must be just and disciplined leaders for citizens and servants to have an orderly life.

He raised his wine glass to Torey and said, "To trusted friends." Torey raised her glass and they drank together.

She was still not sure what the purpose of this time with the king was. She kept waiting for him to make a grand announcement, or to give her a new assignment, but he did not.

Soon King Byron bade her good night, and she rose to take her leave to her chambers.

King Byron remained reposed at the bath, staring up at the heavenlies as a small smile curved the corners of his sensuous mouth. He knew Danu was looking on. He closed his eyes, as Danu, the Prisms, and her champions sang their serenade that came softly to his ears, through the columns of the castle bath.

"The morrow will dawn a whole new day for Torey," King Byron thought to himself as he drifted off to sleep.

The Dawn Brings a New Day

Torey awoke to the sound of Olaf pounding on her door, "Lass, awaken, arise, what keeps you? Make haste! Come to the throne room, the king summons you, for he has a mission for you!"

Torey, sleepy and a little disoriented, stumbled to the door, opening it, "Olaf, stop pounding and shouting, I am not deaf!"

Rubbing her eyes, and trying to awaken, she asked, "What about a mission, what are you talking about?"

Olaf smiled at her affectionately, and gently boxed her shoulder playfully.

Olaf was usually so stoic, that this unusual banter piqued her curiosity. "Alright, Olaf, what's going on? Is it my birthday?" Torey asked. Then she thought again, the sleepy fog lifting, "Wait a minute, 'tis not my birthday, Olaf! What's going on? Why is the king summoning me?" Now she was annoyed.

"Don your gear and make haste, his majesty is waiting!" With that, Olaf darted out of her doorway and down the hall.

"Bloody hell, Olaf, why couldn't you just tell me what is going on?" Torey muttered, annoyed, as she readied herself. She tied her hair back in a leather thong, pulled on her leggings, and the soft leather boots until they hugged her shapely calves. She pulled the gray thigh-length tunic over her head, and tucked her dagger in the waist-belt. She would come back for the rest of her weaponry when she learned what the king wanted her to do. She went to the small table in her chamber whereupon sat a pitcher and bowl of water and splashed her face. She rinsed her mouth with water and swallowed it, enjoying the coolness on her throat, gently pressed a small towel to her face, and headed for the door.

Torey was so concerned about this mysterious mission, was so puzzled over Olaf acting so strangely, and trying to make sense of last night, that she burst into the throne room more forcefully than she had intended, causing everyone to turn their attention to her entrance. Her face reddened as she hastened across the large receiving room to King Byron's throne and bowed.

"My apologies, your majesty, we were up late," Torey stammered, realizing what she was implying, "I mean I was up late."

"Torey." He said softly, almost sadly, with a hint of that special small smile, but with no acknowledgement of the events of the night before.

"Your majesty." Torey replied, looking up wonderingly at the king. She was confused. Did last night really happen, or was it a dream. Was he annoyed? Did he have news? Did something wonderful happen? For the first time, she could not tell, for his countenance bore happiness and pride, but it was mingled with a wistful sadness. Torey dared not ask in such a public setting.

"Torey, it was in this room so long ago that you were brought before me for judgment of your crimes against the Crown. You wore a veil of shame and anger from your life of oppression, and I had grown distrustful and cynical from discerning evil in the hearts of men. It was in this room that we began our journey together, and mettle for mettle, we have learned many good lessons, we two."

His eyes were soft now, and his voice low, as though the two of them were alone on the veranda, talking, as they had so many times. Instead, they were in the throne room, with the entire royal entourage present. She listened in wonderment to the touch of sadness in his voice as he continued. He certainly didn't sound to her as though he was about to give her an important assignment or mission.

"It seems fitting, Torey, that it should be in this room, that your freedom be granted to you this day. My council of advisors agrees unanimously that you have more than paid your debt to your Sovereign, and to the kingdom, and that you are a loyal and faithful citizen on whom we can always depend. I have signed the decree declaring you a free citizen." King Byron hesitated, for he was momentarily overcome by the momentousness of the ocassion. He cleared his throat and gathered his composure. "Olaf, bring me the sword!" The king commanded.

Torey's gaze shifted to Olaf, who wore the most abashed grin she had ever seen. He stepped away from his position next to the king and handed the king a sheathed sword. Torey would have recognized it anywhere.

King Byron handed Torey her own sword, the one Gregg had given to her for her birthday at the tavern so long ago. With great sadness, he said, "As a free citizen who has a past reputation for being a rebel against the Crown," and he smiled ruefully at her as they exchanged knowing glances of that time long ago, "you will, henceforth, be known as Torey the Warrior Woman, Defender of the King's Name and Kingdom. Do you accept this oath to your king for as long as you shall live?"

In complete surprise, Torey glanced at Olaf who was nodding, winking at her, and grinning his approval.

Torey knelt on one knee with her fist over her heart, as was the posture of a sworn soldier. "Aye, my liege, I do."

King Byron straightened his posture, took a deep breath, and raised his eyes to all gathered there, and declared in a loud voice, "It would please the council if you would accept the hunting lodge in the forest as your home. It is not far from the lake where you solved the mystery of the dragon."

Torey blinked and pinched herself, first last night, and now this. Was this real, or was this a dream, too?

King Byron smiled wistfully, and, as though reading her thoughts, he said, "this is real, Torey. You are a free citizen now. You may continue to serve as my castle guard with full pay like the rest of my guards and soldiers; and continue to live here at the castle, or you may live at the lodge, perhaps with the one who waits for you. It is your choice. Now rise, my Warrior Woman, and face the kingdom you have sworn to protect."

Everyone in the throne room rose and applauded the king's decision. Even the Tamlin, who was usually expressionless but observant, stood beside the king's throne, gave Torey a wide smile.

Queen Danu, with Dian at her side, and the Prisms all around her, smiled through misty eyes as she peered through the Pool of Mortals.

Torey could not believe her ears, and Olaf kept grinning at her. She shifted from one foot to the other, still absorbing the king's declaration, and holding her sword. She had formed many friendships here, and had grown in sage wisdom and strength of character, but every slave and every servant longs to be master of their own destiny. She could hardly believe it. She pinched herself again. No, she wasn't dreaming.

Her voice sounded almost apologetic when she asked the king, "In truth, your majesty, in truth, the decision is mine?"

King Byron smiled, not at all surprised at Torey's inability to take it all in.

"On my honor, Torey," his fist went to his heart in the sign of the oath of loyalty and truth. "You are free." The king handed Torey an official document with his seal upon it. "This is the signed decree of your freedom and your position as my sworn subject and defender. Keep it in a safe place, for it is my belief that there are those who would rob you of your freedom, and force you into a position of servitude, if given the chance."

Torey nodded her understanding and pressed the document to her heart, her lips pressed into a tremulous smile.

"May I escort you to your lodge, my lady?" said a familiar, beloved male voice from the back of the throne room behind her.

Torey squealed with delight - she would have known that voice anywhere! She turned, and quickly covered the distance to where he was standing. She flung herself in his arms, Liam, her love, and he twirled her around, kissing and hugging her. It had been a long five years for both of them.

After a joyous reunion, Torey turned from Liam and walked slowly back to the throne, and knelt to King Byron. "I thank you, my Sire, I have not the words to thank you properly." Her tears brimmed over. She wanted to fling herself into his arms and kiss him passionately as she had always dreamed of doing, but propriety forbade it.

She understood now why the king had summoned her to the castle bath, and supped with her, and talked with her as though she were his most respected advisor, and closest friend. He treasured her friendship, and wanted her to know that. It had also been his way of saying goodbye should she decide to leave. She looked up into King Byron's handsome face. He was smiling that small smile that had always been just for her, but now the smile held heavy sadness and his eyes were misted. Torey rose, kissed the back of his hand, and pressed it to her cheek, then turned, and with a last look back, joined Liam where he waited at the massive wooden doors of the throne room.

Then Liam and Torey strolled together, hand in hand, out of the throne room, into the bright, warm sunshine and into her new life as Torey, the Warrior Woman; a free citizen.

Alas, there was one more order of business King Byron felt he must do to balance the scales of justice ...

READER LETTER

1 hope you have found courage and honor in your journey to the 17th century, and may chivalry never be dead.

You don't have to be a mythological entity to live forever. The One Who placed the stars in the sky and made mankind in His Image longs to give us the gift of eternal life with Him through His Son, Jesus Christ, we have only to accept Him: "For God so loved the world that He gave His only Son that whosoever would believe in Him should not perish, but have everlasting life." John 3:16

Find out in the sequel what King Byron's last order of business is that he felt he must do, and meet the courageous and beautiful Wisdoms who help Torey answer a call to a nearly impossible duty.

I would love to hear from readers; you can write to me at geniebear1@sbcglobal.net.

www.ingramcontent.com/pod-product-compliance
Lightning Source LLC
Chambersburg PA
CBHW070808180626
46818CB00001B/161